Great Britain and Ireland

ANGLAIS

1re année

FAST WINGS

Fiona Morel
B. A. (Hons.) Sussex

Martine Bélorgey
Professeur agrégé au collège Condorcet
à la Chapelle-de-Guinchay
Formatrice en IUFM

Graham Bushnell
M. A. (Oxon) R. S. A. Dip (TEFL)

BELIN
8, rue Férou 75278 Paris Cedex 06
http://www.editions-belin.com

EXTRAIT DU PROGRAMME D'ANGLAIS DE QUATRIÈME LV2

(Le programme complet se trouve dans le classeur du professeur.)

SAVOIR-FAIRE À MAÎTRISER EN FIN DE QUATRIÈME LV2

1. Domaine des relations courantes

1.1 Saluer, prendre congé.
1.2 S'excuser, remercier.
1.3 Exprimer voeux et souhaits.
1.4 Demander, proposer, répondre.
1.5 Se donner le temps de réfléchir.
1.6 Téléphoner.
1.7 Écrire une lettre.
1.8 Adapter son niveau de langue à l'interlocuteur et à la situation.

2. Échange d'information

2.1 Présenter quelqu'un, demander et donner des informations relatives à l'identité, la nationalité, la résidence de quelqu'un.
2.2 Décrire, nommer ; demander et donner des informations sur des personnes, des animaux, des objets et des symboles culturels.
2.3 Se renseigner sur ce qu'ont les autres ; parler de ce qu'on a, de ce qu'on n'a pas, de ce qu'on voudrait avoir.
2.4 Demander et donner des informations sur des occupations habituelles, se renseigner sur les habitudes de quelqu'un ; demander, dire ce que quelqu'un fait dans la vie, dire ce qu'on veut faire comme métier.
2.5 Parler de ce qu'on voit, de ce qu'on entend ; poser des questions sur une activité en cours.

3. Domaine des repères dans l'espace et dans le temps

3.1 Repérer dans l'espace : parler de la présence, de l'absence, du nombre, de la quantité. Situer dans l'espace, indiquer une direction, décrire un changement de lieu. Demander ou indiquer un itinéraire. Utiliser quelques repères géographiques simples, situer sur un document iconographique.
3.2 Repérer dans le temps : situer dans le passé, le présent, l'avenir ; dire la date et l'heure. Comprendre les horaires, des programmes simples. Évoquer le passé. Raconter et établir des liens chronologiques simples. Fixer un cadre à un événement passé. Mettre en perspective historique. S'enquérir sur la durée, indiquer la durée. Situer dans l'avenir.

4. Expression de goûts, de réactions et d'opinions personnelles

4.1 Parler de ses goûts, de ce qu'on aime, de ce qu'on n'aime pas, de ce qu'on aimerait (faire), proposer un choix, indiquer sa préférence, dire ce qu'on a décidé de faire / de ne pas faire.
4.2 Réagir à des situations (exprimer la surprise, l'admiration, l'indifférence, la désapprobation, le regret, le reproche, etc.).
4.3 Exprimer une opinion personnelle, un jugement, formuler un doute, une hypothèse.

5. Latitude et contrainte

5.1 Parler de ce qu'on a le droit de faire, de ce qu'on n'est pas obligé de faire, de ce qu'il est interdit de faire.
5.2 Parler de ce qu'on sait / peut / ne sait pas / ne peut pas faire.
5.3 Parler de ce qu'on veut / ne veut pas faire ou laisser faire.

6. Domaine de l'action exercée sur autrui

6.1 Exercer de l'influence sur autrui par des injonctions, des suggestions ou des conseils.
6.2 Parler de l'influence exercée sur autrui.

7. Domaine de l'expression discursive

7.1 Rendre compte de ce que quelqu'un dit, pense, ressent ou fait.
7.2 Exprimer son accord ou désaccord, justifier, commenter, opposer, apprécier.
7.3 Confronter son expérience et sa culture avec celle des autres.

ISBN 2-7011-**2706**-8

PRÉFACE

FAST WINGS est une méthode en deux niveaux, destinée à l'apprentissage de l'anglais en tant que deuxième langue étrangère. Par son approche à la fois variée, dynamisante et réaliste, **FAST WINGS** répond aussi aux besoins des classes qui suivent une année de remise à niveau.

La méthode reprend les principes de la collection **WINGS** :

- Une organisation **thématique** qui encadre des situations toujours **authentiques** et stimulantes.
- Une approche **communicative** et **interactive** où l'élève est au centre de son apprentissage.
- Une **progression** grammaticale **en spirale** qui prend en compte les vrais besoins langagiers, et qui aide l'élève à construire, au fur et à mesure, savoirs et savoir-faire.
- Une **grammaire énonciative** fondée sur un anglais naturel et moderne. La contextualisation authentique des leçons amène les élèves à une vraie réflexion sur la langue.

LE LIVRE DE L'ÉLÈVE

- Au début de l'année, nous proposons quatre pages de **ZERO LESSONS**.
- Ensuite le manuel s'organise en **7 PARTS**.

Chaque **PART** comprend :

- Une double page d'ouverture qui illustre le thème.
- **4 LESSONS** : chacune occupe une double page qui propose une très grande variété d'activités autour des quatre compétences.
- **SPREAD YOUR WINGS** : une double page de civilisation placée entre **Lessons 2** et **3**.
- **HOW TO...** : une double page qui développe l'autonomie et structure la démarche de l'élève en lui apprenant des stratégies d'apprentissage.
- **SOUNDS** : un choix d'activités (et de "raps") qui aident l'élève à mettre au point et améliorer sa prononciation.
- **LET'S PRACTISE!** : un choix d'exercices sur les points de grammaire de chaque **Lesson**.

- **READING CORNER**, à la fin du manuel, fournit de la lecture supplémentaire : poèmes, histoires courtes et une adaptation d'une nouvelle.

LE "WORKBOOK"

- Véritable outil de classe, les activités de **CLASSWORK** permettent une participation active et une prise de parole de tous les élèves.
- Pour chaque leçon, la rubrique **LOOK AND LEARN** amène les élèves à observer leurs productions personnelles et à réfléchir au fonctionnement et aux structures de la langue.
- La trace écrite représente le trésor personnel de chaque élève : son travail en classe, sa réflexion sur la langue, et avec **YOUR WORD BANK**, tout le vocabulaire actif de l'année.

LE CLASSEUR ITINÉRAIRES

Ce classeur est destiné aux enseignants. Vous y trouverez :

- Une introduction à la méthode **Fast Wings**.
- Des notes et suggestions détaillées sur toutes les activités et les textes d'enregistrement.
- Les tests pour chaque Part : **Listening, Reading and writing** *(à photocopier)*.
- Les fiches d'exploitation des pages **HOW TO...** *(à photocopier)*.
- 12 transparents – images du manuel sans texte, illustrations de champs lexicaux importants, et documents authentiques – avec des fiches d'exploitation *(à photocopier)*.

Les auteurs

WORK AND PLAY

COMMENTS

CONTENTS

PART 5

FACT AND FICTION

PART 6

CHOICES

PART 7

PLANS

PART 8

READING CORNER

CONTENTS suite

W E L C O M E   T O   F A S T   W I N G S

Dans les lessons tu suivras Di, ses amis et sa famille dans leur vie de tous les jours à travers trois continents différents.

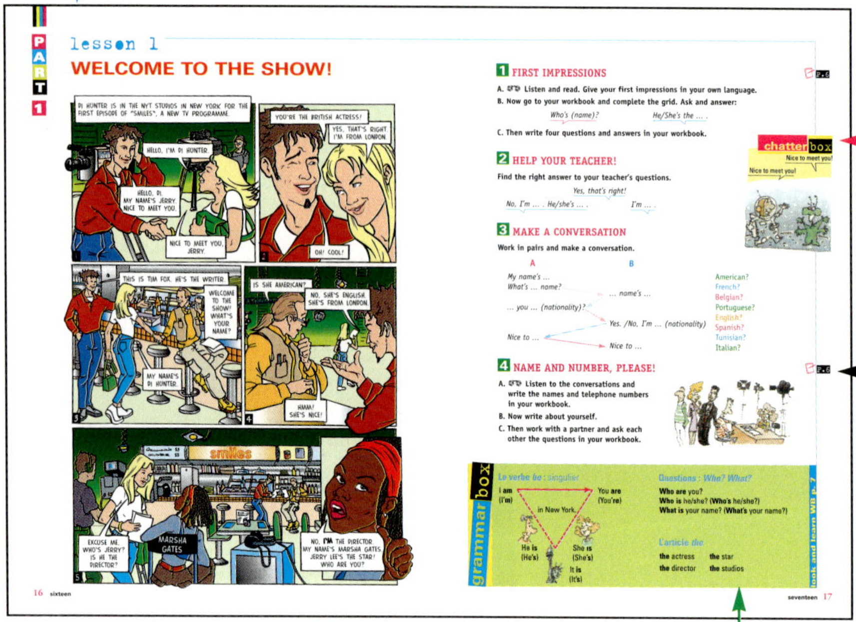
PART 1

lesson 1

WELCOME TO THE SHOW!

16 sixteen

1 FIRST IMPRESSIONS P.6

A. Listen and read. Give your first impressions in your own language.
B. Now go to your workbook and complete the grid. Ask and answer:
Who's (name)? *He/She's the ... .*
C. Then write four questions and answers in your workbook.

chatterbox
Nice to meet you!
Nice to meet you!

2 HELP YOUR TEACHER!

Find the right answer to your teacher's questions.
Yes, that's right!
No, I'm ... . He/she's ... . *I'm ... .*

3 MAKE A CONVERSATION

Work in pairs and make a conversation.

A / B
My name's ...
What's ... name? → *... name's ...*
... you ... (nationality)? → *Yes. /No, I'm ... (nationality)*
Nice to ... → *Nice to ...*

American? French? Belgian? Portuguese? English? Spanish? Tunisian? Italian?

4 NAME AND NUMBER, PLEASE! P.6

A. Listen to the conversations and write the names and telephone numbers in your workbook.
B. Now write about yourself.
C. Then work with a partner and ask each other the questions in your workbook.

grammar box

Le verbe *be* : singulier
I am (I'm) → You are (You're)
in New York.
He is (He's) — She is (She's) — It is (It's)

Questions : *Who? What?*
Who are you?
Who is he/she? (Who's he/she?)
What is your name? (What's your name?)

L'article *the*
the actress — the star
the director — the studios

look and learn WB p. 7

seventeen 17

La chatterbox de chaque lesson t'aidera à retenir des expressions utiles.

Le symbole indique que l'activité se fait à l'aide du WORKBOOK.

La grammarbox résume, avec des exemples, les points de grammaire de chaque leçon.

Dans How to... tu trouveras des conseils pour améliorer ta façon d'apprendre, jeux et activités à l'appui.

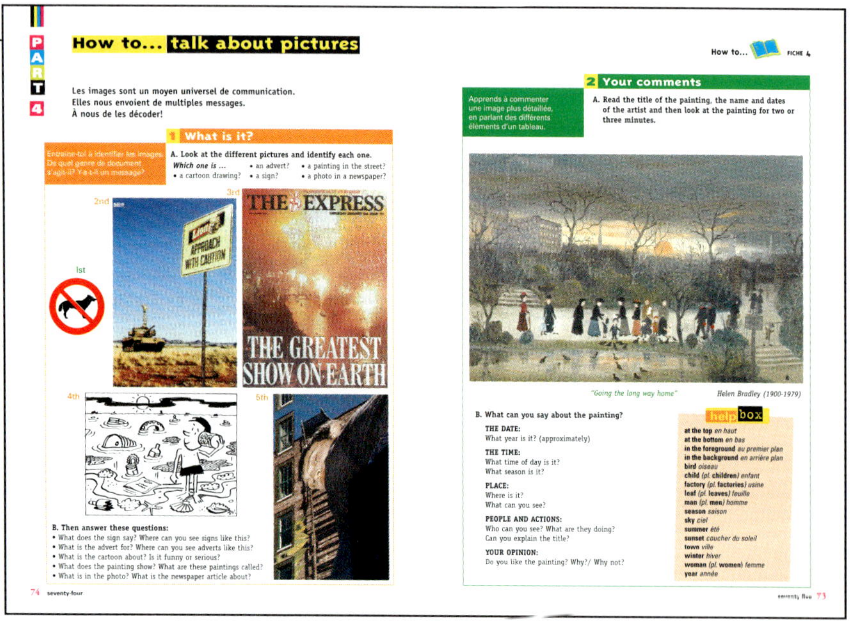
PART 4

How to... talk about pictures

Les images sont un moyen universel de communication.
Elles nous envoient de multiples messages.
À nous de les décoder!

1 What is it?

Entraîne-toi à identifier les images. De quel genre de document s'agit-il? Y-a-t-il un message?

A. Look at the different pictures and identify each one.
Which one is ...
• a cartoon drawing? • an advert? • a sign? • a painting in the street? • a photo in a newspaper?

B. Then answer these questions:
• What does the sign say? Where can you see signs like this?
• What is the advert for? Where can you see adverts like this?
• What is the cartoon about? Is it funny or serious?
• What does the painting show? What are these paintings called?
• What is in the photo? What is the newspaper article about?

74 seventy-four

How to... FICHE 4

2 Your comments

Apprends à commenter une image plus détaillée, en parlant des différents éléments d'un tableau.

A. Read the title of the painting, the name and dates of the artist and then look at the painting for two or three minutes.

"Going the long way home" *Helen Bradley (1900-1979)*

B. What can you say about the painting?
THE DATE:
What year is it? (approximately)
THE TIME:
What time of day is it?
What season is it?
PLACE:
Where is it?
What can you see?
PEOPLE AND ACTIONS:
Who can you see? What are they doing?
Can you explain the title?
YOUR OPINION:
Do you like the painting? Why?/ Why not?

helpbox
at the top *en haut*
at the bottom *en bas*
in the foreground *au premier plan*
in the background *en arrière plan*
bird *oiseau*
child *(pl.* **children**) *enfant*
factory *(pl.* **factories**) *usine*
leaf *(pl.* **leaves**) *feuille*
man *(pl.* **men**) *homme*
season *saison*
sky *ciel*
summer *été*
sunset *coucher du soleil*
town *ville*
winter *hiver*
woman *(pl.* **women**) *femme*
year *année*

seventy-five 75

Les exercices de **Let's practise!** te permettront de t'entraîner et de vérifier tes connaissances.

PART 4

Sounds

1 The silent "r/re"

A. Lorsqu'un mot se termine par **r** ou **re**, cette terminaison ne se prononce pas, sauf si l'on peut faire la liaison avec le mot qui suit. Écoute et entraîne-toi. (Sur la première ligne, les mots de chaque paire se prononcent de façon identique.)

you're/your where/wear hear/hear our/hour
are car near shower

B. Mais on entend bien le **r/re** final si le mot suivant commence par une voyelle, car on fait la liaison. Écoute et entraîne-toi.

1. Your answer is wrong!
2. Where is the airport?
3. Can you hear us?
4. Our address is different.
5. Are all your friends here?
6. The car is outside.
7. Are we near a town?
8. There's a shower upstairs.

2 Stress of long words

Écoute et entraîne-toi à bien marquer l'accent tonique.

L'accent est sur la première syllabe :

• interesting • frightening • difficult
• temperature • probably • popular

L'accent est sur la deuxième syllabe :

• expensive • attractive • computer
• fantastic • remember • photographer

3 "The A-1 rap"

I'm "A-1"! I'm just the best!
I'm bigger and better than all the rest!
I'm taller and faster and heavier too!
I'm much more important than all of you!

Maybe you're bigger and maybe you're fast!
You're the first and we're the last!
But we can tell you how this story ends.
The problem is - you haven't got any friends.

76 seventy-six

Let's practise

Lesson 1 pp. 64-65

A Tu es policier et tu suis un suspect dans New York. Tu parles à un collègue avec ton téléphone portable. Complète ce que tu lui racontes à l'aide des verbes suivants au présent avec be + -ING:
• buy • eat • get • go • happen • leave • look • sit • talk • walk • wear

The suspect ... a black jacket and blue jeans. She ... into an Italian restaurant and she ... to a man. She ... a pizza. Ah! She ... the restaurant with her pizza and she ... to the park. We're in the park now. She ... on the grass and she ... her pizza. Oh! What ...? She ... up! She ... at me! She can see me!

B Regarde les illustrations et réponds aux questions.

1. *Picture 4, page 16.* Who is Tim talking to? Who is he looking at? Can Di hear them?
2. *The small picture, page 33.* Who is Sally talking to? What are they looking at?
3. *Picture 5, page 40.* Who is Marsha talking to? Who is she looking for? Who is she waiting for?
4. *Picture 4, page 64.* Who is James talking to? Who is Di looking at? Can she see Jerry?

C Traduis.

1. "J'entends une voiture!" "C'est notre taxi!"
2. "J'attends Di. Où est-elle?" "Je ne la vois pas!"
3. "Que regardes-tu?" "La carte, mais je ne vois pas l'aeroport."
4. "Est-ce que tu m'entends?" "Pas très bien!"
5. "Vois-tu le policier? Pourquoi nous regarde-t-il?"

Lesson 2 pp. 66-67

D Regarde les quatre photos page 66 et trouve des verbes au présent avec be + -ING (formes affirmative et négative) pour compléter chaque déscription.

1. In the first photo he ... to the crowd. He ... but he ... at the camera.
2. In the second photo he ... next to his father and he ... at the camera. He ... a jacket. He ... jeans.
3. In the third photo he ... a car and he ... next to a driving instructor. They ... .
4. In the fourth photo he ... a young woman but he ... at the camera and he ... .

E Tu es vendeur/vendeuse dans une boutique de farces et attrapes. Tu essaies de persuader une cliente à acheter! Réagis à ce qu'elle te dit avec une phrase au superlatif avec le même adjectif qu'elle emploie. Voici un exemple :
Customer: The sun mask is very attractive, isn't it?
You: *Yes, it's the most attractive mask in the shop!*

1. The clown trousers are quite funny, aren't they?
2. The Chaplin mask is very realistic, isn't it?
3. The Princess costume is very pretty, isn't it?
4. The Pirate hat is very nice, isn't it?
5. The chimpanzee mask is amusing, isn't it?
6. The E. T. costume is good, isn't it?

F Complète chaque phrase avec une "question tag" et puis complète chaque réponse courte.

1. Prince William's quite tall, ... ? Yes, ...
2. The masks are original, ... ? Yes, ...
3. Rob and Carole aren't in London, ... ? No, ... !
4. "Smiles" is a TV series, ... ? Yes, ...
5. Jerry isn't Di's boyfriend, ... ? No, ...!
6. James is English, ... ? Yes, ...

Lesson 3 pp. 70-71

G Regarde l'information dans 1B p. 70 et trouve les réponses aux questions suivantes:

1. Which animal is faster than a pig but slower than an elephant?
2. Which animals aren't as fast as a rabbit but faster than a camel?
3. Which animal is the fastest in the world?
4. Is a human being faster or slower than a cat? Can you remember?

H Regarde à nouveau les photos de gens célèbres, page 32. Pour chacune des phrases suivantes, trouve une autre manière de dire exactement la même chose. Nous te donnons le début de chaque phrase.

1. Celine Dion is older than Ewan McGregor.
Ewan McGregor isn't ...
2. Celine Dion isn't as tall as Nicole Kidman.
Nicole Kidman is ...
3. Ewan McGregor is shorter than Liam Neeson.
Liam Neeson is ...
4. Ewan McGregor is much younger than Liam Neeson.
Liam Neeson is ...

I Regarde les photos dans The Crazy World of Sport, pp. 68-69. Compare chaque fois les deux sports en utilisant le comparatif d'un de ces adjectifs : • amusing • difficult • dangerous • exciting • easy

1. bungy-jumping & surfing.
2. rodeos & human table football
3. scuba-diving & snow-rafting
4. frisbee & cricket
5. ballooning & snow-rafting

Lesson 4 pp. 72-73

J Relis les questions sur Dylan (2A p. 72). Lis les réponses ci-dessous et trouve la question qui correspond à chaque réponse. Ecris les questions et les réponses.

1. No, it's much more difficult.
2. Because it's too late.
3. Because he must finish his Maths homework.
4. Very tired.
5. Because he's doing the wrong exercise.
6. Yes, it's half past ten.

K Pour chaque phrase (1 à 5) trouve la réponse (A à E).

1. I don't feel very well.
2. How do you feel?
3. Do you feel all right?
4. You look tired.
5. Have you got a temperature?

A. Yes, I feel fine. Do I look ill?
B. Oh? What's the matter? You look fine!
C. Tired. I must go to bed.
D. Perhaps. I feel very hot!
E. I know. I feel tired.

L Reformule chaque phrase en utilisant must ou mustn't :

1. Don't speak French! Speak English!
2. Don't write in your book! Write in your workbook!
3. You can't stay in bed! Get up!
4. You can't leave now! Help me with my homework!
5. You can't eat in the library! Go outside!
6. Don't move! Dial 999 and wait for the ambulance!

seventy-seven 77

La partie **Sounds** propose une variété d'activités avec – à chaque fois – un "rap" pour t'aider à mieux prononcer.

Dans les pages de **Spread your wings** tu découvriras la civilisation et l'actualité des pays anglophones.

LE WORKBOOK

Les activités de **CLASSWORK** te permettront de participer activement à chaque étape du cours et de garder une trace écrite de tout ton travail.

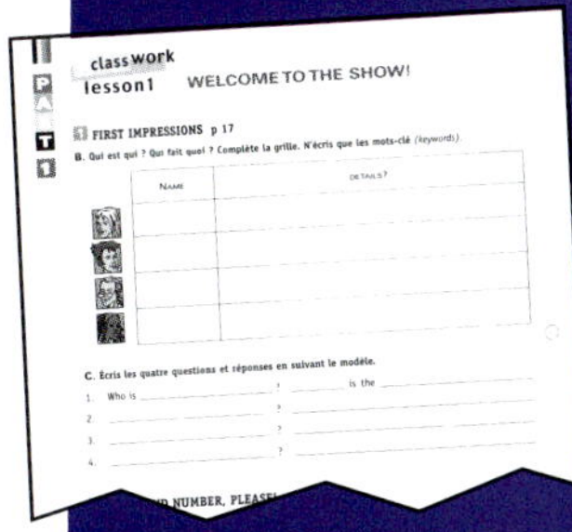

La rubrique **LOOK AND LEARN** t'aidera à observer et réfléchir sur les points grammaticaux nouveaux.

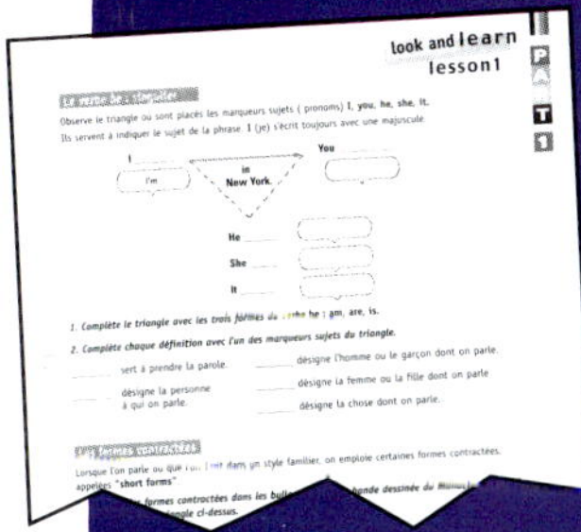

Tu compléteras **YOUR WORD BANK** à la fin de chaque leçon. Cette banque de vocabulaire se trouve à la fin du Workbook.

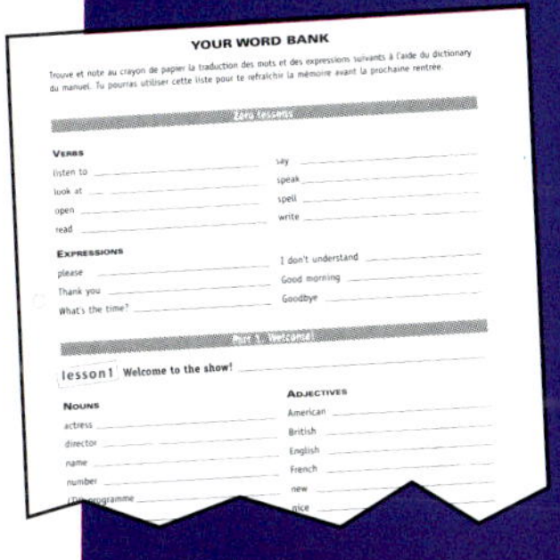

SPEAK ENGLISH! DON'T SPEAK FRENCH!

WORKBOOK P.4

FOLLOW THE INSTRUCTIONS!

WORKBOOK P.5

A. Open your books!

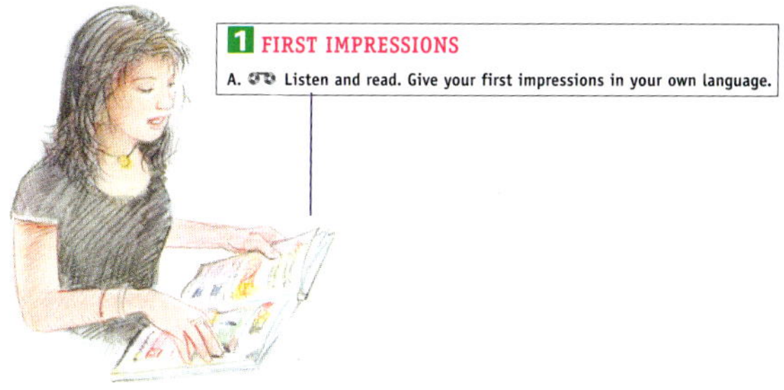

B. Read the instructions!

C. Look at the picture!

D. Talk about the picture!

E. Listen to the tape!

F. Ask and answer questions!

G. Don't write in your textbooks, write in your workbooks!

H. Close your books!

grammar box

Donner un ordre : (V = la base verbale)

V!	Don't + V!
Speak English!	**Don't speak** French!
Write in your workbooks.	**Don't write** in your textbooks.
Close your books!	**Don't open** your books!

look and learn WB p. 5

LEARN THE ENGLISH ALPHABET!

WORKBOOK P.6

1. LISTEN AND SING!

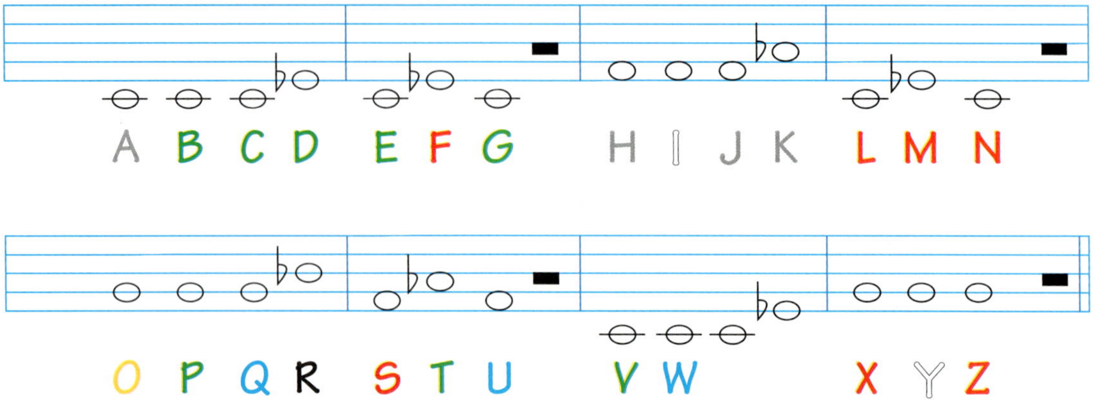

2. READ

a. Read the GREY letters, the GREEN letters, the RED letters, the WHITE letters, the YELLOW letters, the BLUE letters and the BLACK letter.

b. Now read the alphabet from A to Z.

c. Write the colours in your workbook.

3. READ AND WRITE

a. Read these abbreviations.

b. Complete the words in your workbook.

TV USA DJ CD UK GB

4. WORDS AND SOUNDS

a. Listen to these words and practise the sounds.

1 [ɒ] stop, spot	10 [ɪə] theatre, hero
2 [iː] team, metre	11 [e] web, centre
3 [æ] match, taxi	12 [aɪ] site, style
4 [ɪ] film, biscuit	13 [ɛə] square, pair
5 [əu] phone, show	14 [ɑː] dance, star
6 [ɜː] world, person	15 [eɪ] date, skate
7 [ɔː] sport, board	16 [ʌ] jungle, bus
8 [u] foot, look	17 [au] round, mouse
9 [uː] zoo, group	18 [ɔ] boy, toy

b. Can you spell the words? Ask and answer:

Can you spell...? *Yes! ...*

c. Go to your workbook and follow the instructions.

WHAT'S THE TIME?

WORKBOOK P.7

1. LOOK AND LISTEN

Listen and look at the digital clocks. Practise the times.
Then say the times in chronological order!

08:00
It's **eight** *o'clock*.

09:10
It's *ten past* **nine**.

16:15
It's *quarter past* **four**.

11:20
It's *twenty past* **eleven**.

06:25
It's *twenty-five past* **six**.

7:30
It's *half past* **seven**.

11:35
It's *twenty-five to* **twelve**.

12.45
It's *quarter to* **one**.

14:55
It's *five to* **three**.

2. LISTEN AND TICK

Listen and look at the clocks in your workbook. What's the time?

WHAT'S THE DATE?

WORKBOOK P.7

It's (day) **, the** (number) **of** (month).

LISTEN TO THE DATES

Listen and practise the examples.
Then go to your workbook and tick the dates you hear.

DAYS	NUMBERS		MONTHS
Monday	1st first	17th seventeeth	January
Tuesday	2nd second	18th eighteenth	February
Wednesday	3rd third	19th nineteenth	March
Thursday	4th fourth	20th twentieth	April
Friday	5th fifth	21st twenty-first	May
Saturday	6th sixth	22nd twenty-second	June
Sunday	7th seventh	23rd twenty-third	July
	8th eighth	24th twenty-fourth	August
	9th ninth	25th twenty-fifth	September
	10th tenth	26th twenty-sixth	October
	11th eleventh	27th twenty-seventh	November
	12th twelfth	28th twenty-eighth	December
	13th thirteenth	29th twenty-ninth	
	14th fourteenth	30th thirtieth	
	15th fifteenth	31st thirty-first	
	16th sixteenth		

1

2

3

4

5

PART 1

WELCOME!

PART 1

lesson 1

WELCOME TO THE SHOW!

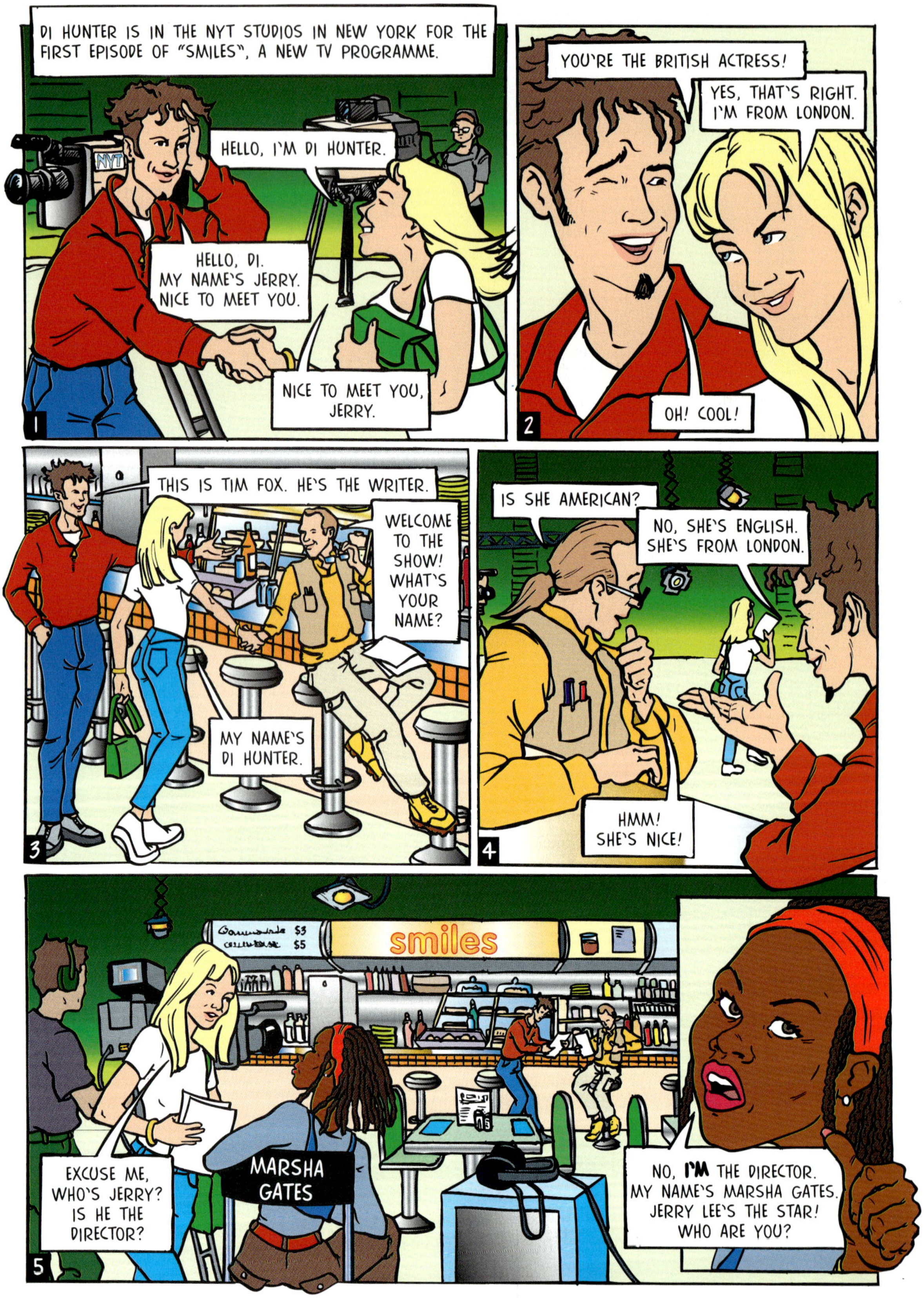

1 FIRST IMPRESSIONS

P.8

A. Listen and read. Give your first impressions in your own language.

B. Now go to your workbook and complete the grid. Ask and answer:

Who's (name)? *He/She's the … .*

C. Then write four questions and answers in your workbook.

chatterbox

Nice to meet you!

Nice to meet you!

2 HELP YOUR TEACHER!

Find the right answer to your teacher's questions.

Yes, that's right!

No, I'm … . He/she's … . *I'm … .*

3 MAKE A CONVERSATION

Work in pairs and make a conversation.

A	B
My name's …	
What's … name?	*… name's …*
… you … (nationality)?	*Yes. /No, I'm … (nationality)*
Nice to …	*Nice to …*

American?
French?
Belgian?
Portuguese?
English?
Spanish?
Tunisian?
Italian?

4 NAME AND NUMBER, PLEASE!

P.8

A. Listen to the conversations and write the names and telephone numbers in your workbook.

B. Now write about yourself.

C. Then work with a partner and ask each other the questions in your workbook.

grammar box

Le verbe *be* : singulier

I am (I'm) — **You are** (You're) — in New York.

He is (He's) — **She is** (She's) — **It is** (It's)

Questions : *Who? What?*

Who are you?
Who is he/she? (**Who's** he/she?)
What is your name? (**What's** your name?)

L'article *the*

the actress — **the** star
the director — **the** studios

look and learn WB p. 9

lesson 2

WHERE ARE THEY?

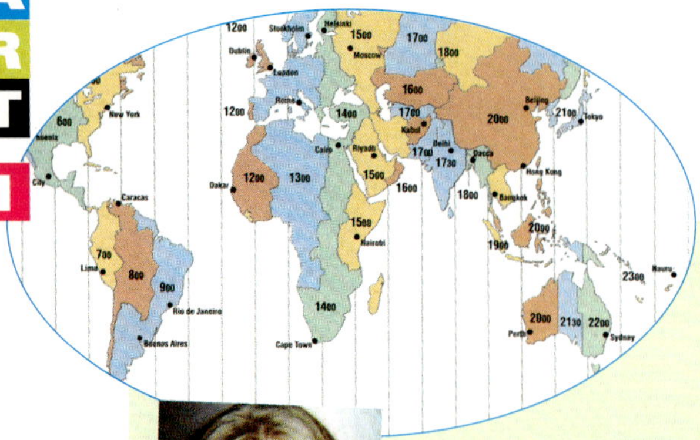

It is eight o'clock in the morning in New York. **Di Hunter** is an actress. She is at work in the NYT studios.

It is one o'clock in the afternoon in London. **Mr and Mrs Hunter** are Di's parents. They are at work at Camden Hospital. Di's father is a doctor. His first name is Colin. Di's mother is a nurse. Her first name is June.

Sally Hunter is Di's sister. She is at school. She is a pupil at Acland Burghley School in London. She is with her friends.

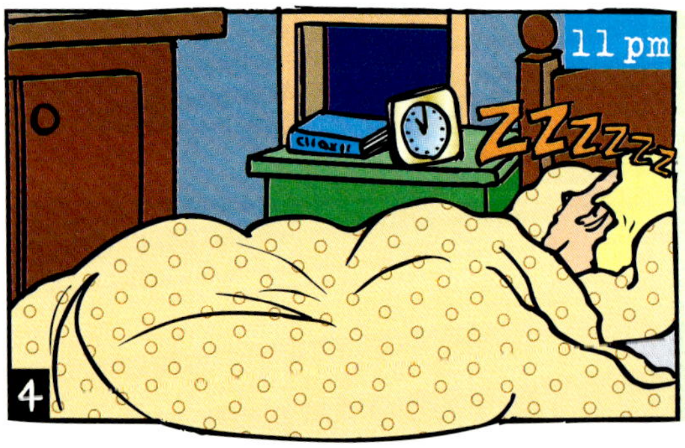

It is eleven o'clock in the evening in Sydney. **Rob Hunter** is Di's brother. He is a journalist in Australia. He is at home in bed and he is asleep!

1 READING AND LISTENING

P.10

A. Read about Di's family and go to your workbook.

B. Now listen. Can you hear the short forms?

C. Read the questions and find the answers in the text.
Write your answers in your workbook.

1. Who are Colin and June?
2. Where are they?
3. What is the time?
4. Who is Rob?
5. Where is he?
6. What is the time?

D. Ask and answer three questions about Sally.

2 LISTEN AND WRITE

P.11

Listen. Can you answer the questions?
Then complete the questions and answers in your workbook.

What's her job?

What's his name?

3 LISTEN AND COMPLETE

A. Listen to the telephone conversation and answer the questions.

1. Where is Rob?
2. Where are his Mum and Dad?
3. What is the time in London?
4. Who is asleep?
5. What is the time in Sydney?

B. Now listen again and complete the conversation in your workbook.

P.11

grammar box

Le verbe *be* : pluriel

We **are** (We'**re**) → You **are** (You'**re**) → They **are** (They'**re**)

at school.

Déterminants possessifs

My → Your → His / Her

school is in London.

Le génitif : *'s*

Di**'s** parents are at home.
Sally**'s** school is in London.

L'article : *a/an*

Sally is **a** pupil.
Colin is **a** doctor.
Di is **an** actress.

Questions : *Where?*

Where are they?
They are (They're) in London.
Where is (Where's) Sydney?
It is (It's) in Australia.

look and learn WB pp. 12-13

PART 1

spread your wings 1

WHAT'S THE WEATHER LIKE TODAY?

P.14

"Good morning everyone. What's the weather like in Europe today?

Well, in Ireland, the north of the United Kingdom, Denmark, Sweden and Finland, it's sunny but it's very cold with temperatures of eight degrees, and it's very windy over the North Sea.

In the south of the UK and the north of France it's very cloudy and quite cold, about twelve degrees, and it's raining in Belgium and the Netherlands. So, if you're in that part of the world today, remember your umbrella!

In Portugal, Spain and the south of France it's cloudy but quite warm with temperatures of eighteen degrees. It's quite windy over the Mediterranean.

To the east, from the north of Germany, through Luxembourg and Austria to Italy, it's fine and sunny and it's quite hot in Greece with temperatures of about twenty-three degrees.

That's all from me. Have a nice day!"

FLAGS OF THE E.U.* COUNTRIES

Austrian
Belgian
British
Danish
Dutch
European
Finnish
French
German
Greek
Irish
Italian
Luxembourgeois
Portuguese
Spanish
Swedish

* The European Union (in 2000)

What's the capital of ... (country)?

What colour is the (nationality) *flag?*

What's the weather like in ... (country/city)?

Where's (city)*?*

PART 1

lesson 3

WHAT'S THE MATTER?

Di Hunter is in her dressing-room at the studios. She is with Helen from the costume department.

Helen: Hi, I'm Helen.
Are you Di Hunter?
Di: Yes, I am.
Helen: Well, this is for you, Di.
Di: Is it my costume?
Helen: Yes, it is.

Di: What is it?
Helen: It's a sweater.
Di: But it's very big!
And what are they?
Helen: They're jeans.
Di: Er… thank you.

Helen: Is the sweater okay?
Di: No, it isn't! It's too big!
Helen: Are the jeans okay?
Di: No, they aren't! Look!
They're too long!

Marsha: Are you ready, Jerry?
Jerry: No, I'm not!
Marsha: What's the matter?
Jerry: Look!
Marsha: But it isn't your sweater, Jerry, and they aren't your jeans! HELEN!

1 FIRST IMPRESSIONS

A. Listen to the conversations and look at the pictures. Look at picture two.
What colour is the sweater? What colour are the jeans?
Now ask the same questions about picture four.

B. Listen again. Look at the adjectives in the chatterbox and ask and answer:
What's the matter with the yellow sweater?
What's the matter with the black jeans?

chatterbox

What's the matter?
It's/They're too ...
BIG
LONG
SHORT
SMALL

2 FIND THE ANSWERS

A. Listen to the questions, look at the pictures on the left-hand page and find the correct short answer.

Yes, she is. *No, it isn't.* *No, he isn't.*
Yes, it is. *Yes, they are.* *No, they aren't.*

B. Then complete the questions and answers in your workbook. P.15

C. Listen again and practise.

3 COLOURS AND CLOTHES

A. Listen and look at the girl and the boy. Ask and answer.

What colour is/are ... ? *It's/they're ... .*

The girl's shoes are black,
her socks are white
and her skirt is green.
Her jacket is black,
her T-shirt is grey
and her hat is pink.

The boy's trainers are white
and his trousers are blue.
His shirt is yellow and blue.
His anorak is brown
and his hat is red.

B. PAIRWORK. Now do the activities in your workbook. P.15

grammar box

L'article *a*/*an*:	What **is it?**	– It's **a** sweater. It's **an** anorak.
L'article *zéro* (ø) + nom pluriel:	What **are they?**	– They're **Ø shoes**. They're **Ø jeans**.
La forme négative du verbe *be*:	It **is not** (It **isn't**) your sweater. They **are not** (They **aren't**) my jeans.	

Questions et réponses courtes

Is it too big? – **Yes**, it **is**./– **No**, it **isn't**.
Are you Di Hunter? – **Yes**, I **am**.
Are they too long? – **Yes**, they **are**./ – **No**, they **aren't**.
Are you ready, Jerry? – **No**, I'm **not**!

look and learn WB p. 16

lesson 4

"LET'S GO TO CENTRAL PARK!"

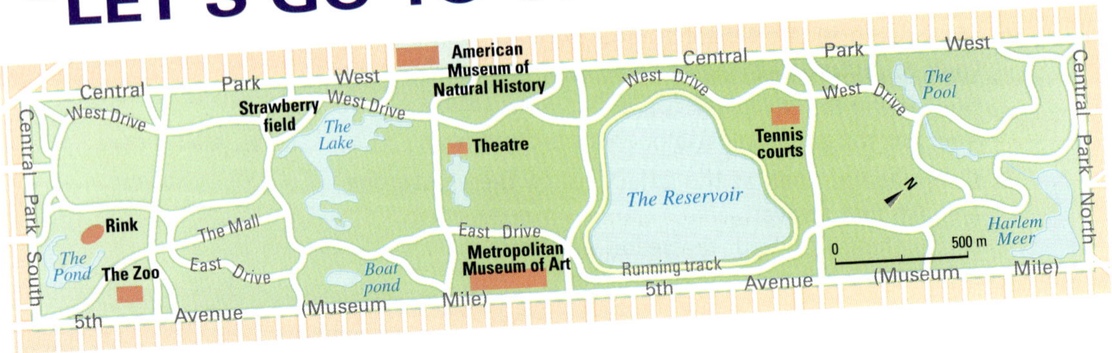

1 There are always a lot of people on the grass in the summer...

CENTRAL PARK is in the centre of Manhattan. The park is very big – about 4 square kilometres. There are about 500,000 trees and a lot of open spaces. The park is very popular with tourists and New Yorkers. **WHY?**

2 ... and a lot of people on the rink in the winter.

BECAUSE YOU CAN DO A LOT OF INTERESTING THINGS...

You can picnic or play your favourite ball games on the grass. You can take a boat on the lakes. You can ice-skate on the rink. There are tennis courts and you can jog on the running track around the reservoir.
If it is sunny, you can sit on the grass and look at the skyscrapers around the park. The views are fantastic!

3 You can rollerblade and cycle on the roads at weekends.

YOU CAN SEE A LOT OF INTERESTING THINGS TOO!

There is a zoo and a theatre and there are two museums: the famous Metropolitan Museum of Art ("The Met") and the enormous American Museum of Natural History with 36 million exhibits including dinosaurs and meteorites! Music fans can listen to concerts at weekends and visit a memorial to John Lennon in Strawberry Field.

PART 1

1 READ AND PREPARE

P.18

A. You can prepare this lesson at home!
Go to your workbook and follow the instructions.

B. Compare your lists of vocabulary. Ask each other questions:

What's the English word for ...?

C. Then listen to the text and practise these words.
The stress is on the first syllable.

- centre
- interesting
- dinosaurs
- thousand
- favourite
- music
- spaces
- theatre
- concert
- popular
- famous
- visit

chatterbox

2 NAMES AND NUMBERS

NAMES

1. What is the park called? *(It's called ...)*
2. What are the inhabitants of New York called? *(They're called ...)*

NUMBERS

3. How many trees are there in the park? *(There are ...)*
4. How many museums are there in the park?
5. How many exhibits are there in the American Museum of Natural History?

3 HOW MUCH CAN YOU SAY?

P.19

A. What can you do in Central Park? Make 5 questions and answers with the words in the boxes. Then write them in your workbook.

Can you	skate play tennis picnic jog cycle	in the park?	Yes, there's Yes, there are	tennis courts. a running track. a lot of roads. a rink. a lot of open spaces.

B. Why is Central Park very popular? Work in groups and write three sentences in your workbook. Then exchange your ideas.

It's popular because ... *you can ...* *there is a ...* *there are ...*

grammar box

There is / There are

There is a theatre.
There are Ø tennis courts.
How many trees **are there**?

There is a zoo.
There are two museums.
About five hundred thousand. (500,000)

There is a memorial.
There are a lot of **people**.

Le modal *can* + V

What **can** you **do**?
You **can do** a lot of things.

Can you **skate** in the park?
Music fans **can listen** to concerts.

look and learn WB p. 20

P A R T 1

How to... listen

Ce n'est qu'en écoutant que l'on apprend à écouter !
Entraîne-toi avec ces quatre activités !

1 First impressions

Il est très rare d'écouter une conversation sans avoir une idée du contexte.
Dans ta classe d'anglais, entraîne-toi à imaginer ce qui se passe, avant d'écouter l'enregistrement, *en regardant les images.*
Place? Time? People? Actions?

A. Look at the picture and give your first impressions in your own language. What can you say in English?

Avant d'écouter, *ferme ton livre.* Il est plus facile de suivre l'évolution de la situation et d'en découvrir la « chute », en te concentrant uniquement sur ce que tu entends.

B. Close your books and listen. Are you surprised? Explain why in your own language.

2 In the dark

Quelquefois on écoute « dans le noir » - sans aucun indice. Ceci peut aussi arriver dans ta classe d'anglais !
Les bruits d'ambiance et/ou les mots-clé peuvent t'aider à identifier le genre de message et à en capter l'essentiel.

A. Close your books and listen. Follow your teacher's instructions!

B. Now listen again and find the right description.

It's...
a. a TV show
b. an announcement in an airport
c. a recorded phone message
d. a sports commentary

C. Listen again and find:

1. sport? teams? score?
2. name? phone number?
3. show? group?
4. flight number? destination?

3 Attitudes

Pendant l'écoute essaie de repérer *les mots-clé* qui t'aident à capter l'essentiel même si tu ne comprends pas tout !

A. **Listen to the three conversations.**
Listen for the keywords.
Where are the people in each conversation?
Choose from A, B or C.

A in a hospital

B at home

C in a restaurant

Sois aussi très attentif à *l'intonation* de la voix. Elle te renseignera sur les *attitudes* des personnes.

B. **Listen again and find the right adjective to describe the attitude of each person.**

The man/boy/woman/girl is ... .

amused

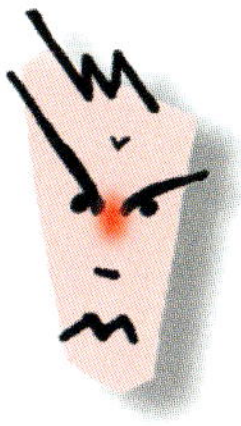

angry

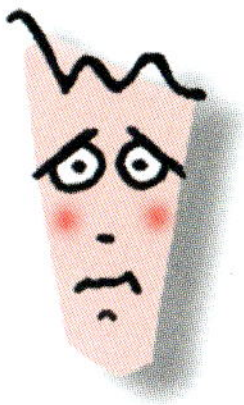

embarrassed

frightened

happy

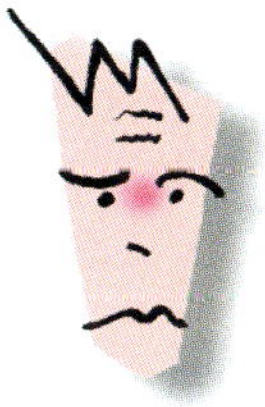

worried

4 Statements

Pendant l'écoute d'une conversation essaie aussi d'identifier le type de phrase. S'agit-t-il d'une phrase affirmative, négative ou interrogative ? S'agit-il d'une salutation ? Entraîne-toi en écoutant ces exemples que nous avons sélectionnés parmi les phrases entendues dans **Part 1**.

A. **Listen to the sentences.**
For each sentence choose the correct symbol.

Is it an affirmative sentence? ✔

Is it a negative sentence? ✗

Is it an interrogative sentence? ?

Is it a greeting?

B. **Listen again and practise the intonation.**

Sounds

1 Vowel sounds

Lis chaque groupe de mots et trouve l'intrus qui n'a pas le même son-voyelle que les autres mots.

1. be	jeans	his	he	green
2. nice	big	fine	my	time
3. who	you	do	blue	go
4. they	home	name	eight	skate
5. her	girl	work	first	where
6. what	from	small	lot	job

Ensuite écoute et vérifie si tu as eu raison.

2 Stress

Un mot peut comporter des syllabes accentuées (●) et des syllabes non-accentuées (•).
Lis chaque mot en faisant attention à l'accent tonique.

● • (l'accent est sur la première syllabe):

actress	**pu**pil	**Brit**ish
colour	**num**ber	**an**swer

• ● (l'accent est sur la deuxième syllabe):

hel**lo**	as**leep**	mu**se**um
a**bout**	to**day**	good**bye**

Ensuite écoute et entraîne-toi.

3 "The weekday rap"

It's **Mon**day **mor**ning! **Look** at the **rain**!

Tuesday, **Wednes**day, it's **rain**ing a**gain**!

Thursday's **wind**y,

Friday **too**!

Saturday's **sun**ny.

Hey! That's **cool**!

On **Sat**urday and **Sun**day we **aren't** at **school**!

Have a **nice** week**end**!

Let's practise!

lesson 1 pp. 16-17

A Observe le modèle et réponds aux questions en utilisant les formes pleines de be:

Is Jerry the writer? No/the star.
No, he is the star.

1. Is Jerry from San Francisco? No/New York
2. Is Marsha Spanish? No/American
3. Is Di English? Yes/from London
4. Is Tim the director? No/the writer
5. Are you American? No/...

B Retrouve les formes contractées:

1. My name is David Fuller.
2. I am in the NYT studios.
3. Who is Pierce Brosnan?
4. What is your telephone number?
5. She is the director.
6. Jerry is the star.

C Écris cinq phrases que tu peux dire à quelqu'un:

1. pour lui demander son nom,
2. pour savoir s'il est anglais,
3. pour lui dire ton nom,
4. pour lui dire ta nationalité,
5. pour lui dire que tu es enchanté(e) de faire sa connaissance.

lesson 2 pp. 18-19

**D Relis la conversation téléphonique dans ton workbook p. 11.
Copie les questions ci-dessous en retrouvant les formes contractées possibles.
Ensuite écris tes réponses.**

1. Where is Rob?
2. Where are his parents?
3. What is the time in London?
4. Who is asleep?
5. What is the time in Sydney?

E Complète les phrases suivantes avec **a** ou **an**:

1. Jerry Lee is ... American star.
2. Di Hunter is ... British actress.
3. Marsha Gates is ... director.
4. Tim Fox is ... writer.
5. Acland Burghley is ... English school.

F Complète les questions et les réponses avec les mots qui manquent: **who, where, what, he's, it's, they're**.

1. ... is the time? – ... 8 o'clock.
2. ... is Sydney? – ... in Australia.
3. ... are the NYT studios? – ... in New York.
4. ... are Mr and Mrs Hunter? – ... Di's parents.
5. ... is Rob? – ... Di's brother.

G Complète les phrases en trouvant les mots qui manquent. Écris les phrases en retrouvant la forme pleine du verbe **be**:

1. He's a journalist in Sydney. ... name's ... .
2. She's Di's sister. ... name's ... .
3. He's the star in "Smiles". ... name's ... .
4. She's a nurse. She's Di's ... . name's ... .
5. He's a ... . Di's father. ... name's ... .
6. This is Mr and ... Hunter. They're Di's ... .

lesson 3 pp. 22-23

H Écris chaque phrase au pluriel.

1. It isn't my sock. It's your sock.
2. What is it? Is it a T-shirt?
3. Is he your friend? Is he at your school?
4. The girl isn't English. She's American.

i Trouve la bonne réponse (A>E) à chaque question:

1. What is it?
2. What are they?
3. Where's Di?
4. What's the matter?
5. Who's Di?

A. In her dressing room.
B. It isn't my costume!
C. She's an actress.
D. A TV programme.
E. My new jeans.

J Relis le texte p. 22 et réponds par une réponse courte:

1. Is Helen an actress?
2. Is she from the costume department?
3. Are Di and Jerry at the studios?
4. Are the black jeans Jerry's jeans?
5. Is the yellow sweater too small for Jerry?
6. Is the red and white sweater too small for Jerry?

lesson 4 pp. 24-25

K Complète chaque phrase avec des mots nouveaux de la leçon 4:

1. ... are a lot of people on the rink in the ... .
2. You can ... on the rink and you can rollerblade on the ... .
3. Music fans can ... to concerts at the ... .
4. ... are about five hundred thousand ... in the park.
5. You ... see a lot of interesting ... .

L Retrouve les questions en mettant les mots dans l'ordre. Ensuite relis le texte p. 24 et réponds aux questions:

1. can/skate/in/people/the/why/winter?
2. park/how many/are/the/in/museums/there?
3. tourists/why/the/popular/park/is/with?
4. can/you/where/picnic?
5. park/are/in/trees/there/how many/the?

M Réponds par une phrase complète en parlant de l'endroit où tu habites:

1. What is your town called?
2. How many inhabitants are there?
3. Is there a park?
4. How many cinemas are there?
5. How many schools are there?
6. How many restaurants are there?
7. What can you do at weekends?

2

FAMILIES

1

5

PART 2

AND FRIENDS

3

4

PART 2

lesson 1

WHO'S THAT?

NAME: **NICOLE KIDMAN** DATE OF BIRTH: **20/06/67**
NATIONALITY: **AUSTRALIAN** HAIR: **RED** EYES: **BLUE**
PROFESSION: **ACTRESS** HEIGHT: **1m 75**

P.25

1 WHAT ARE THEY LIKE?

A. What can you say about the person in the photo?

B. Now read the details in the box and the short description below.

Nicole Kidman is
a well-known
Australian actress.
She has got long red hair
and big blue eyes
and she is quite tall.

C. Ask and answer the questions and then write the answers in your workbook.

1. Who's Nicole Kidman? – She's *(nationality/profession)*.
2. What's she like? – She's got *(hair and eyes)*.
3. How tall is she? – She's one metre *(height)*.
4. How old is she? – She's *(age)*.

D. Work in pairs and ask and answer the same questions about the three people below. Then write a description of your favourite actor, actress or singer.

NAME: **EWAN McGREGOR**
NATIONALITY: **SCOTTISH**
PROFESSION: **ACTOR**
DATE OF BIRTH: **31/03/71**
HAIR: **FAIR**
EYES: **BLUE**
HEIGHT: **1m 78**

NAME: **CELINE DION**
NATIONALITY: **CANADIAN**
PROFESSION: **SINGER**
DATE OF BIRTH: **30/03/68**
HAIR: **BROWN**
EYES: **BROWN**
HEIGHT: **1m 71**

NAME: **LIAM NEESON**
NATIONALITY: **IRISH**
PROFESSION: **ACTOR**
DATE OF BIRTH: **07/06/52**
HAIR: **BROWN**
EYES: **BLUE**
HEIGHT: **1m 92**

2 FIRST IMPRESSIONS

Listen to the first part of the conversation and answer these questions.

1. Who is Sally with?
2. What is the date today?
3. Why is it a special day for Sally?
4. How old is she?
5. What has she got from her sister?

3 BROTHERS AND SISTERS

P.25

A. Now listen to the second part of the conversation and complete the grid in your workbook.

B. Ask and answer questions about Sally, Dylan and Lucy.

Has ... (name) got any brothers or sisters? — *Yes, he/she has.* / *No, he/she hasn't.*

Who's ... (name)? — *He/She's ... (name)'s sister/brother.*

How old is ... (name)? — *He/She's ... (age).*

C. Then complete the four questions and answers in your workbook.

chatter box

Who's that? — **It**'s my sister.

What's that? — **It**'s a birthday card.

4 WHAT ABOUT YOU?

P.26

Work in pairs and complete the questionnaire in your workbook. Then exchange information in class.

Have you got any brothers or sisters?

grammar box

Have got : singulier

I have got (I'**ve got**) — blue eyes. — **You have got** (You'**ve got**)

He has got (He'**s got**)
She has got (She'**s got**)

Have I got — blue eyes or grey eyes? — **Have you got**

Has he got
Has she got

***Any* + N** pluriel — **Have you got any** brothers? – Yes, I **have**./– No, I **haven't**.
She has not (**hasn't**) **got any** brothers or sisters.

How old/tall...? : **How old are you?** — **I am fifteen.**
How tall is she? — **She is one metre sixty-five.**

look and learn WB pp. 26-27

PART 2

lesson 2

AT HOME

THE HUNTERS' HOUSE

Sally and her parents, Mr and Mrs Hunter, live in an old house near the hospital in Camden. It is a big house with a garage and a nice garden. It has got four bedrooms and two bathrooms. The Hunters like their house but it is too big now because Di and Rob do not live at home!

THE TATES' FLAT...

Dylan's family, the Tates, live in a modern flat opposite a park in Camden. Their flat is on the top floor. It is small but very sunny and there is a nice view of the park. They have got three bedrooms and one bathroom. Mr and Mrs Tate like their flat but it is not very big for a family with four children!

P.28

1 READ AND FIND OUT

A. Look at the two pictures and read the first paragraph.
Find the answers to these questions.

1. Do the Hunters live in a house or a flat?
2. Where is it?
3. What is it like?
4. How many bedrooms are there?
5. How many bathrooms has it got?
6. What is the problem?

B. Now read the second paragraph and ask the same questions about the Tates.

C. Listen and choose the right short answer.

Yes, they do. *No, they don't.*

Then complete the questions and answers in your workbook.

2 AT SALLY'S

P.28

Look at the plans of the Hunters' house.

A. Listen to the questions and practise the answers. Then continue!

Where's the living-room?

It's downstairs on the right.

Where's Sally's bedroom?

It's upstairs on the left.

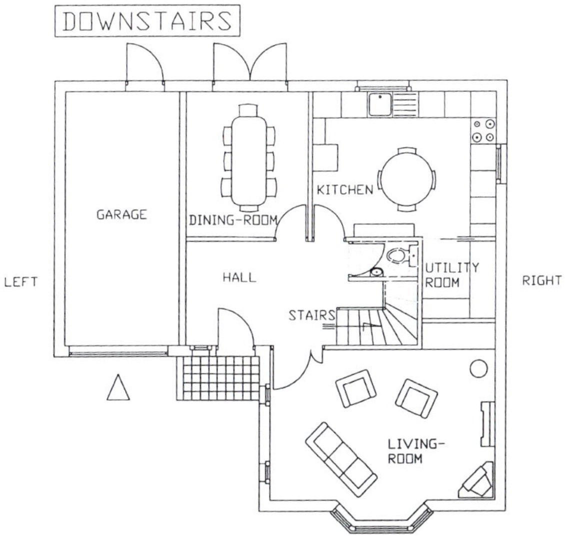

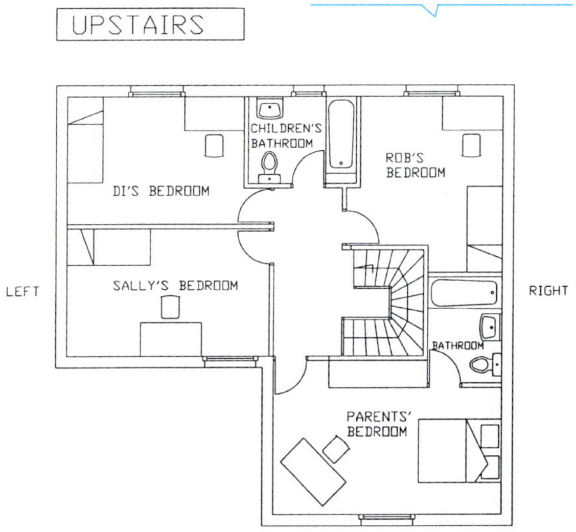

B. Look at these prepositions and use them to complete the sentences in your workbook.

above under next to between in front of behind

3 WHAT ABOUT YOU?

P.28

Make conversations like these. Then write about where you live in your workbook.

Do you live in a house or a flat? — *I live in a ... .*

Do you live near our school? — *Yes, I do./No, I don't. I live near/next to/opposite ... .*

grammar box

Le présent simple

They live in Camden. **They like** their house. **Di and Rob do not** (do**n't**) **live** at home now.

Do you live in a house or a flat? — **I live** in a flat.

Do you live near the school? — Yes, **I do**. / No, **I don't**.

Le génitif : *'s* ou *'*

N singulier : Sally**'s** bedroom — N pluriel irrégulier : the children**'s** bathroom

N pluriel qui se termine en ***s*** : the Hunters**'** house; her parents**'** bedroom

Pour traduire **"chez"** : at Sally**'s**; at the Hunters**'**

look and learn WB p. 29

LIFE AT AN ENGLISH SCHOOL

What is life like at an English secondary school?
Is it very different from life at your school?

Acland Burghley is a mixed state school.

1 London is a multi-ethnic city. Pupils here come from many different countries.

2 All English schools teach I.T. (Information Technology). This school has got 130 computers linked to the Internet.

3 All the pupils participate on Sports Day, in June.

Newstead Wood

is a girls' state school for very good pupils. It is called a grammar school.

4 There are school orchestras.

5 Drama is a school subject and there are school productions.

6 Hockey is a popular sport for girls.

Millfield
is a mixed independent school.

7 There are boarders at Millfield. This room is for two girls.

8 School clubs offer a lot of different activities *after* school: photography, music, games, computing...

9 The swimming pool...

10 ... and the school library.

Trinity is a boys' independent school.

11 Trinity pupils wear a uniform with a school blazer and badge, and a school tie.

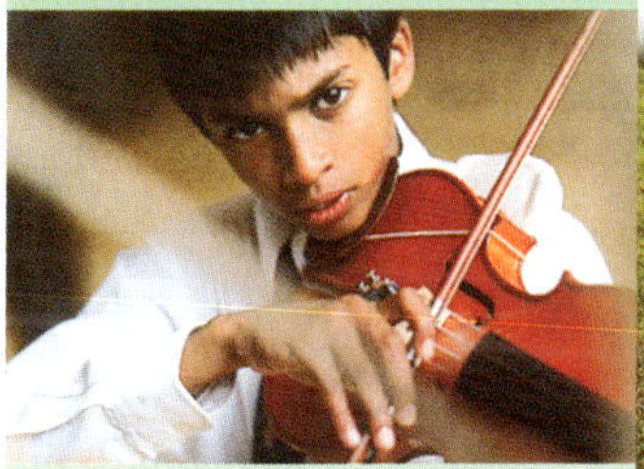

12 At all English schools, you can learn to play a musical instrument.

13 School teams play against other schools. Rugby and cricket are traditional sports for boys.

PART 2

lesson 3

SALLY'S FAVOURITE DAY!

ACLAND BURGHLEY SCHOOL

Timetable: Friday
year: 10
class: 10D
name: *Sally Hunter*

9.00am - 9.55am	English
9.55am - 10.35am	Drama
10.35am - 11.20am	Geography
Break: 11.20am - 11.40am	
11.40am - 12.20pm	Maths
12.20pm - 1.00pm	Science
Lunchtime: 1.00pm - 2.00pm	
2.00pm - 2.45pm	Information technology (IT)
2.45pm - 3.30pm	Art

Sally goes to school from Monday to Friday. School starts at nine in the morning and finishes at three thirty in the afternoon.

When the weather is nice, she walks to school because she lives quite near. When the weather is bad, she goes by bus.

Sally stays at school all day and she has lunch in the canteen.

After school she goes home or to a friend's. She always does her homework before dinner.

P.31

1 READ AND MATCH

Read about Sally and look at the sentences in blue.
Look at the four pictures in your workbook and choose the right sentence to describe each picture. Then write it under the picture.

P.31

2 TALK ABOUT SALLY'S SCHOOL DAY

A. It's Friday today. Look at Sally's timetable. What lessons has she got today?

B. Now listen to Sally and go to your workbook.
Number the times you hear in order (1 to 8).

C. Ask and answer these questions. Then write the answers in your workbook.
1. When does school start and finish?
2. When is the morning break?
3. When do they have lunch?
4. When is Art today?

D. Answer the questions. Say as much as you can.
1. Why can Sally walk to school?
2. How does she go to school when the weather's bad?
3. Where does she have lunch?
4. Does she do her homework at school?

P.32

3 LISTEN AND FIND OUT

A. Listen to Sally, Dylan and Lucy and complete the grid in your workbook.

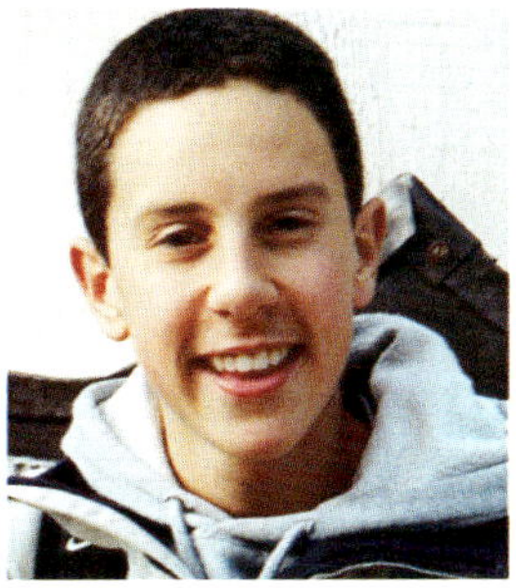

B. Compare your information.
Ask and answer questions like these:

How does ... go to school?

What is his/her favourite day?

What subjects does he/she like?

Is he/she happy today?

C. Listen to the questions and find the right short answer.

Yes, he does. *No, he doesn't.* *Yes, she does.* *No, she doesn't.*

Listen again and practise. Then complete the questions and answers in your workbook.

chatterbox

I walk to school!

I go by bus.

I go by car.

I go by train.

I go by bike.

I go by tube.

4 A QUESTIONNAIRE: WHAT ABOUT YOU?

P.32

A. Work in pairs and do the questionnaire. Then report back to the class.

B. Write four sentences about yourself and your partner.

grammar box

Le présent simple : 3e personne du singulier

When **does** school **start**?	It **starts** at nine o'clock.
When **does** it **finish**?	It **finishes** at three-thirty.
How **does** Lucy **go** to school?	She **goes** to school by tube.
Does she **like** Games?	**Yes,** she **does.** / **No,** she **doesn't**!

Les verbes *do* et *have*

When **do** you **have** lunch?	We **have** lunch between one and two.
Where **does** Sally **have** lunch?	She **has** lunch at school.
When **does** she **do** her homework?	She **does** her homework before dinner.

When **: mot interrogatif ou conjonction**

When do you do your homework? **When** the weather is nice, she walks to school.

look and learn WB pp. 33-34

lesson 4

HE'S VERY FRIENDLY!

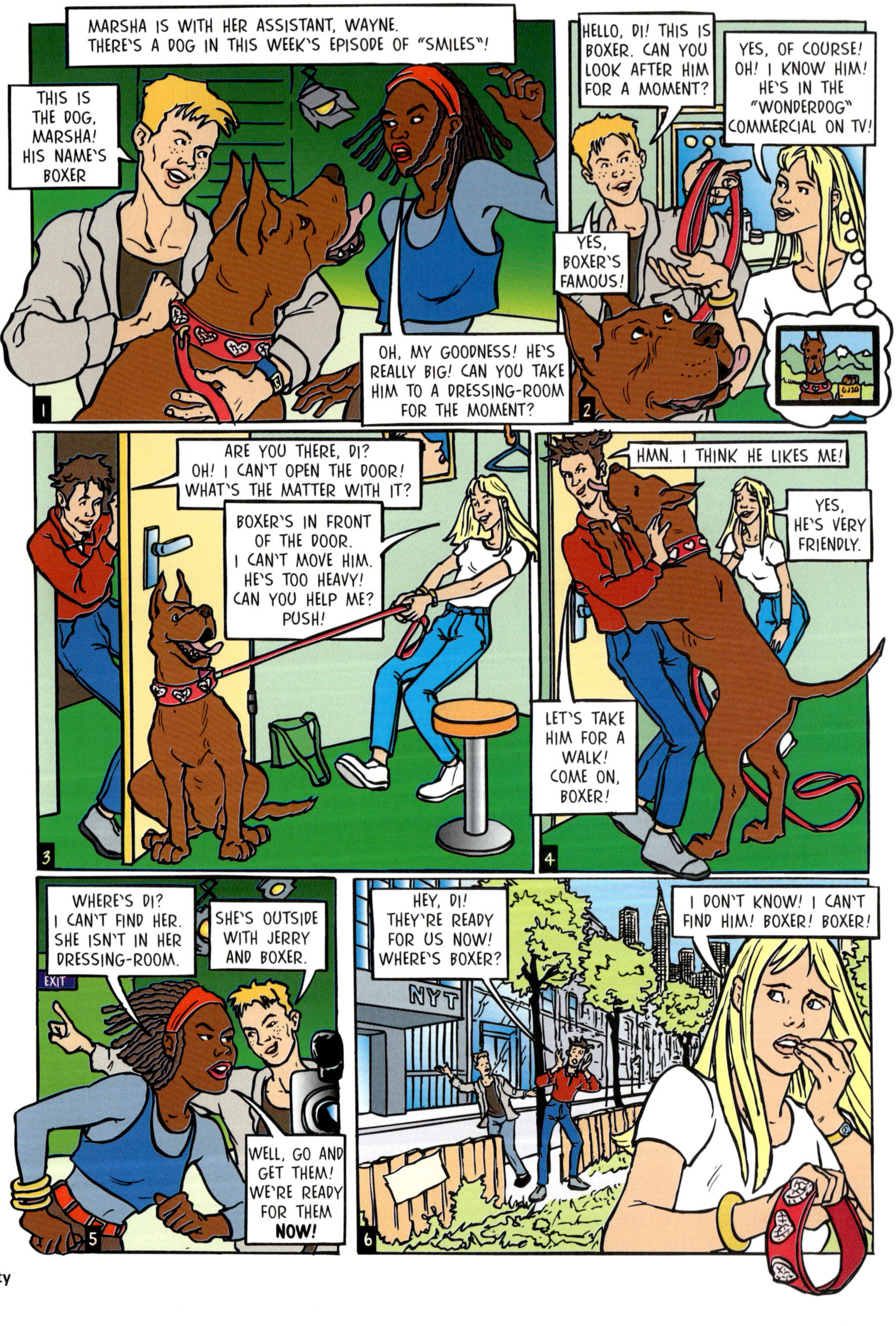

1 HOW MUCH CAN YOU SAY?

A. Listen and look at the pictures. Find adjectives to describe Boxer.

B. Listen again and find the answers:

1. Where does Wayne take Boxer?
2. Why does Di know him?
3. Why can't Jerry open the door?
4. Why can't Di move Boxer?
5. Why can't Marsha find Di?
6. What's the problem in picture 6?

2 LISTEN AND CONTINUE

Listen to the examples and practise. Then take the role of Marsha and continue. Choose the right word each time:

• it • them • him • her

"Where's my script?" "I don't know!"
"Can you find it?" "Okay!"

"Where are my glasses?" "I don't know!"
"Can you find them?" "Okay!"

3 WHAT'S THE PROBLEM?

P.35

A. Go to your workbooks and look at the four pictures. Can you imagine the text for each bubble?

B. Now read the sentences in the boxes. Choose <u>two</u> boxes for each bubble and write them in your workbook.

a. I've got a problem with my car.

b. It's too heavy for you!

c. I can't open the window!

d. It's raining, Dad!

e. Can you take us to the cinema?

f. Can you push?

g. You can't move the piano.

h. You're tall. Can you help me?

4 BOXER'S FRIENDS!

P.35

Look at the picture of Boxer and the other dogs and cats in your workbook and follow the instructions.

grammar box

Les marqueurs compléments

me → **you**
us

him **them**
her
it

Le modal *can*: demandes polies

Can you find them?
Can you help me?

Le modal *can't*: l'impossibilité

I can't open the door!
I can't find her.

look and learn WB p. 36

PART 2

How to... learn vocabulary

À noter ! On ne retient que 20% de ce qu'on entend !
On retient 35% de ce qu'on voit.
On retient 50% de ce qu'on lit et entend.
On retient 75% de ce qu'on lit, entend et écrit.
Mais on retient 95% de ce qu'on lit, entend, écrit et dit !

1 Associations

Chacun d'entre vous aura une stratégie personnelle pour mémoriser des mots nouveaux. Cette activité teste votre mémoire visuelle.

A. Cover picture N° 2 and look at picture N° 1 for 5 seconds. Then close your book and write a list of objects you remember. How many can you remember?

1

B. Now look at picture N° 2 for 5 seconds. Close your book and write a list of objects you remember. How many can you remember this time? Why?

2

2 Categories

On retient mieux les mots à apprendre si on les classe en « champs lexicaux » ou catégories grammaticales.

A. Read the 24 words in the boxes and put them into six categories. There are 4 words in each category.

B. Find a title for each category and compare with your friends.

sister — kitchen — shoe — actor

sweater — brown — mother — brother — bathroom

black

yellow — hat — green — dining-room — play tennis

singer — hall — nurse

cycle — doctor — jeans — skate

father — jog

3 Grammatical families

Il est important de faire le bilan, de temps en temps, de tous les verbes, noms, adjectifs, ou prépositions… que tu connais. Entraînez-vous par équipes !

A. Work in four teams. Each team chooses one grammatical family and writes a list of words from Part 1 and Part 2. Use YOUR WORD BANK in your workbooks!

B. Each team tests another team and asks them questions. Look at the examples in the bubbles.

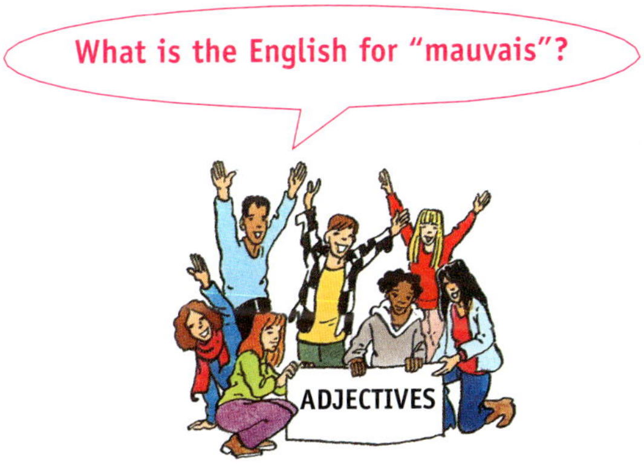

PART 2

Sounds

1 Vowel sounds

A. Écoute les mots dans chaque colonne. Les trois mots en bleu contiennent tous les lettres **oe**, mais le son-voyelle de chacun est bien différent !

[əu]	[ʌ]	[uː]
GOES	DOES	SHOES
don't	**come**	**who**
know	**one**	**two**
boat	**us**	**new**
home	**number**	**blue**
road	**front**	**move**

2 The plural

A. ***Le pluriel en « s ».*** En anglais, la majorité des noms font leur pluriel en **s**. On le prononce de trois façons différentes.
Écoute, le **s** final se prononce-t-il [s], [z] ou [ɪz] ?

- **socks** • **parents** • **cats** • **flats**
- **rooms** • **eyes** • **friends** • **dogs**
- **houses** • **ages** • **garages** • **badges**

Lis à voix haute et retrouve le singulier de chaque mot. À quels mots ajoute-t-on une syllabe au pluriel ?

B. ***Le pluriel en « es ».*** Les noms qui se terminent en **-ch**, **-sh**, **-x**, ou **-ss** font leur pluriel en **-es.** Cette opération ajoute également une syllabe.
Écoute et entraîne-toi : **sandwich** ➞ **sandwiches**, **box** ➞ **boxes**, **actress** ➞ **actresses**

3 "The autograph rap"

Look behind you! He's an actor.
What's his name?
I don't know. I can't remember!
Is he well-known?
Yes, he is!
Well, ask him for an autograph!
Excuse me, please.
Can I have an autograph?
An autograph?
Yes, of course! Who am I?

Let's practise!

Lesson 1 pp. 32-33

A **Observe les 's dans les phrases et réécris chaque phrase avec la forme complète du verbe quand cela est possible. Ensuite entoure le génitif 's :**

1. It's Sally's birthday today.
2. She's got a brother and a sister.
3. Sally's sister's called Di.
4. Sally's brother's 24.
5. He's got a job in Australia.
6. Sally's with Lucy and Dylan.
7. She's got a birthday card from her sister!

B **Relis les fiches d'identité des acteurs, p. 32, et réponds par une réponse courte. Quand cela est nécessaire donne l'information correcte :**

1. Are Ewan McGregor and Liam Neeson actors?
2. Is Ewan McGregor Australian?
3. Has Liam Neeson got brown hair?
4. Is he tall?
5. Has he got blue eyes?
6. Are his eyes grey?

C **Trouve la bonne réponse (A > G) à chaque question :**

1. How old is Nicole Kidman?	A. No, she hasn't.
2. What's her hair like?	B. Yes, she is.
3. How tall is Liam Neeson?	C. Yes, she has.
4. Is Céline Dion well-known?	D. No, she isn't.
5. Has she got brown eyes?	E. She's (age).
6. Is she French?	F. He's very tall!
7. Has she got fair hair?	G. It's long and red.

Lesson 2 pp. 34-35

D **Réponds en disant la vérité :**

1. Do you live near the school?
2. Do you live in a house or in a flat?
3. Is it old or modern?
4. How many bedrooms are there?
5. Has it got a garage?
6. Have you got any brothers or sisters?
7. How old are you?
8. What are you like?

E **Complète les questions et les réponses :**

1. Where … the Hunters …? They … near the hospital in Camden.
2. … the Tates … in Camden too? Yes, ….
3. … Di and Rob … at home now? No, ….
4. … … children … the Tates …? They have got ….
5. … their flat … big? No, ….
6. … they … their flat? Yes, ….
7. … … bedrooms … the Tates' house …? It … … three.

F **Imagine que tu interroges Sally. Écris ses réponses :**

1. Where do you live?
2. What's your house like?
3. Do you like your house?
4. What's your mother's job?
5. What's your father's job?
6. Have you got any brothers or sisters?
7. Do they live at home too?

Lesson 3 — pp. 38-39

G **Retrouve la question (au sujet de Sally ou Dylan) pour chaque réponse :**

1. Because she lives quite near.
2. When the weather's bad.
3. No, he doesn't. He goes to school by bike.
4. Between one and two.
5. In the canteen.
6. Drama and Art.

H **Complète chaque phrase avec un de ces verbes : • do • go • finish • have • like • live • stay • walk**

1. Sally … in Camden.
2. Dylan doesn't … to school. He goes by bike.
3. Sally … at school all day.
4. She … lunch at the canteen.
5. School … at 3.30 pm.
6. Sally … Friday. It's her favourite day.
7. Sally doesn't … her homework at school. She … it at home before dinner.
8. Lucy … to school by tube.
9. We don't … to school on Wednesday afternoon.
10. We … school at twelve thirty on Wednesday.

I **Complète les phrases (1 > 8) avec la fin qui correspond (A > H).**

1. Di and Rob don't live
2. The Hunters' house is
3. Dylan's flat
4. It is too small
5. Dylan goes to school
6. He isn't very happy
7. Lucy is happy today
8. School finishes

A. by bike.
B. because it's raining.
C. for a family of six.
D. too big now.
E. at home.
F. because it's Saturday tomorrow.
G. at 3.30 in the afternoon.
H. has got three bedrooms.

J **Interviewe un/une camarade. Rédige tes questions et ses réponses. Demande-lui :**

1. si il/elle habite une maison ou un appartement,
2. où l'appartement/la maison est situé(e),
3. combien de chambres il y a chez lui/elle,
4. si il/elle a des frères et sœurs (si oui, lui demander des détails),
5. comment il/elle va à l'école,
6. quand et où il/elle fait ses devoirs,
7. son jour préféré dans l'emploi du temps et pourquoi.

Lesson 4 — pp. 40-41

K **Réponds aux questions sur la situation, page 41 du manuel, par une phrase complète et en remplaçant les noms (soulignés) par les marqueurs de personne sujets et compléments :**

1. Where does <u>Wayne</u> take <u>Boxer</u>? *He takes him to …*
2. Why does <u>Di</u> know <u>Boxer</u>?
3. Why can't <u>Jerry</u> open the <u>door</u>?
4. Why can't <u>Di</u> move <u>Boxer</u>?
5. Why can't <u>Marsha</u> find <u>Di</u>?

L **Imagine que tu as un robot personnel à la maison ! Demande-lui poliment…**

1. d'ouvrir la porte,
2. de t'emmener à l'école,
3. de déjeuner avec toi,
4. de s'occuper de ton chien,
5. d'aller chercher une pizza,
6. de rester à la maison et de faire tes devoirs !

2

1

PART 3

WORK AND PLAY

3

4

5

lesson 1

AN UNUSUAL FAMILY

Rob Hunter is a journalist. He works for a Sunday newspaper in Sydney. Every week he chooses people with interesting or unusual jobs and writes an article about them for the colour magazine.

The amazing Boehmers!

Larry and Judy with their children at home in Jerseyville, Illinois.

The Boehmer Family Jugglers: the only family of jugglers in the world with 13 members!

How many brothers and sisters have you got? Margaret Boehmer (pronounced "bermer") has got ten – four brothers and six sisters! They live in a big house in Jerseyville, Illinois, with their parents, Larry and Judy, and their dog, Bosco.

But the Boehmers aren't an ordinary American family. They're very famous jugglers and acrobats. They perform all over America so they have to travel a lot in their motor home – about 25,000 miles every year.

The children have to work very hard. They have to practise every day, but it's great fun and they don't go to school! Larry and Judy teach them at home.

Margaret doesn't work hard in the show – she doesn't juggle and she isn't an acrobat. She just has to stand on Judy's hand. Well, she's very young – she's only two!

chatterbox

1 FIRST IMPRESSIONS

P.41

Look at the pictures and the captions. What can you say about the Boehmers? Fill in the grid in your workbook.

2 READ THE ARTICLE

P.41

A. Read about Rob and read his article. Then answer these questions.

1. What does Rob do?
2. What do the Boehmers do?
3. What do the children have to do every day?
4. Why don't the children go to school?
5. Why doesn't Margaret juggle?

B. Make more questions with the words in the boxes. Ask and answer them then write the questions and answers in your workbook.

How many miles Where What Why	does Margaret don't the children do the Boehmers	live? travel every year? go to school? have to do in the show?

3 A TV INTERVIEW

P.41

A. Jonathan Boehmer is 13. He is on a TV programme called "Questions for Famous Kids". Listen to the interview and take notes in your workbook.

B. Listen again. Use your notes and take Jonathan's role.

4 JOBS

P.42

Look at the people in the photos and answer the questions in your workbook. Compare your ideas.

a

b

c

grammar box

***Have to* + V :**
exprimer une obligation

The children **have to practise** every day.
Margaret **has to stand** on Judy's hand.
Do they **have to practise** every day?
Does she **have to juggle**?

Le présent simple :
la forme interro-négative

Why **don't** the children **go** to school?
Why **doesn't** Margaret **juggle**?

look and learn WB p. 43

lesson 2

MONDAY TO FRIDAY

1

From Monday to Friday, Di gets up early, at 6.45. She always has a cup of tea and a piece of toast for breakfast.

2

She leaves home at 7.30 and walks to the subway. She often buys a newspaper on the way. She always gets to the studios on time, before 8.15. She is never late.

3

In the morning, the actors get their scripts. They have to learn their words before lunchtime.

4

Between midday and 1.00 they have lunch. Di usually has a snack: an omelette or a salad. She never eats meat because she's a vegetarian.

5

After lunch, they film. They never finish before 5.30 in the afternoon and they often have to work very late.

6

When Di gets home, she is always tired. She has dinner and then she usually watches TV, but she sometimes goes to bed early with a good book.

7

Di doesn't have to work at the weekend. She usually goes to a club with some friends on Saturday evening and dances all night.

8

And on Sunday... she sometimes stays in bed all day!

1 FIRST IMPRESSIONS

P.44

Look at the pictures and the times. Choose a title for each picture.
Write the titles in the grid in your workbook.

- Saturday night
- Breakfast at home
- Sunday morning
- On the way to work
- A snack in the canteen
- An evening at home
- An afternoon at work
- The actors learn their words.

2 LISTEN

P.44

A. Listen to the text and find the times.

B. Then listen again and complete the grid.

3 READ AND FIND OUT

P.45

A. Read the texts. Then read the questions in your workbook and choose the correct answers.

Yes, she is.

No, she doesn't.

Yes, sometimes.

Yes, they do.

Yes, usually.

Yes, she does.

B. Now work in pairs and make your own questions for the answers in your workbook.

4 WHAT DO YOU DO AT THE WEEKEND?

P.45

Work in pairs and do the questionnaire in your workbook.

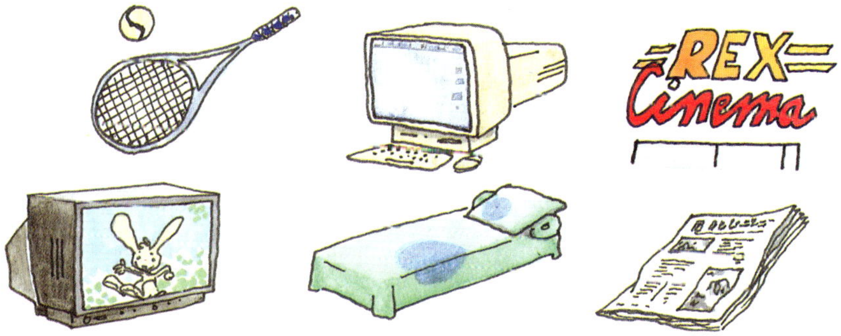

help box

always	● ● ● ● ●
usually	● ● ● ●
often	● ● ●
sometimes	● ●
never	

grammar box

Le présent simple et les adverbes de fréquence

– avec le verbe ***be***:
She **is never** late. She **is always** tired.
Is she **usually** tired in the evening?

– avec d'autres verbes:
She **usually has** a snack. They **never finish** before 5.30.
Does she **often buy** a newspaper?

Have to : la forme négative, absence d'obligation

She **doesn't have to** get up early on Saturday.
They **don't have to** work at the weekend.

look and learn WB p. 46

spread your wings 3

Worksheet P.47

THEY LOVE PARADES!

When Americans have a national holiday, they often celebrate with a parade. There are bands, majorettes, floats, giant balloons, celebrities... It's a lot of fun!

1

2

The Rose Parade

In Pasadena, California, they celebrate New Year's Day with a parade called the Tournament of Roses and a special American football match (between two university teams) called the Rose Bowl Game. The tradition is over 100 years old and people watch the parade and the match all over the USA.

3

4

Macy's Parade

The last Thursday of November is a public holiday in the USA called Thanksgiving. People celebrate the first harvest of the Pilgrim Fathers, one year after their arrival in America in 1620. Every family has a special dinner – with turkey on the menu – and Macy's, a large department store in New York, organises a magnificent parade from Central Park to Broadway. This tradition is over 70 years old.

5

The New York Easter Parade

On Easter Sunday, in New York, a lot of people put on fancy clothes and extravagant hats and parade from 49th Street, along Fifth Avenue, to 57th Street. This is a tradition that dates from the Civil War, 1859-1865.

6

7

The Washington Independence Day Parade

The 4th of July is Independence Day. It celebrates the signing of the Declaration of Independence on 4th July, 1776. There are celebrations all over the USA and in the capital, Washington, there is an enormous parade. About 400,000 people stand in the streets and watch it!

lesson 3

WHAT SORT OF PERSON ARE YOU?

TEEN'ZINE

EARTH, FIRE, AIR or WATER?

Everyone knows about the 12 signs of the Zodiac but Maria Morgan, a regular reader of Teen 'zine, believes you can also divide people into the 4 elements: earth, fire, air and water. The following tables are the result of 400 answers to a questionnaire for teenagers on her website. The four elements are in all of us, says Maria, but there is usually one very strong element. So... what's your element?

EARTH PEOPLE are practical, confident and like being leaders...

GAMES AND SPORTS	football, chess, table-tennis.
SPARE TIME	cooking, decorating, shopping.
COLOURS	yellow, brown.
FOOD	cheese, chips, chocolate.
NO!	being late, fish, science fiction.

FIRE PEOPLE are adventurous, impatient and like taking risks...

GAMES AND SPORTS	basketball, karate, skateboarding.
SPARE TIME	computer games, dancing, acting.
COLOURS	red, black.
FOOD	steak, spicy food, tomatoes.
NO!	watching the news, milk, classical music.

AIR PEOPLE are imaginative, creative and don't like making decisions...

GAMES AND SPORTS	running, ice-skating, tennis.
SPARE TIME	surfing the Internet, reading, photography.
COLOURS	blue, white.
FOOD	chicken, fruit, green vegetables.
NO!	doing the housework, insects, gardening.

36

1 FIRST IMPRESSIONS

Look at the magazine page and find the following information as quickly as possible.

1. What's the name of the magazine?
2. Who reads it?
3. Who is the photo of?
4. Where does Maria's information come from?
5. This is page 36 of the magazine. What is at the top of page 37?

2 LISTEN AND FIND OUT

P.48

A. Listen to Maria.
She is talking to Jason on the Internet.
Complete the grid in your workbook.

B. Listen again and complete the conversation in your workbook.

C. Then ask and answer questions about Jason.

What ... does he like? / What ... doing? / What is/are his favourite ...? — He likes ... .

Does he like ...? — Yes, he likes ... a lot. / No, not much. / No, he hates ... .

3 WHAT DO YOU LIKE?

P.49

Look at the pictures and write four sentences in your workbook.

I love ... I like ... I don't like ... I hate ...

4 WHAT'S YOUR ELEMENT?

P.49

Work in pairs and go to your workbook. What sort of person is your partner?

grammar box

Exprimer ses goûts

Like, love, hate + N

I **like** football.	She **loves** cheese.	They **hate** insects.
Do you **like** chips?		

Like, love, hate + V-ING

I **like** cook**ing**.	He **loves** danc**ing**.	They **hate** garden**ing**.
Do you **like** shopp**ing**?		

L'article zéro (Ø)

I like **Ø** football.	He loves **Ø** shopping.	They hate **Ø** insects.

look and learn WB p. 50

PART 3

lesson 4

NEXT, PLEASE!

Di is at an audition. Julia Wallace, the star of the film *Danger Woman*, is ill and can't make the sequel, *Danger Woman II*. Mr Silverman, the producer, has to find a new star. Perhaps Di is the right actress...

1 FIRST IMPRESSIONS

Look at the poster. What can you say about the film and its heroine?

2 THE INTERVIEW

P.51

A. Di is with Mr Silverman and his assistant, Anna. Listen to the interview and complete Anna's notes in your workbook.

B. Use the notes and the list of verbs and make as many true sentences as possible. Then write four sentences in your workbook.

- She can … .
- She can … very well.
- She can … a little.
- She can … quite well.
- She can't … .

C. Listen to the questions about Di and find the answers. There are sometimes two possible answers. Then write the answers in your workbook.

Yes, she can. No, she can't. Yes, but not very well.

Yes, she is. Yes, she does. No, she doesn't.

Yes, quite well. Yes, very well. Yes, very good. Yes, a little.

3 WHAT ARE YOU GOOD AT?

P.52

Work in pairs and do the activities in your workbook. What is your partner good at?

grammar box

Parler de ce que l'on sait faire

Can + V

Can you **swim**?
– Yes, I **can**.
I **can sing** very well but I **can't dance**.

Know how to + V

Do you know how to ride a motorbike?
– Yes, I **do**.
I **don't know how to play** the piano.

Be good at + N/ + V-ING

Are you good at swimm**ing**?
– Yes, I **am**.

Are you good at karate?
– No, **I'm not very good at** it.

look and learn WB p. 52

How to... find information

Sur cette page il y a cinq brochures distribuées dans différents offices de tourisme en Angleterre.
Comment savoir si l'une d'elle peut t'intéresser?
De quoi parlent-elles? Procède par étapes...

EASY

1 What's it about?

Il faut d'abord identifier le document. De quoi s'agit-il? Il suffit de repérer les mots que tu connais et de bien observer les images.

Look at each brochure for 10 seconds and look at the list below. You have got 1 minute to identify all the brochures.

Number ? is about
- a sort of zoo.
- a restaurant.
- public transport.
- a trip to France.
- a show.

1

2

3

4

5

2 What's important?

NOT SO EASY

Il faut maintenant repérer les informations essentielles.

Work with a partner and look for the important information. Then look at the four sentences below and decide if the endings are true or false.

A. The Ashford Gardens Tea Rooms
1. serve lunch and tea.
2. don't serve dinner.

B. At Combe Martin Park
1. all the animals are real.
2. you can see prehistoric animals.

C. The Lion King
1. is a show with music.
2. finishes on 24th September.

D. A day trip to Lille costs £39
1. by train.
2. by boat.

3 Words I don't know

QUITE DIFFICULT

Il est souvent possible de déduire le sens des mots de leur contexte !

Look at the brochures again and guess the meaning of the words you don't know. Then read the words below (1-7) and find their French equivalents (A-G).

1. Greater London
2. Devon
3. free
4. on sale
5. homemade
6. wildlife
7. fares

A. le prix des billets de transport
B. la faune (les animaux sauvages)
C. fait maison
D. un comté de l'Angleterre
E. Londres et sa banlieue
F. en vente
G. gratuit

4 Look up the word!

DIFFICULT

Si tu n'arrives pas à comprendre certains mots, ou si tu veux en vérifier le sens, sers-toi d'un dictionnaire !

This is an extract from a dictionary entry for *free*. Read the extract and the remarks, then answer the questions.

A. Is *free* an adjective? What can it be?

B. What are the two principal meanings of the adjective *free*?

C. Do you always translate an English adjective by a French adjective? Give an example.

D. How do you translate these sentences?
1. He's a free man.
2. It's a free ticket.
3. You can come in free.
4. Free the prisoner!

free [friː] *adj.* **1.** libre ; **you are ~ to leave** vous être libre de partir ; **a ~ press** une presse libre ; **to set ~** libérer, remettre en liberté ; **is that seat ~ ?** est-ce que ce siège est libre ? ; **are you ~ for lunch today?** êtes-vous libre pour déjeuner aujourd'hui ? **2.** [at no cost] gratuit ; **– admission** entrée *f* gratuite ; **~ gift** *(comm.)* cadeau *m.*
adv. gratuitement ; **they deliver ~ of charge** ils livrent gratuitement ; **children under twelve travel ~** les enfants de moins de douze ans voyagent gratuitement.
vt. **1.** relâcher, libérer ; [animal] détacher. **2.** [disengage] dégager, libérer ; **they can't ~ the driver from the car** ils ne peuvent pas dégager le conducteur de la voiture. **3.** [unblock – pipe] déboucher.

abréviation : adjectif
la place de "free" dans l'expression
transcription en symboles phonétiques
l'infinitif d'un verbe est précédé par "to"
abréviation : langage commercial
nom féminin
abréviation : adverbe
nom masculin
abréviation : verbe transitif
chaque chiffre indique un sens différent
précision de contexte

PART 3

Sounds

1 The same sound

A. There, their et they're se prononcent de la même façon. Écoute et entraîne-toi.

- **He isn't there.**
- **Their garden is very big.**
- **They're at school.**

B. Écoute les quatre questions et réponses. Quel mot se trouve dans chaque réponse ?

1. there **2. their** **3. they're**

2 Intonation in questions

A. Les questions fermées, qui commencent par un mot interrogatif (**who, what, when, where, how, why**), ont en général une intonation descendante. Les questions ouvertes, auxquelles on peut répondre par oui ou non, ont une intonation montante. Écoute les exemples et entraîne-toi.

What do you do? **Do you like swimming?**

B. Écoute et répète les questions suivantes. Ont-elles une intonation descendante ou montante ?

1. Can you ride a bike?
2. What do you do in the evening?
3. Do you have to get up early?
4. Are you good at cooking?
5. Where do you go to school?
6. How many sisters have you got?

3 "The clever brother rap"

I've **got** a clever **bro**ther; his **name** is **Mike**.

He **can't** kick a **ball** and he **can't** ride a **bike**.

He **does**n't like **sport** or **wat**ching **TV**.

He **does**n't like my **friends**
and he **does**n't like **me**!

He **al**ways does his **home**work
and he's **ne**ver late for **school**.

His **room** is always **ti**dy
and his **clothes** are never **cool**.

He **isn't** good at **swim**ming
and he **isn't** good at **gym**.

Why do I **have** to have a **bro**ther like **him**?

Let's practise!

Lesson 1 pp. 48-49

A Tu interviewes Larry et Judy Boehmer. Complète les questions et les réponses avec les mots et expressions de l'article page 48 et les verbes suivants :
do – go – juggle – live – perform – practise – travel

1. What … you … ? – *We are … and … .*
2. Why … you … all year in Jerseyville, Illinois? – *Because we … all over America.*
3. How many miles … you … every year? – About … .
4. Why … your children … to school? – *Because they … … … .*
5. … your children have to … a lot? – *Yes, … .*
6. What about Margaret? Why … she …? – *Because … .*

B Sally écrit à sa correspondante française. Voici quelques phrases tirées de sa lettre. Complète-les avec **have**, **have got** ou **have to**.

1. I … a sister and a brother.
2. My mother's a nurse and my father's a doctor. They … work very hard.
3. My sister … an exciting job. She's an actress.
4. We … learn French in my class this year.
5. My favourite day is Friday because we … Drama and Art.
6. Every day, I … lunch in the school canteen.
7. My mum says I … do my homework before dinner!

C Que fais-tu les jours de classe ? Raconte :

1. à quelle heure tu dois être à l'école,
2. comment tu vas à l'école,
3. combien de matières tu dois apprendre,
4. si tu manges chez toi ou à la cantine,
5. ce que tu dois faire après l'école.

Lesson 2 pp. 50-51

D Suis l'exemple en écrivant l'heure de deux manières différentes : *07.15 > seven fifteen am > quarter past seven in the morning*

1. 08.00	4. 17.00
2. 11.15	5. 21.45
3. 12.45	6. 02.30

E Complète les phrases en ajoutant le métier de chacun, have to à la forme affirmative ou négative, et en utilisant les mots entre parenthèses, comme dans l'exemple :

Colin Hunter ... (work/very hard) =
Colin Hunter is a doctor.
He has to work very hard.

1. June Hunter ... (wear/uniform)
2. Di Hunter ... (work/weekend)
3. The Boehmer children ... (go/school)
4. Rob Hunter ... (write/article/every Sunday)

F Explique à un correspondant australien ce que tu fais pendant la semaine et dis-lui

1. à quelle heure tu te lèves d'habitude et aussi le weekend,
2. ce que tu prends d'habitude pour le petit déjeuner,
3. à quelle heure tu quittes la maison pour l'école,
4. ce que tu fais toujours après l'école,
5. ce que tu regardes parfois à la télévision,
6. si tu fais toujours tes devoirs avant le dîner.

Lesson 3 pp. 54-55

G Regarde la page 54 du manuel et la page 49 du workbook et complète les huit phrases.

1. Earth people like ... .
2. They don't like ... .
3. Fire people love ... .
4. They hate ... .
5. Air people like ... .
6. They hate ... .
7. Water people love ... .
8. They don't like ... .

H Complète chaque phrase en utilisant Ø + V + -ING et/ou Ø + N.

1. I like ... and I love ... .
2. My favourite sport is ... . I really love ... to the swimming-pool!
3. I don't like ... and I hate ... .
4. At the weekend I like ... .
5. At school I like ... but I don't like ... .
6. After school I love ... but I hate ... .

I Complète ces phrases avec a, the ou Ø.

Jason has got ... bike. He loves ... cycling. He also likes ... swimming. He goes to ... swimming-pool a lot. He likes ... salads but he hates ... red meat. He is ... vegetarian. He is ... very shy person. Maria believes he is ... typical water person.

Lesson 4 pp. 56-57

J Remets les mots dans l'ordre pour en faire une phrase complète. Attention ! Le mot en majuscules est un « mot caché » : les lettres sont dans le désordre.

1. how Di NGIS to knows
2. the LYAP little piano can a she
3. helicopter she a how LYF doesn't to know
4. DRIE a she motorbike can't
5. at is good she NGSMWIMI
6. karate can ALREN she

K Lis l'interview de Jason dans le workbook p. 48 et réponds par une réponse courte. Ensuite justifie chaque réponse par une autre phrase.

1. Can Jason swim?
2. Does he know how to play scrabble?
3. Is he good at cycling?
4. Is he good at football?
5. Does he like going to parties?
6. Can he paint pictures?

L Réponds à ce questionnaire.

1. Are you good at tennis?
2. Can you swim one kilometre in thirty minutes?
3. Can you sing well?
4. Do you know how to ride a horse?
5. Can you do martial arts?
6. Do you know how to play chess?
7. Can you play the guitar?
8. Are you good at cooking?
9. Are you good at English?
10. Can you do everything?

2

1

3

4

PART 4

COMMENTS

5

PART 4

lesson 1

SURPRISE! SURPRISE!

1 HOW MUCH CAN YOU SAY?

Where?
Who?
What?

A. Read the introduction. Ask and answer questions about James.
B. Look at the pictures. Where is everyone?
Ask and answer questions about each picture.

2 LISTEN AND TALK ABOUT THE PICTURES

P.58

A. Listen to the conversation and ask and answer these questions.

Picture 1
1. What is James doing?
2. Why can't Di hear him?

Picture 2
3. Where is the taxi going?
4. What can James see?

Picture 3
5. What is the problem?

Picture 4
6. Can Di see James? Why?
7. What is James looking for?
8. Where is Di's flat?

Picture 5
9. Who is Di talking to?
10. Why is she suprised?
11. Does James know Jerry?

B. Now work in pairs and write a caption for the pictures in your workbook.

3 WHAT'S HAPPENING?

P.58

A. Look at each photo and find a question with the words in the boxes.

Who What	are is	she they he	waiting talking looking	to for at	?

1

2

3

B. Now write a question and answer for each photo in your workbook.

grammar box

Le présent avec *be* + -ING

I am
We are
You are
waiting for the bus.
He is
She is
They are

Le modal *can* + *hear* / *see*

I **can't hear** you.
He **can see** the Twin Towers.

Can you **hear** me?
Yes, I **can.** / No, I **can't.**

look and learn WB p. 59

PART 4

lesson 2

WHICH ONE'S THE BEST?

Ist

2nd

3rd

4th

P.61

1 PHOTO PUZZLE

A. Look at the photos.
Do you know the young man? What can you say about him?

B. You can play this game in teams. Go to your workbooks. Read the clues and find the right photo. You have got five minutes!

C. Then compare your answers with the other teams. Ask and answer:

Is he (V-ING) in the first photo? — Yes, he is. / No, he isn't.

D. Now make questions with the words in the boxes and practise the questions and answers.

In which photo is he ...

driving	some flowers?		The	first	one.
standing	to the crowd?			second	
wearing	next to a driving instructor?			third	
looking	next to his father?			fourth	
holding	jeans?				
talking	a car?				
sitting	at the camera?				
	to a young woman?				

2 LISTEN AND FIND OUT

P.61

Rob is talking to Carole, another journalist.
She has to choose one of the photos for an article.
She's asking Rob for his opinion.

A. Listen and complete the grid in your workbook.

- **What does Rob think about the photos?**
  Which one is the most interesting?
  Which one is the funniest?
  Which one is the nicest?
  Which one is the best?
- **What do you think?**

B. Listen again and complete the conversation in your workbook.

3 WHICH ONE DO YOU LIKE?

P.62

Look at these masks and identify each one. Then work in pairs and complete the grid in your workbook. Exchange your ideas in class.

Ist

2nd

3rd
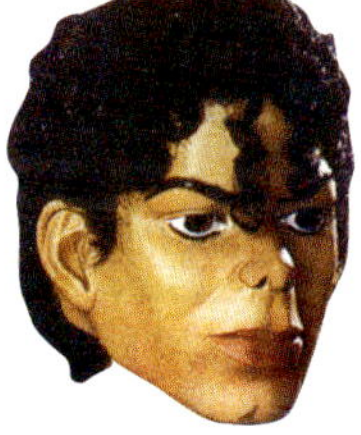

4th

A. Prince Charles
B. The sun
C. Madonna
D. The Screamer
E. The pig
F. The moon
G. Michael Jackson
H. Frankenstein

5th
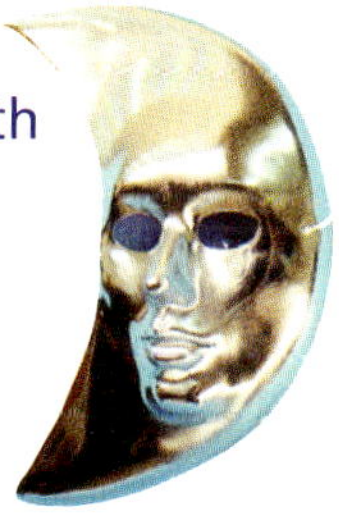

6th

7th

8th

grammar box

Le présent avec *be* + -ING

forme négative :	He **isn't** smil**ing**.	They **aren't** look**ing** at the camera.
réponses courtes :	**Is** he wear**ing** a jacket?	–**Yes, he is.** / –**No, he isn't.**

Le superlatif

adjectifs courts :	It's **the** nic**est**.	It's **the** funn**iest**.	He's **the** tall**est** in the family.
adjectifs longs :	It's **the most** interesting.	It's **the most** frightening.	

One

	Which one do you like?	**This one** or **that one?**
		The first **one**. **The one** on the left.

look and learn WB p. 63

THE CRAZY WORLD OF SPORT...

Worksheet P.65

A 98% of the Australian population live on the coast, so water sports are very popular. Scuba-diving is one example!

B Rafting on the rivers is a popular sport in Canada. In the winter, you can go snow-rafting!

C Rodeos, originally a pastime for Texan cowboys in the 19th century, now attract spectators all over America.

D Golf, football, rugby, tennis and cricket are all British inventions. Human table football is the latest invention!

E Bungy-jumping is a recent craze all around the world. It's very exciting but a little dangerous perhaps?

F Frisbee, originally a beach game, is now an international team sport!

G Cricket is played in England, India, Pakistan, Australia and South Africa. It is often exciting and players now wear helmets!

H Hawaii, the last state to join the United States (in 1959), is the surfing capital of the world!

I New Zealand has wonderful scenery and ballooning is the most amusing way to see it!

PART 4

lesson 3

A WORLD OF DIFFERENCE!

P.66

1 GIVE YOUR OPINION

You can do this activity in teams of three or four.

A. The four squares A, B, C and D represent the size of four countries:

AUSTRALIA THE UNITED KINGDOM
CANADA THE UNITED STATES

• **Read the text in the box and give your opinion.**
Which country is A? Which country is B?
Which country is C and which country is D?

• **Now listen to the answers and complete the sentences in your workbook.**

HOW BIG are they?

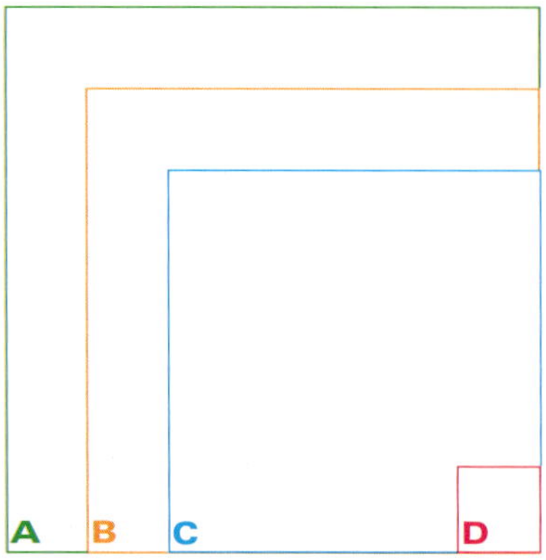

A is the biggest country and D is the smallest. C is much bigger than D but it isn't as big as B.

B. This scale shows the speed of nine animals.
Which animal is the fastest? Which one is the slowest?

HOW FAST are they?

?

chicken pig camel elephant cat rabbit kangaroo lion cheetah

• **How fast is a human being in comparison? Read the text in the box and give your opinion.**

• **Now listen to the answer and complete the sentences in your workbook.**

A pig is faster than a chicken but slower than a camel. A kangaroo isn't as fast as a lion but it's faster than a rabbit.

C. This scale shows the weight of eight balls.
Which ball is the heaviest? Which one is the lightest?

HOW HEAVY are they?

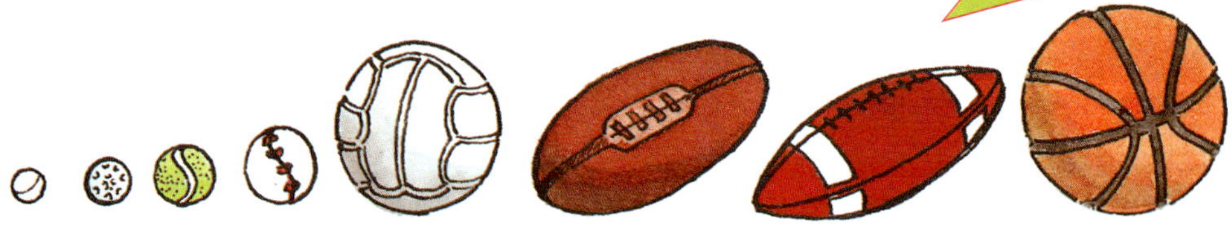

ping-pong ball golf ball tennis ball baseball volleyball rugby ball American football basketball

• **How heavy is an English football? Read the text in the box and give your opinion.**
• **Now listen to the answer and complete the sentences in your workbook.**

?

Is a volleyball as heavy as a rugby ball?
No, it isn't! It's lighter. But a rugby ball isn't as heavy as an American football and an American football is much heavier than a ping-pong ball.

2 GO SHOPPING!

chatterbox

Look at the prices in the four cities.
The products are the same but the prices are different!

price in dollars, January 2000	a bottle of Coca Cola 	a Mars bar 	Levi jeans(501) 	a CD 
LOS ANGELES	**$ 0.99**	**$ 0.55**	**$ 45.46**	**$ 16.22**
LONDON	**$ 2.09**	**$ 0.63**	**$ 72.90**	**$ 22.66**
PARIS	**$ 1.55**	**$ 0.79**	**$ 78.34**	**$ 23.39**

A. Practise the prices. Ask and answer questions like these:

How much is a Mars bar in Paris? — *It's 79 cents!*

How much are Levi jeans in London? — *They're 72 dollars and 90 cents.*

B. Now answer these questions:

1. Is a Mars bar cheaper in London or in Paris?
2. Are Levi jeans more expensive in Paris or in London?
3. Where are Levi jeans the cheapest?
4. Where is a CD the most expensive?

C. Read the sentences in your workbook. Are they true or false?
If they are true, translate them. If they are false, correct them in English!

P.66

3 PREFERENCES

Work in pairs and do the questionnnaire in your workbook.

P.67

... favourite TV series?

... favourite comedians?

... favourite restaurants?

... favourite video games?

grammar box

Le comparatif

adjectifs courts : A cat is fast**er than** an elephant. Is Canada bigg**er than** Australia?
A basketball is **(much)** heav**ier than** a tennis ball.

adjectifs longs : A CD is **(much) more** expensive **than** a Mars bar!

Good : A pizza **is better than** a hamburger!

As... as : Is a golf ball **as** heavy **as** a tennis ball?
No. A golf ball **isn't as** heavy **as** a tennis ball.

look and learn WB p. 67

lesson 4

DON'T BE SILLY!

Dylan is doing his homework in the kitchen tonight because he shares a bedroom with his younger brother Mark, and Mark's asleep. It's late and Dylan's very tired...

Mrs Tate: Dylan! Why aren't you in bed? It's half past ten and you look very tired.
Dylan: I *feel* very tired but I must finish this Maths exercise!
Mrs Tate: It looks very difficult! Are you sure you're doing the right exercise?
Dylan: Er,... page 23, exercise 5.

Mrs Tate: No, look! Page 23 exercise 3! You're doing the wrong exercise! You must be more careful!
Dylan: Oh! Exercise 3 is much easier. I can do that in two minutes!
Mrs Tate: Don't be silly! You can't do it now. It's too late. Go to bed!

The next morning...

Mrs Tate: Dylan! Get up! You mustn't be late!
Dylan: What's the time?
Mrs Tate: Ten past eight! Oh dear! You don't look very well. How do you feel?
Dylan: I feel ill. I've got a sore throat and a headache.
Mrs Tate: Hmm. Wait a minute...

Dylan: Have I got a temperature?
Mrs Tate: Yes! You can't go to school today.
Dylan: Good! I can do my Maths.
Mrs Tate: Don't be silly! You mustn't get up! You must stay in bed. You're ill!
Dylan: Oh, all right.

1 FIRST IMPRESSIONS

Read the introduction and look at the pictures. How much can you say about each picture? What's the problem?

2 LISTEN AND FIND OUT

P.69

A. Listen to the first part of the conversation and ask and answer these questions:

1. Why isn't Dylan in bed?
2. Is it late?
3. How does Dylan feel?
4. Is exercise 5 easier than exercise 3?
5. Why must Dylan be more careful?
6. Why can't he finish his homework tonight?

B. Listen to the second part of the conversation and complete the grid in your workbook. Then write the answers to the questions.

3 READ AND FIND OUT

P.70

Read the information on this poster and do the activities in your workbook.

HOME ALONE

You come home and find someone from your family motionless on the floor. It looks like an accident! Don't panic, just follow these rules...

1. BE CAREFUL!
Don't run into the room. Look for dangers first. Is there smoke? Can you smell gas? Is the electricity working?

2. STAY CALM!
NEVER move the person. Look for important signs: Can the person hear you? Can you see any injuries?

3. DIAL 999...
Find the nearest phone. Ask the operator for an ambulance. ALWAYS give your complete address.

4. STAY THERE!
Don't leave the person alone. Talk to him/her and be patient. Wait for the ambulance.

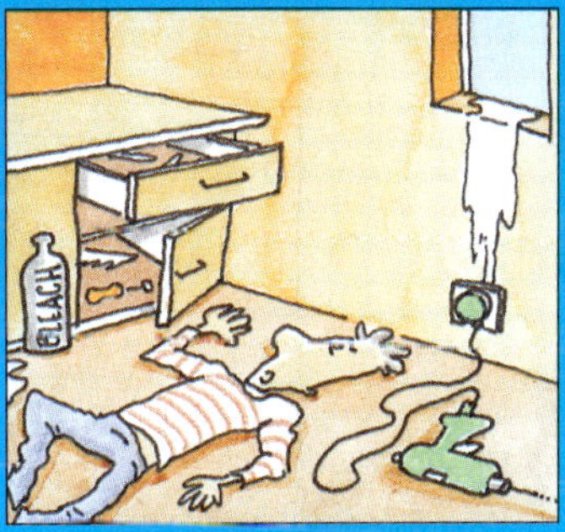

grammar box

Le modal *must* – exprimer l'obligation

I **must finish** my Maths. You **must stay** in bed and **rest**.

Mustn't / can't – exprimer l'interdiction

You **mustn't be** late! You **mustn't get up**! You **can't go** to school!

Les verbes *look / feel* + adjectif

You **look** very tired. How **do** you **feel?** – I **feel** very tired!
You **don't look** very well. – I **feel** ill.

look and learn WB p. 71

PART 4

How to... talk about pictures

Les images sont un moyen universel de communication.
Elles nous envoient de multiples messages.
À nous de les décoder !

1 What is it?

Entraîne-toi à identifier les images. De quel genre de document s'agit-il ? Y a-t-il un message ?

A. Look at the different pictures and identify each one.

Which one is ...
- a cartoon drawing?
- an advert?
- a sign?
- a painting in the street?
- a photo in a newspaper?

Ist

2nd

3rd

THE NEWSPAPER FOR THE NEW MILLENNIUM
THE EXPRESS
SATURDAY JANUARY 1st 2000
THE GREATEST SHOW ON EARTH

4th

5th

B. Then answer these questions:
- What does the sign say? Where can you see signs like this?
- What is the advert for? Where can you see adverts like this?
- What is the cartoon about? Is it funny or serious?
- What does the painting show? What are these paintings called?
- What is in the photo? What is the newspaper article about?

2 Your comments

Apprends à commenter une image plus détaillée, en parlant des différents éléments d'un tableau.

A. Read the title of the painting, the name and dates of the artist and then look at the painting for two or three minutes.

"Going the long way home" — *Helen Bradley (1900-1979)*

B. What can you say about the painting?

THE DATE:
What year is it? (approximately)

THE TIME:
What time of day is it?
What season is it?

PLACE:
Where is it?
What can you see?

PEOPLE AND ACTIONS:
Who can you see? What are they doing?
Can you explain the title?

YOUR OPINION:
Do you like the painting? Why?/ Why not?

help box

at the top *en haut*
at the bottom *en bas*
in the foreground *au premier plan*
in the background *en arrière plan*
bird *oiseau*
child *(pl.* **children***) enfant*
factory *(pl.* **factories***) usine*
leaf *(pl.* **leaves***) feuille*
man *(pl.* **men***) homme*
season *saison*
sky *ciel*
summer *été*
sunset *coucher du soleil*
town *ville*
winter *hiver*
woman *(pl.* **women***) femme*
year *année*

PART 4

Sounds

1 The silent "r/re"

A. Lorsqu'un mot se termine par **r** ou **re**, cette terminaison ne se prononce pas, sauf si l'on peut faire la liaison avec le mot qui suit. Écoute et entraîne-toi. (Sur la première ligne, les mots de chaque paire se prononcent de façon identique.)

you're/your where/wear hear/here our/hour
are car near shower

B. Mais on entend bien le **r/re** final si le mot suivant commence par une voyelle, car on fait la liaison. Écoute et entraîne-toi.

1. **Your answer is wrong!**
2. **Where is the airport?**
3. **Can you hear us?**
4. **Our address is different.**
5. **Are all your friends here?**
6. **The car is outside.**
7. **Are we near a town?**
8. **There's a shower upstairs.**

2 Stress of long words

Écoute et entraîne-toi à bien marquer l'accent tonique.

L'accent est sur la première syllabe :

- **interesting**
- **frightening**
- **difficult**
- **temperature**
- **probably**
- **popular**

L'accent est sur la deuxième syllabe :

- **expensive**
- **attractive**
- **computer**
- **fantastic**
- **remember**
- **photographer**

3 "The A-1 rap"

I'm "A-1"! I'm just the best!
I'm bigger and better than all the rest!
I'm taller and faster and heavier too!
I'm much more important than all of you!

Maybe you're bigger and maybe you're fast!
You're the first and we're the last!
But we can tell you how this story ends.
The problem is - you haven't got any friends.

Let's practise!

Lesson 1 pp. 64-65

A **Tu es policier et tu suis un suspect dans New York. Tu parles à un collègue avec ton téléphone portable. Complète ce que tu lui racontes à l'aide des verbes suivants au présent avec be + -ING:**
• buy • eat • get • go • happen • leave • look • sit • talk • walk • wear

The suspect ... a black jacket and blue jeans. She ... into an Italian restaurant and she ... to a man. She ... a pizza. Ah! She ... the restaurant with her pizza and she ... to the park. We're in the park now. She ... on the grass and she ... her pizza. Oh! What ...? She ... up! She ... at me! She can see me!

B **Regarde les illustrations et réponds aux questions.**

1. *Picture 4, page 16.* Who is Tim talking to? Who is he looking at? Can Di hear them?
2. *The small picture, page 33.* Who is Sally talking to? What are they looking at?
3. *Picture 5, page 40.* Who is Marsha talking to? Who is she looking for? Who is she waiting for?
4. *Picture 4, page 64.* Who is James talking to? Who is Di looking at? Can she see Jerry?

C **Traduis.**

1. « J'entends une voiture! » « C'est notre taxi! »
2. « J'attends Di. Où est-elle? » « Je ne la vois pas! »
3. « Que regardes-tu? » « La carte, mais je ne vois pas l'aéroport. »
4. « Est-ce que tu m'entends? » « Pas très bien! »
5. « Vois-tu le policier? Pourquoi nous regarde-t-il? »

Lesson 2 pp. 66-67

D **Regarde les quatre photos page 66 et trouve des verbes au présent avec be + -ING (formes affirmative et négative) pour compléter chaque description.**

1. In the first photo he ... to the crowd. He ... but he ... at the camera.
2. In the second photo he ... next to his father and he ... at the camera. He ... a jacket. He ... jeans.
3. In the third photo he ... a car and he ... next to a driving instructor. They ... .
4. In the fourth photo he ... at a young woman but he ... at the camera and he ... .

E Tu es vendeur/vendeuse dans une boutique de farces et attrapes. Tu essaies de persuader une cliente d'acheter ! Réagis à ce qu'elle te dit avec une phrase au superlatif avec le même adjectif qu'elle emploie. Voici un exemple :

Customer: The sun mask is very attractive, isn't it?
You: *Yes, it's* the most attractive mask *in the shop!*

1. The clown trousers are quite funny, aren't they?
2. The Chaplin mask is very realistic, isn't it?
3. The Princess costume is very pretty, isn't it?
4. The Pirate hat is very nice, isn't it?
5. The chimpanzee mask is amusing, isn't it?
6. The E.T. costume is good, isn't it?

F Complète chaque phrase avec une question tag et puis complète chaque réponse courte.

1. Prince William's quite tall, ... ? Yes, ...
2. The masks are original, ... ? Yes, ...
3. Rob and Carole aren't in London, ... ? No, ... !
4. "Smiles" is a TV series, ... ? Yes, ...
5. Jerry isn't Di's boyfriend, ... ? No, ... !
6. James is English, ... ? Yes, ...

Lesson 3 pp. 70-71

G Regarde l'information dans 1B p. 70 et trouve les réponses aux questions suivantes :

1. Which animal is faster than a pig but slower than an elephant?
2. Which animals aren't as fast as a rabbit but faster than a camel?
3. Which animal is the fastest in the world?
4. Is a human being faster or slower than a cat? Can you remember?

H Regarde à nouveau les photos de gens célèbres, page 32. Pour chacune des phrases suivantes, trouve une autre manière de dire exactement la même chose. Nous te donnons le début de chaque phrase.

1. Celine Dion is older than Ewan McGregor.
   Ewan McGregor isn't ... .
2. Celine Dion isn't as tall as Nicole Kidman.
   Nicole Kidman is ... .
3. Ewan McGregor is shorter than Liam Neeson.
   Liam Neeson is ... .
4. Ewan McGregor is much younger than Liam Neeson.
   Liam Neeson is ... .

I Regarde les photos dans The Crazy World of Sport, pp. 68-69. Compare chaque fois les deux sports en utilisant le comparatif d'un de ces adjectifs : • amusing • difficult • dangerous • exciting • easy

1. bungy-jumping & surfing
2. rodeos & human table football
3. scuba-diving & snow-rafting
4. frisbee & cricket
5. ballooning & snow-rafting

Lesson 4 pp. 72-73

J Relis les questions sur Dylan (2A p. 72). Lis les réponses ci-dessous et trouve la question qui correspond à chaque réponse. Écris les questions et les réponses.

1. No, it's much more difficult.
2. Because it's too late.
3. Because he must finish his Maths homework.
4. Very tired.
5. Because he's doing the wrong exercise.
6. Yes, it's half past ten.

K Pour chaque phrase (1 à 5) trouve la réponse (A à E).

1. I don't feel very well.
2. How do you feel?
3. Do you feel all right?
4. You look tired.
5. Have you got a temperature?

A. Yes, I feel fine. Do I look ill?
B. Oh? What's the matter? You look fine!
C. Tired. I must go to bed.
D. Perhaps. I feel very hot!
E. I know. I feel tired.

L Reformule chaque phrase en utilisant must ou mustn't :

1. Don't speak French! Speak English!
2. Don't write in your textbook! Write in your workbook!
3. You can't stay in bed! Get up!
4. You can't leave now! Help me with my homework!
5. You can't eat in the library! Go outside!
6. Don't move! Dial 999 and wait for the ambulance!

1

FACT

5

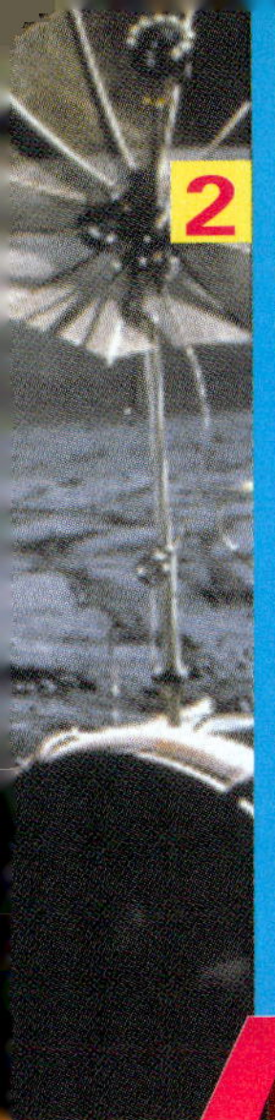

2 3

PART 5

AND FICTION

4

PART 5

lesson 1

VOICES FROM THE PAST

Jerry: Look at the man on the right. He's my great-grandfather. His name was Luigi.

Di: Where was he from? Was he Italian?

Jerry: Yes, he was. He was born in Naples in 1890 but he emigrated to the States with his brothers in 1908. They were all musicians. The Stromboli brothers were quite famous! Luigi played the violin.

Di: When did he die?

Jerry: He died in 1965 and my grandfather changed his surname to Lee.

Di: How interesting!

Di: Were all your family Italian?

Jerry: Oh no! My great-grandmother, Luigi's wife, was Irish! Her name was Rose. She was born in Dublin in 1894 and she emigrated with her sister Mary on the Titanic! She survived but her sister died.

Di: How terrible!

Jerry: Yes, Rose was only 18 and she was all alone in New York. But she married Luigi four years later. She worked in the same theatre. She was a dancer!

Di: Oh! How romantic!

1 HOW MUCH CAN YOU SAY?

P.76

A. Look at the picture and listen to Jerry and Di.
What are they looking at? Who is Jerry talking about?

B. Listen again and answer these questions about Luigi.

1. Where was he from?
2. When was he born?
3. When did he emigrate to the States?
4. How old was he when he emigrated?
5. Who were the Stromboli brothers?
6. What instrument did Luigi play?
7. When did he die?
8. How old was he when he died?

C. Now read about Rose and complete the questions in your workbook. Then ask and answer the questions.

chatterbox

How romantic!

2 WHO ARE THE "GHOSTS"?

P.76

A. Listen to the "voices" from the past and look at the five pictures.

a

b

c

d

e

Who is talking?

Charlie Chaplin
Queen Victoria
Alexander Graham Bell
John Lennon
Captain Cook

B. Listen again and complete the grid in your workbook. Then ask and answer questions about each famous person.

3 WHAT ABOUT YOU?

P.77

Work in pairs and ask each other the questions in your workbook. Then write about yourself and your family.

grammar box

Le prétérit de *be*

I **was** / We **were** → You **were**

very famous.

He **was** / She **was** — They **were**

Le prétérit des verbes réguliers

V + -D/-ED

I live**d** in the 20th century.
He play**ed** the violin.
She reign**ed** for 64 years.

Where **did** she **work**? She work**ed** ...
When **did** he **die**? He die**d** ...
When **did** she **marry** him? She marri**ed** ...

look and learn WB p. 78

lesson 2

WHAT HAPPENED?

A lucky man!

Ten years ago, Fred Dickinson opened a junk shop in Sydney. He bought and sold all sorts of things and he sometimes exchanged things too. Unfortunately, he wasn't a good businessman and he didn't make a lot of money. But two months ago, something changed his life. What happened? Well, one morning, an old couple came into his shop. The old man had a small parcel under his arm. He opened it and Fred saw a very dirty old painting. He didn't usually buy paintings but the old couple were very poor so Fred exchanged the painting for a coat and a pair of shoes. The old couple were very pleased. In the evening, he cleaned it and found the signature: Picasso! Fred wasn't an expert on art but he knew the name and realised the painting was very valuable. What happened next? It's a mystery, but Fred made a fortune. He left Sydney a month ago and went to a Caribbean island. He bought an enormous house there and now lives in luxury...

You're a lucky man, Fred; you made a fortune – but who bought the Picasso?

Rob Hunter

A recent photo of Fred Dickinson in the Caribbean.

Fred Dickinson's junk shop in Sydney.

Fred's Picasso.

chatterbox

1 FIRST IMPRESSIONS

Look at the left-hand page. What is it? What is it about? Say as much as you can.

P.80

2 READ THE ARTICLE

A. Read the article and choose the correct short answer for the questions. Then write the answers in your workbook. Find sentences in the article to justify your answers.

1. Was Fred's shop in Sydney?
2. Was he a good businesman?
3. Did he sell junk?
4. Did the old couple come to his shop?
5. Was the painting new?
6. Were the old couple rich?
7. Did Fred buy the painting?
8. Were the old couple happy?
9. Did Fred's life change?
10. Did he stay in Sydney?

Yes, ... was.
No, ... wasn't.
Yes, ... were.
No, ... weren't.
Yes, ... did.
No, ... didn't.

B. Then complete the questions and answers in your workbook.

C. Find the preterite of the irregular verbs in the article. Complete the grid in your workbook.

P.81

3 WHAT REALLY HAPPENED?

A. Rob gets a phone call at his office. Listen to the conversation and complete it in your workbook.

B. Work in pairs.
Compare the information in the conversation with the information in Rob's article.
What is not true in Rob's article?
Exchange your ideas in class.
What are your conclusions?

grammar box

Le prétérit des verbes irréguliers: forme affirmative

FIND	He **found** the signature.	KNOW	He **knew** the name.
SELL	He **sold** the picture.	BUY	He **bought** a house.

Le prétérit: forme négative

BE	He **wasn't** a good businessman.	The old couple **weren't** rich.
Autres verbes :	He **didn't buy** pictures.	He **didn't make** a lot of money.

Réponses courtes: contredire

It **was** a Picasso.	**No, it wasn't!**
The old couple **weren't** pleased.	**Yes, they were!**
Picasso **painted** the painting.	**No, he didn't.**
Fred **didn't sign** the painting.	**Yes, he did!**

look and learn WB pp. 82-83

THE STORY OF LONDON

A

Londinium was an important port in the Roman Empire.

When the Romans invaded Britain in AD 43 they founded "Londinium" and built the first "London Bridge" over the river Thames. The Romans stayed in Britain for 400 years. They built many roads and towns and brought Roman civilisation to the island of Britain.

B

William built a fortress called The White Tower to defend London. It is now part of the Tower of London.

William the Conqueror invaded England in 1066 and became King William I. The Normans ruled England for 300 years and introduced a lot of French words into the English language.

C

The fire started in a baker's shop. Over 200,000 people lost their homes but only six people died.

In the summer of 1666, the Great Fire of London destroyed about 70% of the buildings. But after the fire, architects designed a more modern city with wide streets and stone houses.

D

London was the first city to build an underground railway in 1900, but buses were still pulled by horses!

From 1800 to the middle of the 20th century the British Empire included Canada, India, Australia, New Zealand, the West Indies and vast regions of Africa. London was one of the most important cities in the world.

E

Many Londoners lost their homes during the terrible Blitz of 1940.

During World War II (1939-1945) German planes bombed London again and again. The bombs destroyed many buildings and killed thousands of people but the city survived.

F

London was a favourite city for young people in the "Swinging Sixties".

London was the capital of pop culture during the 1960s.

G

The "London Eye" was built to celebrate the new millennium.

From this gigantic wheel you can see all of London. It opened in February 2000.

PART 5

lesson 3

QUIZ NIGHT

Yesterday there was a "Quiz Night" at school.
It was a competition between Sally's class and their parents.
The quizmaster was Mr Blake, Sally's history teacher.

P.85

1 LISTEN AND FIND OUT

A. Listen to the first part of the quiz.

1. Who gave two correct answers?
2. Who gave a wrong answer?
3. How many points did Lucy score?
4. How many points were scored by the pupils?

B. Listen again and read the questions on the cards. Then, in teams, find the answers from the words in the boxes in your workbook. Ask the other teams the questions.

Who invented television?

Who built the first motorised aeroplane?

Name the spacecraft that landed on the moon on 21st July, 1969.

Name the explorer who discovered Australia.

Name the writer who wrote "Huckleberry Finn".

C. Now write the answers in your workbook.

chatterbox

2 HELP THE PARENTS!

A. Read the five questions for the parents.
Do you know the answers? Exchange your ideas.

1. Who built the first London Bridge?
2. Name the famous ship that sank on 15th April 1912.
3. Who invented the electric light bulb?
4. Name the Beatle who wrote the song "Yesterday".
5. Who produced the first family car and what was it called?

B. Now complete the answers in your workbook.

P.86

3 A CLASS QUIZ

P.86

You can do this quiz in teams. Go to your workbook and circle a. b. or c. (the correct answer or the correct ending). You score 2 points for each correct choice.

grammar box

Pronoms relatifs : sujet

pour les personnes : ***who***	Name the explorer **who** discovered Australia.
pour les choses : ***that***	Name the spacecraft **that** landed on the moon.

La forme passive : *be* (conjugué) + participe passé

The telephone **was invented** by Alexander Graham Bell.
How many points **were scored** by the pupils?

look and learn WB p. 87

lesson 4

WHAT WENT WRONG?

The actors are rehearsing a scene for this week's episode. "Amy" is a regular customer at "Smiles" and it's her 80th birthday!

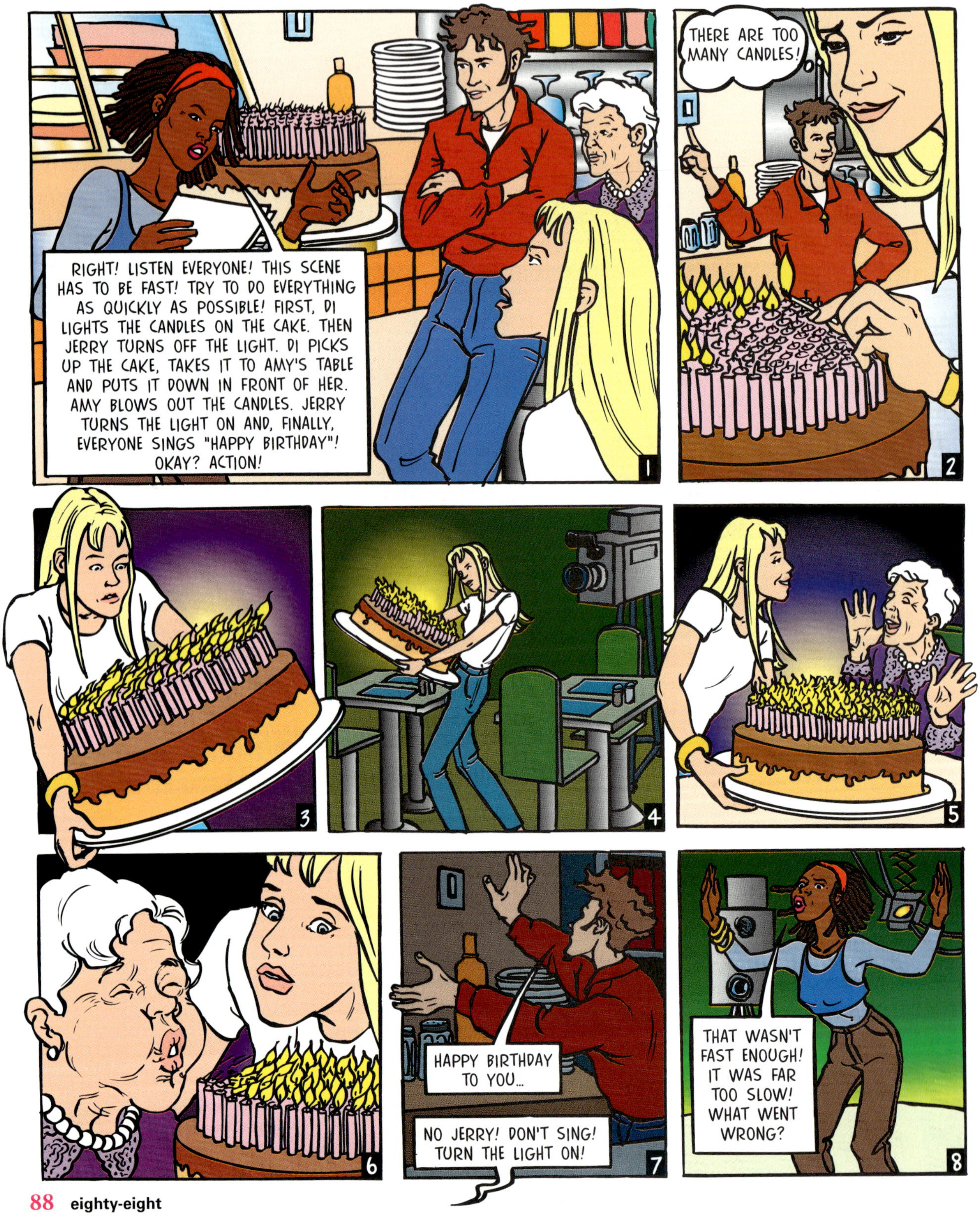

1 HOW MUCH CAN YOU SAY?

A. Read Marsha's instructions to the actors. What does everyone have to do?

B. Now look at everyone. What are they trying to do? What are the problems?

2 LISTEN AND FIND OUT

P.89

A. Listen to the conversation at the end of the rehearsal and find the answers to the questions. Then write the questions above the answers in your workbook.

1. Was the scene fast enough?
2. Could Di light the candles?
3. Could Di pick up the cake?
4. Why couldn't Di move quickly?
5. Are there too many candles?
6. Did Jerry turn on the light?

B. Now listen again and complete the conversation in your workbook.

3 READ THE LETTER

P.90

Di is very disappointed. This morning she got a letter from Mr Silverman's assistant, Anna. Read the letter and do the activities in your workbook.

21st April

Dear Miss Hunter,

Mr Silverman and I were very pleased to meet you in March.

Unfortunately, we cannot offer you the role of "Danger Woman". You are a talented young actress but we think you are a little too young and not experienced enough for the role.

In fact we are looking for a well-known American actress for the film. The television series "Smiles" is very popular but, unfortunately, your accent is very British, and you are perhaps too well-known as the English waitress in the series!

However, thank you for coming to the audition last month and good luck for the future.

Best wishes,

Anna Benton

Anna Benton.

grammar box

Les verbes à particule:	**Turn on** the light. / **Turn** the light **on. Turn it on.** **Blow out** the candles. / **Blow** the candles **out. Blow them out.**
***Too, enough*:**	It was (far) **too slow.** It wasn't **fast enough.** You are (a little) **too young**. You are not **experienced enough**.
Le prétérit de *can*:	**Could** she **light** the candles? **Yes, she could. / No, she couldn't.** I **could pick up** the cake but I **couldn't move** very quickly.
Le verbe *try + to* + V:	**Try to do** everything as quickly as possible. What **are** they **trying to do**? I **tried to blow** them **out**!

look and learn WB p. 91

PART 5

How to... tell a story

Apprendre à raconter une histoire, c'est apprendre à construire des phrases plus longues et aussi à relier une phrase à une autre.

1 Read a story

Entraîne-toi à identifier les mots de liaison : conjonctions, adverbes, pronoms relatifs.

Listen to this well-known story. Then read the story. Can you say what the BLUE words mean? Are they conjunctions, adverbs or relative pronouns?

"THE THREE LITTLE PIGS"

Once upon a time, there were three little pigs who lived with their mother and father. They were very happy together but they decided they were old enough to live on their own, so they said goodbye to their parents and left the family home.

Pinky, the youngest one, was very lazy so he made a house of straw. It only took him one day but it was very fragile. Porky wasn't as lazy as Pinky so he made a house of sticks. It took him two days but he was very pleased with the result. However, Perky, the oldest and cleverest pig, built a house of bricks that was very solid. It took him a week and he was very tired because he worked very hard.

Unfortunately, there was a big, bad wolf who lived very near and he could see the three little pigs in their new houses. First he went to Pinky's house because it was the most fragile. He blew and blew and blew until the house fell down. Luckily, Pinky escaped and ran to Porky's house. Then the wolf went to the house of sticks. He blew and blew and blew but, before the house fell down, Pinky and Porky ran to Perky's house.

Finally, the wolf went to the house of bricks, where the three little pigs were all together. Although Pinky and Porky were very frightened of the wolf, Perky felt quite happy because he knew his house was much stronger.

The wolf blew and blew but the bricks didn't move, so he climbed onto the roof and looked down the chimney. When Perky heard the wolf on the roof, he said "Quick! Let's light a fire!", so they made a big fire in the chimney. Suddenly the wolf fell down the chimney and into the fire. "Aaagh!" he screamed because his ears and his tail were on fire!

He ran out of the house and never came back again! The three little pigs lived happily ever after in the house of bricks.

2 Tell the story

À toi de raconter une autre histoire très connue. Il faut lier le récit en choisissant les mots de liaison.

A. This is a summary of a well-known story .
Where you see the symbol ❖ choose a linking word from the BLUE words on the left-hand page.

"CINDERELLA"

Once upon a time, there was a young girl called Cinderella ❖ lived with her two ugly sisters. ❖ , her sisters didn't like Cinderella ❖ she was much prettier than them. They were very cruel to her ❖ Cinderella was very unhappy.

One evening the three sisters were invited to a ball at the palace, ❖ her sisters told Cinderella she couldn't go ❖ she didn't have the right clothes, ❖ she stayed at home on her own.

❖, a fairy appeared ❖ transformed Cinderella's clothes into a wonderful dress. Cinderella couldn't walk to the ball ❖ the fairy transformed a pumpkin ❖ was in the kitchen into a magnificent coach. ❖ she left, the fairy told her "You must be home before midnight!"

The prince danced with Cinderella all evening ❖ she was the most beautiful girl at the ball, ❖ at midnight she had to leave. ❖ she ran out of the ballroom, she lost her shoe ❖, ❖, the prince found it ❖ picked it up.

The next day, the prince looked everywhere for the mysterious girl ❖ had the other shoe ❖ he couldn't find her. ❖ he looked in the palace. ❖ he looked in the town. ❖ he came to the house ❖ Cinderella and her sisters lived.

❖ their feet were very big, the ugly sisters tried on the shoe ❖ it was far too small for them. ❖, the prince saw Cinderella ❖ said "You must try on the shoe too!" ❖ Cinderella tried it on ❖ it was the perfect size!

The prince married Cinderella ❖ they lived happily ever after.

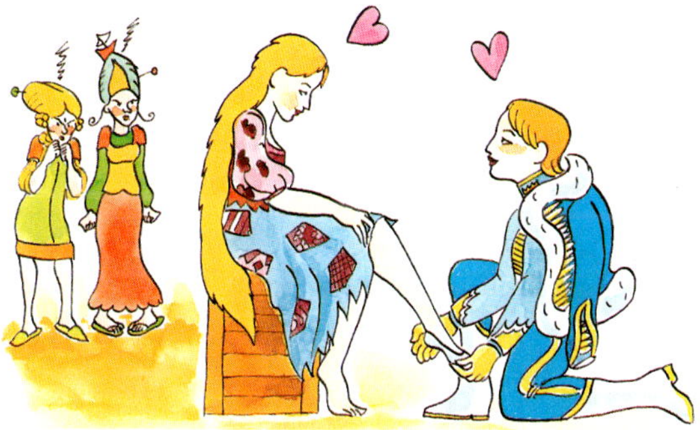

B. Now listen to the story and compare!

PART 5

Sounds

1 1 or 2 syllables?

Lis les réponses courtes. Les mots en vert sont-ils composés d'une syllabe ou de deux? Ensuite écoute la réponse et entraîne-toi.

No, he isn't. No, they aren't. No, it wasn't.
No, we weren't. No, she hasn't. No, I haven't.
No, he doesn't. No, we don't. No, they didn't.
No, I can't. No, you mustn't. No, she couldn't.

2 [t] [d] or [ɪd]?

Au prétérit, la terminaison en ed des verbes réguliers peut se prononcer de trois manières différentes: [t], [d], [ɪd].

Écoute les phrases suivantes. Comment se prononce la terminaison de chaque verbe régulier?

1. **Yesterday we stayed at home.**
2. **We invited our friends to dinner**
3. **They liked our house.**
4. **We watched a good film.**
5. **It started at nine o'clock.**
6. **We played a game of chess.**

Ensuite, écoute à nouveau et entraîne-toi. En faisant la liaison entre le verbe et la voyelle qui suit, tu entendras mieux la différence entre [t] et [d].

3 "The lazy day rap"

I **leave** home every **mor**ning
at **quar**ter to **eight**.

But this **mor**ning, when I **got** up,
it was **ve**ry, very **late**!

I **did**n't have a **show**er
and I **did**n't get **dressed**.

I **stayed** in my py**ja**mas
and I **did**n't look my **best**!

I had **break**fast at **one**
and **lunch** at half past **three**.

I **read** a maga**zine**
and **then** I watched T**V**.

My **pa**rents were quite **an**gry,
but **what** could they **say**?

It's the **first** day of my **ho**lidays
– a **love**ly, lazy **day**!

Let's practise!

Lesson 1 pp. 80-81

A À l'aide de la conversation p. 80 retrouve les questions pour ces réponses concernant Luigi et Rose:

1. In Naples, Italy.
2. In 1890.
3. He was 18.
4. They were musicians.
5. The violin.
6. In 1965.
7. He was 75.
8. In Dublin.
9. In 1912.
10. No, she survived.
11. In 1916.
12. In the same theatre.

B En t'aidant de la grille du workbook (2B p. 76), réponds aux questions suivantes:

1. When was Queen Victoria born?
2. How old was she when she died?
3. Where was Charlie Chaplin born?
4. What was his occupation?
5. How old was John Lennon when he died?
6. When did Captain Cook die?
7. How old was he?
8. What was his occupation?

C Il est lundi matin. Jerry parle à Di. Complète chaque phrase de leur conversation avec was ou were:

Jerry: ... you at home on Saturday night?
Di: No, James and I ... at a restaurant.
Jerry: Oh! Where ... you yesterday afternoon?
Di: I ... at the cinema.
Jerry: ... James with you?
Di: No, he ... at the airport!
Jerry: Oh! ... he pleased with his visit?
Di: Yes, he ... very pleased, thank you!

Lesson 2 pp. 82-83

D Relis l'article de Rob p. 82. Toutes les affirmations suivantes sont fausses. Contredis chaque phrase avec une réponse courte puis donne les renseignements justes:

1. Rob is an actor. *No, he isn't. He's ...* .
2. He lives in London.
3. Fred Dickinson had a clothes shop.
4. He opened his shop twenty years ago.
5. Fred left Sydney a year ago.
6. He went to America.
7. Now he's poor.
8. He lives in a small hotel.

E Reporte-toi à la conversation entre Rob et le vieil homme dans le workbook p. 81 et réponds aux questions suivantes :

1. Did the old man and his wife go to Fred's shop?
2. When did Fred come to their house?
3. Where did Fred find the painting?
4. Did he exchange the painting for some old clothes?
5. Who painted the painting?
6. Who wrote the signature?

F C'est lundi matin. Pose des questions à Dylan au sujet du week-end dernier pour savoir :

1. ce qu'il a fait samedi soir,
2. s'il est allé au cinéma,
3. s'il a regardé la télévision hier,
4. s'il a joué au football pendant le week-end,
5. quand il a fait ses devoirs,
6. s'il est allé chez Sally,
7. s'il a passé un bon week-end.

G Trouve le prétérit de ces verbes irréguliers pour compléter le récit de Sally :

• buy • come • do • go • have • leave • make • see • write

Lucy and I ... shopping yesterday afternoon. I ... a new pair of shoes. Then we ... to the cinema. We ... a very good film. After the film, Lucy ... to my house and I ... dinner. We ... spaghetti bolognese. Lucy ... at nine o'clock and I ... my French homework. I ... two pages in French about my hobbies!

Lesson 3 pp. 86-87

H Choisis entre who et that et termine chaque phrase :

1. The Wright brothers were the men ... .
2. Apollo 11 was the spacecraft ... .
3. Thomas Edison was the scientist ... .
4. Mercury is the planet ... .
5. John F. Kennedy was the American president ... .
6. The Titanic was the famous ship ... .

I Exprime la même chose à la forme passive :

1. The Romans built the first London bridge.
2. Columbus discovered America in 1492.
3. William the Conqueror invaded England in 1066.
4. Celine Dion sang the song in the film "Titanic".
5. Henry Ford produced the first family car.
6. Paul McCartney wrote "Yesterday".

J Complète les question tags et réponds à chaque question par une réponse courte pour confirmer ou pour contredire.

This exercise is very easy, *isn't it? No, it isn't!*
Jerry wasn't born in Italy, *was he? No, he wasn't!*

1. Marsha is an actress, ... she?
2. Tim Fox writes the script for "Smiles", ... he?
3. James visited Di in New York, ... ?
4. Jerry likes Di, ... ?
5. Sally and Lucy are friends, ... ?
6. Sally's team scored a lot of points, ... ?
7. The questions weren't very easy, ... ?
8. It was an interesting quiz, ... ?

Lesson 4 pp. 88-89

K Réponds en remplaçant les mots soulignés par un marqueur de personne complément. Attention à l'ordre des mots :

1. Could <u>Di</u> pick up <u>the cake</u>?
2. Where did <u>Di</u> put down <u>the cake</u>?
3. What did <u>Amy</u> try to do with <u>the candles</u>?
4. Why couldn't <u>Amy</u> blow out <u>the candles</u>?
5. Why couldn't <u>Jerry</u> turn on <u>the light</u>?

L Exprime la même idée en utilisant l'adverbe enough et un des ces adjectifs :

• American • experienced • light • short • fast • old

1. The actors were too slow.
2. The scene was too long.
3. The cake was too heavy!
4. Di is too young for the role of Danger Woman.
5. Her accent is too British.
6. She is too inexperienced.

M Complète les phrases suivantes avec les mots appris dans Part 5.

1. No! That isn't the ... answer! It's the ... answer!
2. No! Don't turn the ... on! Turn it ... !
3. Put the ... on the cake and then ... them!
4. Did Sally's team ... the quiz? How many points did they ... ?
5. Don't pick the cake ... ! Put it ... !
6. "Rose's sister ... on the Titanic!" " ... terrible!"
7. John Lennon was ... in 1940. He wrote a lot of ... .
8. The old couple weren't rich. They were ... . They didn't have a lot of ... .

2

1

4
POWELL & HYDE Sts.
tommy
SAN FRANCISCO MUNICIPAL RAILWAY

PART 6

CHOICES

lesson 1

DON'T MISS THE CONCERT!

There is a concert this week at Sally's School. Ray, who is in one of the bands, is selling tickets. It's Monday lunchtime.

1 FIRST IMPRESSIONS

Read the introduction and look at the poster and the picture.

1. When's the concert?
2. Where's the concert?
3. What day is it today?
4. Who's Ray?
5. What's he doing now?
6. How much are the tickets?
7. Who looks enthusiastic?
8. Who looks disappointed?

chatterbox

P.96

2 LISTEN TO THE CONVERSATION

A. Listen to the conversation and complete the grid in your workbook.

B. Use the information in your grid to ask and answer the questions in your workbook. Then write the answers.

3 LISTEN AND FIND OUT

P.97

A. Lucy's talking to Ray. Listen to their conversation.

- Do you know ...when Ray is leaving school?
  ...what he wants to do?
  ...what Lucy's father does?
  ...where Lucy's father works?
  ...why he is going to the concert?
  ...if Ray can meet him?

- **Ask each other the questions.**

Either: *Do you know when Ray is leaving school?* **or:** *When is Ray leaving school?*

B. Now listen again and complete the conversation in your workbook.

4 PATTERN PRACTICE

Sally's talking to Mike about her summer holidays. Listen and practise the examples. Then take the role of Mike and choose the right "tag question" from the box.

TAG QUESTIONS
Did you?
Do you?
Does he?
Has she?
Is it?
Is she?

5 A QUESTIONNAIRE: "MY SUMMER HOLIDAYS"

Work in pairs and do the questionnaire in your workbook.

P.97

grammar box

Le présent avec *be* + -ING : exprimer le futur

Lucy **is going** to the concert **next Friday.** The Michigans **are playing at 9 o'clock.**
What **is** Ray **doing tonight**? Where **is** Sally **going** on holiday **this summer?**

***Want* + *to* + V : exprimer une volonté**

I **want to go** to the concert. I **don't want to go.** What **does** he **want to do?**

Interrogatives indirectes

Do you know when **Ray is leaving** school?
Do you know what **Ray wants** to do?
Ask your friend where **he/she went** last summer.

et directes

When **is Ray leaving** school?
What **does Ray want** to do?
Where **did you go** last summer?

look and learn WB p. 98

PART 6

lesson 2

HOLIDAY IDEAS!

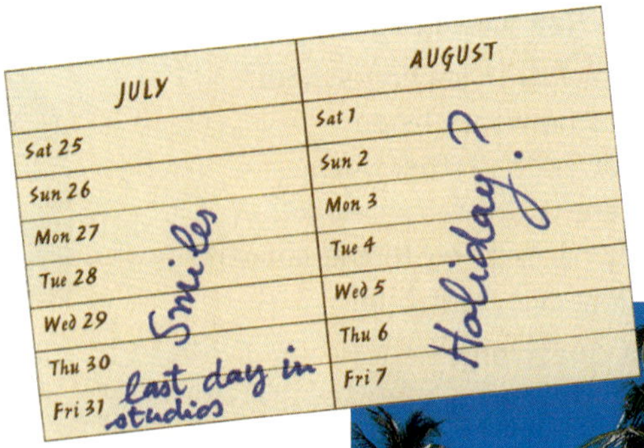

Palm Beach, Miami, Florida

Sea World, Orlando, Florida

The Grand Canyon

Las Vegas

San Francisco

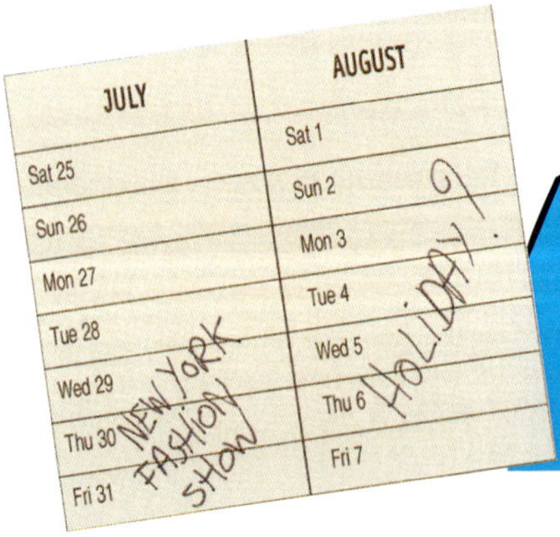

1 FIRST IMPRESSIONS

Look at the pictures and photos. What are Di and James talking about? What do they want to do? Say as much as you can.

2 LISTEN AND FIND OUT

P.100

**A. Listen to the first part of the phone conversation.
Then ask and answer four questions about Di and James. Then complete the questions and answers in your workbook.**

What sort of holiday would … like?

What would … like to do?

She'd He'd	like like to	see everything in New York. an exciting holiday. a real holiday. go to the beach and relax.

B. Listen again and look at the boxes. The sentences in box A are not true! Contradict each sentence with a sentence from box B and then find the correct information about James in box C. Write your answers in your workbook.

A	B	C
Di is on holiday in July. Di doesn't like the sun. Di isn't free in August. Di wants to go to the beach every day.	Yes, she does! No, she doesn't! No, she isn't! Yes, she is!	So does James. Neither does James. Neither is James. So is James.

**C. Listen to the second part of the conversation and complete it in your workbook.
Do Di and James agree? Answer the questions in your workbook.**

chatterbox

3 SUGGESTIONS FOR A SCHOOL TRIP

P.101

Work in pairs and make suggestions for a trip abroad with your class. Do you agree? Then report back to the class and exchange your ideas.

grammar box

***Would like* + N / + *to* + V :** exprimer ses désirs

What sort of holiday **would** you **like**? — I **would (I'd) like** a real holiday!
Where **would** you **like to go**? — We **would** (We'**d) like to go** to London!

Suggérer une activité :
Let's go on holiday together!
Why don't we go to Florida?
How about driv**ing** to the West Coast?

***So… ; neither…* :** exprimer les points communs

I **am** free. – **So am** I.
I **like** the sun. – **So do** I.
I'**d** like to go to London. – **So would** I.

Di **isn't** free. **Neither is** James.
James **doesn't like** crowds and **neither does** Di.

look and learn WB p. 102

The Main

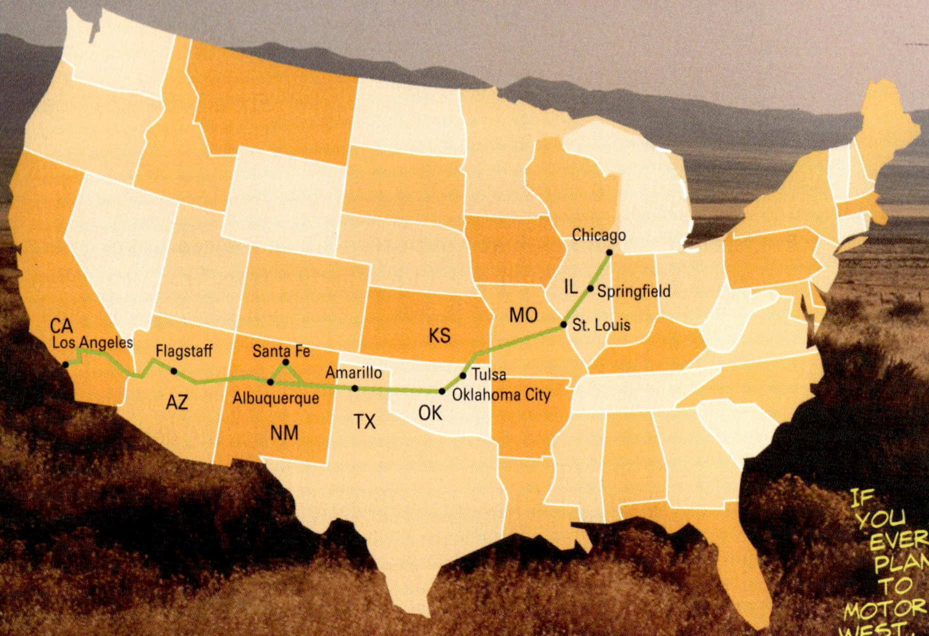

Route 66, the most famous road in America, was built between 1926 and 1939. It was 2,448 miles long (about 4,000 kms) and went from Chicago to Los Angeles. It crossed 8 states and 3 time zones. It linked rural communities with towns and cities and, because it was very flat, truck drivers loved it.

During the Great Depression of the 1930s, a lot of people in the East lost their jobs and many farmers in the Mid-West had to leave their farms. More than 200,000 people took the "Road of Opportunity" and went to California where there were jobs and a pleasant climate.

Travellers needed food and gas, so lots of restaurants and service stations were built, and cheap hotels appeared along Route 66 – the first motels.

About twenty years ago, wider highways with different names replaced Route 66 and you can't find it on a map now. However, you can often see "Historic Route 66" signs on the new roads and tourists can still follow sections of the old route and discover America's past.

IF YOU EVER PLAN TO MOTOR WEST, TRAVEL MY WAY, TAKE THE HIGHWAY THAT'S THE BEST. GET YOUR KICKS ON ROUTE 66. IT WINDS FROM CHICAGO TO L.A., MORE THAN 2,000 MILES ALL THE WAY.

from a song by Bobby Troupe

help box

across *(prép.)*	*à travers*	link *(v.)*	*lier*
flat *(adj.)*	*plat*	motor *(v., fam.)*	*rouler en voiture*
gas *(n., US)*	*essence*	truck driver *(n., US)*	*routier*
"get your kicks" *(expr.)*	*"prends ton pied"*	wide *(adj.)*	*large*
highway *(n., US)*	*route principale*	wind *(v.)*	*serpenter*

Worksheet P.104

Street of America

a The Pacific Ocean, Los Angeles, (the end of Route 66).

b The Sears Tower, Chicago: the world's tallest building.

c The Cadillac Ranch, near Amarillo.

d The Wigwam Village Motel, Arizona.

e Acoma Pueblo (also called Sky City), a 12th century Indian village near Albuquerque, New Mexico.

f Traditional steamboats on the Mississippi river at St Louis, Missouri.

PART 6

lesson 3

CRUMBLE AND CUSTARD!

INGREDIENTS FOR THE FRUIT CRUMBLE...

FOR 6 PEOPLE

* EASY

Fruit filling

- 4 large apples,
- 4 pears,
- 250 grams of raspberries,
- 3 cloves
- 1 teaspoon of cinnamon powder.

The crumble

- 275 grams of flour,
- 180 grams of brown sugar,
- 100 grams of butter.

Homemade custard

See recipe on page 89. Homemade custard is delicious but you can use instant custard powder from a packet. It's easier!

FIRST...

- Heat the oven to 180 degrees.
- Peel the apples and pears and cut them into small pieces.
- Put them in a dish with the raspberries.
- Add the cloves and the cinnamon powder.

THEN...

- Mix the flour and the butter in a large bowl and rub with your fingers.
- Add the sugar and rub until the mixture is crumbly.
- Cover the fruit with the crumble mixture.
- Place the dish in the top of the oven and cook for 40 minutes.

FINALLY...

- Serve hot with real custard! "Bon appétit!"

P.105

1 READ THE RECIPE

A. You can prepare this activity at home. Read the recipe and look at the picture.
- What ingredients do you need? Complete the grid in your workbook.
- Put the pictures in chronological order and write the correct instructions under each picture.

B. In class, use the information in your workbook to ask and answer questions about the different ingredients and the instructions.

What is the ... for? *What are the ... for?*

How much ... do you need? *How many ... do you need?*

What do you do with the ... ?

P.106

2 WHAT'S MISSING?

Rob is having a dinner party this evening for Carole and other journalists he knows at the office. He wants to make crumble and custard. He's looking at the recipe book his mother sent him. Carole lives in the same building and she wants to help...

A. Listen to the conversation. In your workbook ✔ tick the ingredients Rob has got and underline the ingredients Carole can go and get.

B. Make sentences like these:

Rob has got some ... but he hasn't got any ... .

Carole has got some ... but she hasn't got any ... .

C. Listen again and complete the conversation in your workbook.

3 PATTERN PRACTICE

Rob's giving his friends steak and chips, and cheese too! Listen to Rob and Carole and practise the examples. Then take the role of Carole and continue.

Oh! I haven't got enough milk. Have you got any?

Yes, I've got some. I'll go and get **it**!

And we need some eggs!
I haven't got enough. Have you got any?

Yes, I've got some. I'll go and get **them**!

grammar box

Exprimer une quantité :
noms indénombrables

How much butter do you need?
I've got **some** butter.
Have you got **any** brown sugar?
There isn't **any** brown sugar.
Is there **enough** milk?

Exprimer un nombre :
noms dénombrables

How many apples do you need?
I've got **some** apples.
Have you got **any** pears?
There aren't **any** pears.
There aren't **enough** eggs.

***Some, any, enough*: déterminants et pronoms**

I need **some** sugar. There's **some** on the shelf. – I can't see **any**!
We need **some** eggs. I haven't got **enough**. Have you got **any**? – Yes, I've got **some**.

look and learn WB p. 107

lesson 4

WHOSE IS IT?

It's 1.15 pm in the studios and Marsha is looking for something...

Marsha: Where did you put my mobile, Helen? I gave it to you before lunch.

Helen: Oh, er… I don't remember.

Marsha: Well, find it, Helen, and turn it off. We're filming in ten minutes.

Helen: Whose is that phone, Di?

Di: It's mine. James sent it to me for my birthday.

Helen: It's exactly like Marsha's. Are you sure it isn't hers?

Di: Yes. I know ours are the same colour but this is definitely mine.

Helen: Well, don't leave it on the bar, Di. We're filming in five minutes.

Marsha: Whose phone is that? I think it's in one of those bags.

Jerry: One of these bags?

Marsha: Yes. Whose are they? Are they Tim's?

Jerry: No, I don't think they're his.

Marsha: Well, whose bags are they? Oh, never mind! Just find the mobile and turn it off!

Jerry: Here it is! Oh! It's yours, isn't it?

Marsha: Mine? No, I gave mine to... Wait a minute. Show it to me, Jerry! Oh, Sorry! I think you're right.

P.109

1 WHAT'S THE STORY?

A. Look at the pictures. What's happening?

B. Then read the sentences in your workbook. Put them in chronological order and tell the story. What happened?

P.109

2 LISTEN AND FIND OUT

A. Listen to the conversation and answer the questions.

1. What happened before lunch?
2. Did Di buy her mobile?
3. What did Di do with her mobile?
4. Why did Marsha call Di?

B. Who are he, she, her and it in these sentences? Change all the pronouns to nouns and write the sentences in your workbook.

- She gave it to her.
- He sent it to her.
- He showed it to her.

C. Complete the questions in your workbook with who or whose. Ask and answer them (one-word answers) and write the answers in your workbook.

D. Listen to the four questions and find the answer for each one. Then write the questions and answers in your workbook.

Yes, it was hers. No, it wasn't his.

No, they weren't his. No, it wasn't hers.

chatterbox

3 TIDY UP!

Follow your teacher's instructions and make conversations like these.

A: Whose is this/that ...? ... yours?
B: No, ... mine. It's ...'s. Give it to him/her!

A: Whose are these/those ...? ... yours?
B: No, ... mine. They're ...'s. Give them to him/her!

grammar box

L'appartenance :

Whose is that phone? – It's Marsha**'s**.
Whose phone is that? – It's Di**'s**.
Whose (bags) are they? – They're Tim**'s**.

Les marqueurs de propriété pronoms :

It's **mine**.
It's **ours**.
It's **yours**.

It's **his**.
It's **hers**.
It's **theirs**.

Les marqueurs compléments : objet direct/indirect

I gave **it to you**. He sent **it to me**. Show **it to me**. Give **them to her**.

look and learn WB pp. 110-111

PART 6

How to... react

1 A quick reaction!

Entraîne-toi à réagir vite à ce que l'on te dit.

A. AGREE!

Listen to the examples and practise the stress and intonation.
Now listen and continue. Take the role of the young Indian and show that you agree.

Then listen to the complete conversation.

B. DISAGREE!

Listen to the examples and practise the intonation. Then listen and continue. Take the role of the young person. Use a short answer to show that the policeman is wrong!

Then listen to the complete conversation.

2 What's important?

Lorsque quelqu'un te pose une question fermée pour obtenir un renseignement précis, il faut bien comprendre de quel renseignement il s'agit. Apprends à capter le mot-clé dans la question.

Listen to the journalist's questions. He says exactly the same words four times but the question is different each time!

- **What does he want to know?**
  1. He wants to know **when** the President is flying to Chicago.
  2. He wants to know **who** is flying to Chicago on Friday.
  3. He wants to know **where** the President is going on Friday.
  4. He wants to know **how** the President is going to Chicago.

- **Give the right information and stress the important word!**
  a. No, he's flying to Boston.
  b. No, he's going on Thursday.
  c. No, he's going by car.
  d. No, his wife is going.

Then listen to the questions and answers.

3 How do YOU feel?

Lorsque l'on reçoit des informations intéressantes on a souvent envie d'exprimer son point de vue.

A. SHOW INTEREST!

Listen to the example and practise the intonation. Then listen and continue. Take the role of the young passenger. Use a tag question to show you are interested.

Then listen to the complete conversation.

B. GOOD NEWS OR BAD NEWS?

Listen to the four people and choose the right reaction to show what you think.

How exciting!

How awful!

How strange!

How original!

PART 6

Sounds

1 The same sound [huːz]

Whose, Who's (Who is), et Who's (Who has) se prononcent exactement de la même façon.

A. Écoute et entraîne-toi :

- Whose mobile is that?
- Who's on the phone?
- Who's got my phone?

B. Écoute les 6 phrases et dis ce que tu entends :

a. Whose
b. Who's (Who is)
c. Who's (Who has)

2 "th" – [θ] or [ð]?

A. « th » se prononce de deux façons différentes. Écoute et entraîne-toi à faire la différence entre les deux sons.

- « th » se prononce [θ]

think theatre thank thing throat third
bath fourth month birthday south north

- « th » se prononce [ð]

there this that these those their
brother weather together neither father

B. Lis ces phrases à voix haute en faisant la distinction entre les deux sons [θ] et [ð].

1. It's my birthday this month.
2. I think the weather is nicer in the south.
3. Thanks for these tickets to the theatre!
4. Tidy up those things over there!

3 "The fish and chips rap"

Hmm. I'm hungry!

So am I!

I'd like some fish and chips!

So would I!

Have you got any money?

Not very much!

I haven't got enough!

Neither have I!

Why don't we go home
and look in the fridge?

That's a good idea!
Come on! Let's go!

Let's practise!

Lesson 1 pp. 96-97

A Un couple d'Écossais en vacances envoient une carte postale à leurs enfants. Complète-la en utilisant la forme be + -ING des verbes suivants :
• come • go • leave • take • stay • visit

Hello from London! This morning we ... shopping and this afternoon we ... the Tower of London. This evening we ... to the theatre! We ... London tomorrow. We ... the Eurostar train to Paris. We ... there for three days. Then we ... back to Edinburgh on Monday. See you then! Love, Mum and Dad.

B Choisis la bonne réaction à chaque question ou affirmation.

1. I'm leaving school in June.	A. Do they?
2. The tickets are £10.	B. Yes, I do.
3. Do you want to leave now?	C. Do you?
4. I want to go to university.	D. Are you?
5. Are you disappointed?	E. Did you?
6. I wanted to play in the band.	F. Are they?
7. My parents want to come to the concert.	G. Yes, I am.

C Une amie te téléphone. Elle vient de voir dans son jardin un petit garçon habillé en pyjama ! Il a l'air perdu. Elle ne sait pas quoi faire. Transforme tes conseils en questions directes que ton amie va poser au garçon.

1. Ask him what his name is.
2. Ask him where he lives.
3. Ask him if he knows his phone number.
4. Ask him why he is in the garden.
5. Ask him who he is looking for.
6. Ask him why he is wearing pyjamas.

Lesson 2 pp. 98-99

D Complète chaque conversation en utilisant would ... like.

1. – What ... for your birthday? – I ... a dog.
 – What sort of dog ...? – I ... a St Bernard!
2. – ... eat? – ... a hamburger and chips please.
 – ... a glass of orange juice? – No, I ... a Coke please.
3. – What ... do this summer? – I ... to America.
 – Where ... go? – I ... see the Grand Canyon.

E Deux amis sortent du cinéma. Trouve la bonne réaction (A-E) à chaque affirmation (1-5) et écris leur conversation.

1. I didn't understand the story.
2. But I liked the actors.
3. I like Brad Pitt.
4. I'd like a pizza.
5. But I haven't got enough money.

A. Neither have I.
B. Neither did I.
C. So did I.
D. So do I.
E. So would I.

F Complète chaque phrase avec des mots nouveaux de la leçon 2.

1. I don't like beaches in the summer. They're always too … .
2. I'm sorry I can't go to the cinema on Saturday. I'm not …
3. I've got good … for you! You're in the school football team!
4. When they got to New York, they … a car and drove to California.
5. Did you have a nice … ? You went to Spain, didn't you?

G Trouve la suite logique (A-E) à chaque phrase (1-5).

1. This isn't the right road!
2. We've got six eggs.
3. It's raining.
4. It's so hot today!
5. The walls look very dirty.

A. Why don't we stay at home and watch TV?
B. How about washing them?
C. Let's go to the beach!
D. Why don't we stop and ask a policeman?
E. How about making an omelette?

Lesson 3 pp. 102-103

H Complète les phrases.

1. How … butter do you need?
2. How … pieces of toast would you like?
3. Is there … milk in the fridge?
4. Would you like … tea?
5. There aren't … eggs in the fridge.
6. Can I have … chips, please?

I Trouve la bonne réponse (A>E) à chaque phrase (1> 5).

1. Do you need any milk?
2. How many potatoes are there?
3. Have we got any steak knives?
4. I'll buy some bread.
5. Can you get some serviettes?

A. About three kilos, I think.
B. Okay. How much do we need?
C. No, thanks. There's enough in the fridge.
D. Okay. How many do we need?
E. Yes, they're on the table.

J Traduis.

1. Cut the meat into pieces and put it in a bowl with some flour.
2. Don't peel the potatoes. Put them in the top of the oven and cook for one hour.
3. How much cheese would you like?
4. I don't want any custard, thanks.
5. – What's missing? – We need some brown sugar.

Lesson 4 pp. 104-105

K Change tous les noms en pronoms et réécris les phrases, comme dans l'exemple :
Tim gave Di his address. > He gave it to her.

1. Jerry gave Di some flowers.
2. Di gave the actors her phone number.
3. Tim showed Marsha the script.
4. Rob sent his newspaper article to his parents.
5. Helen is showing Di and Jerry their new costumes.

L Traduis ces conversations.

1. – À qui est cette veste ? Est-ce à toi, Tim ?
   – Non, celle-là n'est pas à moi. La mienne est noire.
2. – Ceci est mon script, n'est-ce pas ?
   – Non, ce n'est pas le tien. C'est à Marsha.
3. – Tim a des lunettes comme celles-là. Elles sont peut-être à lui.
   – Non, les siennes sont plus petites.
4. – Je pense que ce pull est à Di.
   – Oui, c'est le sien. Je le lui donnerai !
5. – Ces chaussures-là sont à Jerry. Mais à qui sont celles-ci ? – Je ne sais pas !

2

1

4

3

PART 7

PLANS

5

PART 7

lesson 1

WHAT WILL BE, WILL BE!

YOUR FUTURE IN THE STARS... JUNE HOROSCOPE

GEMINI
22nd May – 21st June

Geminis are energetic but very impatient and they don't like making decisions! Jupiter will be in your sign on 10th June and something will interrupt your everyday life or your career. You will have to make an important decision!

LIBRA
24th September – 23rd October

Librans are unpredictable! They can be lazy but they can be very passionate! In June there will be problems with your family or friends and you will disagree about future plans. You will have to be patient because everything will be all right in July!

AQUARIUS
21st January – 18th February

Aquarians are fascinated by the future. They are artistic and clever and they hate routine! But in June nothing extraordinary will happen and life will seem quite boring! You will have to wait for July when you will be able to make exciting holiday plans!

CANCER
22nd June – 22nd July

Cancerians are sensitive and they are often worried and depressed. But the month of June will be relaxed and easy. You will make new friends and you will be able to relax and have a good time. You will get some good news from a friend on 4th June.

SCORPIO
24th October – 22nd November

Scorpios are independent and seem confident, but they don't often show their feelings. Mars will be in your sign this month and things won't be very easy for you. Your friends will give you some advice – but will you listen to them?

PISCES
19th February – 20th March

Pisceans are imaginative and like dreaming. They are quite shy but friendly. In June you will need a lot of patience. Friends will be difficult and you won't agree with them! Try to understand their feelings because you won't be able to change anything.

LEO
23rd July – 23rd August

Leos are leaders and they like controlling everyone. But they are quite romantic and very charming. Venus will be in your sign on 1st June and you will meet someone important! Be ready for a new romance with someone you won't be able to resist!

SAGITTARIUS
23rd November – 21st December

Sagittarians are confident, very energetic and popular! But they hate rules! This month you will travel but you will have to be careful because there will be risks! You won't be able to do everything you want - so don't be too ambitious!

ARIES
21st March – 20th April

Arians are leaders. They are generous and sincere but they don't like taking orders from anyone! Saturn will cross your sign this month and life will be exciting. You will want to make plans but no one will follow you. Try to be persuasive!

VIRGO
24th August – 23rd September

Virgos are perfectionists. They are clever and well-organised but they don't like crowds and like being on their own. Nothing will be easy for you in June and you will have to work hard, but you will be pleased with the results!

CAPRICORN
22nd December – 20th January

Capricorns are careful and quite conventional but they can be too serious sometimes! Mercury will be in your sign on 13th June and there will be a lot of surprises! You will have to follow other people's decisions.

TAURUS
21st April – 21st May

Taureans are practical and calm but they can be very obstinate! Neptune will be in your sign this month and you will make new friends. Together you will be able to make exciting plans for the future but you will have to listen to their ideas!

1 THE STARS AND YOU!

P.116

A. Prepare this activity at home. Read YOUR horoscope and complete the grid in your workbook.

B. Then compare your horoscopes in class. Ask questions like these:

What sign are you? *What are ... like?* *What will happen in June?*

2 LISTEN AND FIND OUT

P.116

A. Listen to Di and Jerry. They're reading their horoscopes.

What sign is Di?

Does she agree with her horoscope?

Does she believe in horoscopes?

What about Jerry?

B. Listen again and complete the conversation in your workbook.

3 WHAT DO YOU THINK?

P.117

A. What will happen in the next hundred years? For each of the following predictions, tick one of the boxes in your workbook.

• CERTAIN • PROBABLE • POSSIBLE • IMPOSSIBLE

1. Cars won't exist. We will fly everywhere.
2. No one will go to school. We will be able to learn at home.
3. We won't be able to feed everyone on earth.
4. There will be too many people. We will have to live in space.
5. We won't have to do the housework. Robots will do it!
6. Scientists will be able to control pollution.
7. No one will go shopping. We will buy everything by Internet.
8. People won't go out to work. They will work from home.

B. Then ask each other the questions in your workbook and give your opinion.

grammar box

Le modal *will* : exprimer le futur

Friends **will be** difficult!
Will you **listen** to their advice?
You **will not (won't) agree** with them.
What **will happen** in June?

Will + be able to + V

You **will be able to relax.**
You **won't be able to change** anything.
Will scientists **be able to control** pollution?

Les mots composés de *every, some, any, no*

everyone	**someone**	**anyone**	**no one**
everything	**something**	**anything**	**nothing**

look and learn WB p. 118

PART 7

lesson 2

A DIFFICULT DECISION!

It's Saturday afternoon. Di's talking on the phone to her agent, Ed Marcus, in London.

Ed: Di? It's Ed! I've got some great news!
Di: What?
Ed: You know the musical "Romeo and Juliet"?
Di: Yes! By Alan Rice – with Pattie Vito?
Ed: Yes. Pattie's going to leave the show and Alan wants you to replace her!
Di: What? You're joking!
Ed: No, I'm serious! Alan saw you in "Cats" two years ago and he knows "Smiles". He asked me to ring you today.
Di: But when does he want me to start?
Ed: October. You'll have to start rehearsals in September.
Di: But what about "Smiles"?
Ed: Look Di! You must accept! You won't get an offer like this again. Alan wants you to make a decision today.
Di: Today? But I'll have to talk to Marsha and Tim! And Jerry will be very upset!
Ed: No, he won't!
Di: And Marsha won't understand!
Ed: Yes, she will! They'll be able to find someone to replace you, Di.
Di: Well, I *would* like to go back to London…
Ed: Yeah!
Di: And I *would* like to do a musical…
Ed: So, what's the problem?
Di: Nothing – but it's a difficult decision! Can you give me a little time?
Ed: I'll give you twenty-four hours! Give me your answer tomorrow evening!
Di: I'll send you an email.
Ed: I know you'll say yes!
Di: I don't think I can refuse!

1 WHAT'S THE PROBLEM?

P.120

A. Look at the picture. Can you guess what the conversation is about? Say as much as you can.

B. Now listen to the conversation.
- Why is it a difficult decision?
- What is Di going to do tomorrow evening?
- Is she going to say yes or no? How do you know?

C. Then read the conversation and make six sentences with the words in the boxes. Write them in chronological order in your workbook.

chatterbox

Alan Ed Di	tells asks wants	Ed Di	to	give him her answer tomorrow. accept the offer. make a decision now. replace Pattie Vito. start in October. give her a little time.

2 WRITING

P.120

A. Now read Di's email to Ed.

From: dhunter@hello.com
Date: 6th June
To: emarcus@globe.com
Re: decision

Dear Ed - Well, you won't be surprised to hear that the answer is YES! I talked to Jerry on the phone last night. He was a little disappointed but very pleased for me. He told me to "go for it"! I'm going to tell Marsha and Tim tomorrow! Thanks for all your help, best wishes, Di.

1. What's Di's decision?
2. Does Jerry know?
3. Was he upset?
4. What was his advice?
5. What's Di going to do tomorrow?

B. What is Di going to say to Marsha and Tim about her plans? Work together and make four sentences for Di starting with: "I'm going to..."

C. Now work in pairs and use the four sentences to write a short conversation in your workbook between *either* Di and Marsha ***or*** Di and Tim.
Compare your ideas and act out the conversations in class.

grammar box

Want / ask / tell someone to + V

Alan **wants you to make** a decision.
He **asked me to ring** you today.
Jerry **told me to "go** for it".

Be going + to + V: exprimer ses intentions

Pattie **is going to leave** the show.
What **is** Di **going to do**?
She **is going to tell** Marsha and Tim.

look and learn WB p. 121

Worksheet P.122

Send a card!

In Britain, America and Australia people send cards to celebrate all sorts of special occasions. Look at these cards. Can you find the message inside each card?

1

2

3

4

The messages

A. *very very much.*

B. Hope you're back to normal soon.
GET WELL!

C. ... it's
"I'm thinking-About-You Day"

D. Well done!

E. *... in your driving test!*

F. **Neither do I.**
HAPPY MOTHER'S DAY!

G. Wishing you new faces
and great places
GOOD LUCK!

H. *Dad! I can't find any milk!*
Mum! Where are the cups?
Oh no!... CRASH!!!

lesson 3
A SCOOP?

It's 8.30 in the morning. Rob's friend, Carole Short, is in her office at the *Sydney Herald*. She's having a strange telephone conversation.

P.123

1 WHAT'S THE STORY?

A. Look at the picture and say as much as you can.
What's the scoop? Does Carole look interested?
How do the man and his family look?
Is there anything strange about the boy?

B. Now listen to the conversation.
Imagine you are Carole and take notes as you listen.
Write the keywords in your workbook.

C. Ask each other these questions. Use your notes to find the answers and then complete the summary in your workbook.

1. What happened to the boy and when?
2. What happened this morning?
3. Are there any signs of the kidnapping?
4. Why doesn't the farmer want to call the police?
5. Why is Carole going on her own?
6. Where is Cobra Bridge farm?
7. How long will it take to get there?
8. Why will she need a map?

chatterbox

How far is it from...?

It's... from...

(1 mile = 1.6 km)

2 LISTEN AND MAKE SENTENCES

P.124

A. Rob is talking to Carole outside the newspaper offices. Listen and find out:

- if Rob wants to go with Carole,
- why Carole wants to go on her own,
- why Rob thinks it's crazy,
- why Carole wants to go,
- what Rob wants Carole to do.

B. Now make five sentences with the words in the boxes and write them in your workbook.

If Carole If Rob	doesn't go, goes with Carole, gets lost, speaks to Steve, hasn't got a good map,	she'll get lost. Steve won't say anything. she'll ring Rob. she'll never find out if it's true. he'll tell her everything.

C. Ask each other questions. Write two examples of questions and answers in your workbook.

What will happen if ... ?

What will Carole do if ... ?

3 MAKE PLANS FOR NEXT WEEKEND!

P.124

Work in pairs and do the questionnaire in your workbook.

grammar box

Faire une hypothèse sur l'avenir:

If... + présent simple ⟶ (conséquence) *will / won't* + V

If I **leave** now, ⟶ **I'll be** there by lunchtime.
If she **doesn't take** a map, ⟶ **she** won't **find** the farm.

Questions:

What **will happen if Rob goes** with her?
If the weather**'s** nice, what **will** you **do**?

look and learn WB p. 125

PART 7

lesson 4

THERE'S A LOT TO DO!

It is 3.30 on Friday afternoon. Mr Blake, the History teacher, is talking to his pupils. He is organising an end-of-term party for all Year 10 pupils. The party is taking place at 6.30 tomorrow evening in the school hall.

1 FIRST IMPRESSIONS

Read the introduction and look at the picture.
What is Mr Blake talking about? Why does he look worried?
What does he want the pupils to do? Do you think there's a problem?

P.126

2 LISTEN AND FIND OUT

A. Listen to the conversation and complete the grid in your workbook.

B. Use your grid to answer the questions about Sally. Then ask and answer questions about Dylan, Lucy and Mike.

What has Sally got to do tomorrow? When?
Can she help Mr Blake? When? What does Mr Blake want her to do?

C. Then find the questions for the answers in your workbook. Practise the questions and then write them in your workbook.

3 AT THE PARTY

P.127

A. Read the eight bubbles and look at the pictures in your workbook. Can you put each bubble in the right place?

Hey! Don't take the food away! I'm hungry!

We've got to tidy up! Can you help?

What's the matter, Mr Blake?

I'm thirsty! I must have something to drink!

Sorry! I've got to go!

I've got to. Mr Blake told me to!

The music's too loud! You must turn it down!

Sorry! All the bottles are empty!

B. Now listen to the conversations. Were you right? Can you describe the problem in each picture?

4 AN END-OF-TERM PARTY

P.127

Work together and organise an end-of-term party. Look at this check list of things you have got to do and decide who is going to do what. Write your plans in your workbook.

CHECK LIST

- *fix a date and time*
- *find a room*
- *send invitations*
- *make posters*
- *decorate the room*
- *make some food*
- *buy some drink*
- *bring music (CDs, cassettes)*
- *tidy up after!*

We've got to … .

Someone's got to … .

Why don't we … ?

Let's … !

How about … ?

Can anyone … ?

Who will … ?

I'll … !

I can … .

grammar box

***Have got + to + V*: exprimer une obligation**

Mr Blake **has got to organise** the party.

I **have got to get** everything **ready**.

Someone **has got to help**!

What **has** Sally **got to do** tomorrow?

look and learn WB p. 128

PART 7

How to... use numbers

Dates, sommes d'argent, numéros de téléphone, dimensions...
Les nombres et les chiffres sont partout ! Faisons le point !

1 Dates

TIPS

Speaking

- Say "the ... of": the fourteenth of October
- Divide a year into two parts.
  1980 = 19/80 = nineteen eighty.
- For the years 01-09, the "0" is pronounced "oh".
- 1900 = nineteen hundred, 2000 = two thousand.

Writing

- Don't write "the" or "of", just write the day and the month: 14th October.
- Note the abbreviations for days of the month: 1st, 2nd, 3rd, 4th, 5th, etc.

A. Say these dates. They are all from the 20th century.
Then check your answers with the tape.

a. 15/3/86 b. 22/6/48 c. 12/4/99 d. 9/7/09
e. 1/2/77 f. 3/9/60 g. 13/8/02 h. 30/12/55

B. Do you know the dates for these events? Find the date for each one.

- The Second World War started on ...
- We celebrated the new millennium on ...
- William of Normandy invaded England on ...
- Neil Armstrong and Buzz Aldrin walked on the moon on ...
- Napoleon lost the Battle of Waterloo on ...
- The Declaration of Independence was signed on ...

4/7/1776
14/10/1066
18/6/1815

3/9/1939
21/7/1969
1/1/2000

2 Phone numbers

TIPS

- Say each number separately: 751 = seven, five, one.
- When two numbers are the same, say "double...": 44 = double four.
- For 0, say either "oh" (UK) or "zero" (US).

Listen to the four messages on Mr Silverman's answering machine in Los Angeles and write down the numbers. Where are the people calling from?

3 Big and small numbers

TIPS

Speaking

- In precise numbers, "million", "thousand" and "hundred" are singular: 2,500 = two thousand, five hundred.
- Use "and" (a) between the hundreds and the tens: 550 = five hundred and fifty, (b) if there are no hundreds between the thousands and the tens: 5,020 = five thousand and twenty.
- For decimals, say "point": 4.5% = four point five per cent. But don't say "point" for money: £5.50 = five pounds fifty.

Writing

- Use a comma to separate thousands from hundreds, and millions from thousands: 2,500; 1,550,000.
- For money, put the dollar or the pound sign before the number: $100; £5.50.
- Use a full stop to show a decimal: 4.5%; £5.50.

Say these numbers.
Check your answers with the tape.

a. 720 b. £9,523 c. 78.5% d. $1,000,000
e. 6,050 f. 6,256.8 g. 355,470,201 h. £904.50

4 Measurements

TIPS

Sydney Harbour Bridge

Nelson's column

The Statue of Liberty

Big Ben

- Ask questions with "How + adjective":
- Give information like this: "It is 10 metres high/wide..." etc. But be careful! You can't use "big", "far" or "heavy" in this way:

– "How big is your bedroom?"
– "It's 15 square metres./It's 5 metres by 3 metres./It's quite big."

– "How far is the post office?"
– "It's 200 metres from here./It's not far."

– "How heavy is your suitcase?"
– "It weighs 15 kg."

Listen to the descriptions on tape and match each one to the right picture.

PART 7

Sounds

1 Different sounds

A. Lis la phrase suivante et fais bien la différence entre le son de voyelle de **whose** [uː] et celui de **those** [əu]. **Whose are those?** Ensuite lis à voix haute les dix mots. Quels sont ceux qui ont le même son-voyelle que **whose**? Quels sont ceux qui ont le même son-voyelle que **those?**

- **own** • **show** • **lose** • **joke** • **move**
- **know** • **road** • **food** • **news** • **choose**

B. Écoute les deux listes et entraîne-toi.

2 Lost sounds

Lorsque l'on parle vite, un **t** ou **d** final passe inaperçu s'il est suivi d'un mot qui commence par **t** ou **d.** Écoute et entraîne-toi à ne pas prononcer la lettre entre parenthèses.

1. There's a lo(t) to do.
2. Have a goo(d) time!
3. Someone's go(t) to help!
4. I talke(d) to him las(t) Tuesday.
5. Wha(t) do you wan(t) to do?
6. I don'(t) think he aske(d) Dylan to help.

3 Stress

A. Lis les mots. Quelle est la syllabe accentuée, la première ou la deuxième?

- **upset** • **future** • **always** • **career** • **enough**
- **believe** • **boring** • **relax** • **patient** • **advice**

B. Écoute les deux listes et entraîne-toi.

4 "The gotta, gonna, wanna rap!"

I *gotta* run, I'm *gonna* leave,
I *wanna* find a new place.

I *gotta* go, I'm *gonna* change,
I *wanna* find a new face.

I *gotta* run, I'm *gonna* fly,
I *wanna* try a new space.

I don't *wanna* stay, I don't *wanna* play
the same game every day.

I'm *gonna* change direction,
make new connections
– be a different "me" when I'm on holiday!

(Dans les chansons que tu écoutes, tu entends souvent: *"gotta"* = have got to; *"gonna"* = going to; *"wanna"* = want to).

Let's practise!

Lesson 1 pp. 112-113

A Imagine que tu es le père de Lucy (producteur de disques). Écris cinq phrases avec will / won't que tu peux dire à Ray du groupe "The Michigans" pour lui dire:

1. que tu viendras au concert samedi prochain,
2. que tu ne pourras pas venir avant 9 heures,
3. que tu lui parleras pendant le concert,
4. que tu lui donneras de bonnes nouvelles,
5. qu'il faudra que tu partes à 11 heures.

B Lis les prédictions 1 > 5 et trouve la bonne réponse courte A > E pour *contredire* chacune.

1. Life will be more exciting in 2100.
2. Cars won't exist.
3. There will be too many people.
4. There won't be enough food for everyone.
5. We'll be able to work from home.

A. No, we won't!
B. Yes, there will!
C. Yes, they will!
D. No, it won't!
E. No, there won't!

C Complète chaque phrase avec un des mots suivants en l'utilisant une seule fois.

- **anyone** • **anything** • **no one**
- **nothing** • **someone** • **something**

1. You'll meet ... interesting next week.
2. I'll have to buy ... for Dad's birthday.
3. I won't know ... at the party!
4. There's ... interesting on TV. Let's go out!
5. I'll talk to them but ... will listen to me!
6. I'll come shopping with you but I won't buy ...

Lesson 2 pp. 114-115

D Sally et Lucy sont invitées à une fête chez Ray demain soir. Trouve les questions que Sally pose à Lucy pour savoir:

1. ce qu'elle va porter,
2. si elle va apporter des CDs,
3. à quelle heure elle va partir de la maison,
4. si elle va aller en métro chez Ray,
5. qui va être à la fête.

E **Suis l'exemple en choisissant à chaque fois entre le verbe tell et le verbe ask:**
"Send me an email, Di!" said Ed.
Ed told Di to send him an email.

1. "Can you help me, Sally?" said Dylan.
2. "Turn off the television, Dylan!" said Mr Tate.
3. "Please ring me, Di", said James.
4. "Can you go and get a pizza, Lucy?" said Ray.
5. "Relax, Di!" said Marsha.

F **Complète le résumé de la conversation téléphonique entre Di et Ed avec ces verbes. (Il est maintenant 10 heures du matin, le lendemain.) • ask • give • make • phone • ring • say • send • talk • tell • want**

Ed ... Di yesterday afternoon with some great news. Alan Rice ... Di to replace Pattie Vito so he ... Ed to ... her. Alan ... Di to ... a decision yesterday but Di ... Ed to ... her a little time. Ed ... her to ... him an answer this evening. Di ... to Jerry last night and he ... her to ... yes, so Di is going to ... Ed an email tonight.

Lesson 3 pp. 118-119

G **Lis ce que Di a fait dimanche dernier. Elle fera la même chose dimanche prochain s'il fait beau. Raconte ce qu'elle fera en commençant par:**
Next Sunday, if the weather's nice...

Last Sunday the weather was nice. Di didn't stay in bed. She got up early and left her flat at 9.30. She took the subway to Central Park and then she ran around the reservoir. Then she went to a café and bought a sandwich and a newspaper. She sat on the grass and ate her sandwich and read the paper. Then she went home and had a shower.

H **Trouve une conséquence à chaque hypothèse.**

1. If I go to bed early ...
2. If we don't look at the map ...
3. If I do my homework on Saturday ...
4. If you don't have any breakfast ...
5. If I go to England this summer ...
6. If you don't want to go on your own ...

I **Réponds à chaque question en exprimant tes propres idées.**

1. What will Carole do if she thinks Steve's story is true?
2. What will Di say if Marsha asks her to stay in New York?
3. What will happen if Ray signs a contract with Lucy's father?
4. What will James do if someone offers him a job in New York?

Lesson 4 pp. 120-121

J **Complète les phrases avec has / have got + to suivi d'un verbe de ton choix.**

1. Jerry ... to the hairdresser's. Marsha says his hair is far too long!
2. Sally, Lucy and Dylan ... Mr Blake. They ... everything ready for the party.
3. Carole ... very late tonight. She ... her article about the UFO.
4. This week Marsha ... a lot of actresses for Di's role in "Smiles".
5. I won my tennis match but I ... another match tomorrow.

K **Traduis.**

1. The room is empty! Where is everyone?
2. The concert takes place on 15th July.
3. We're having a party because it's the end of term.
4. I'd like to make an appointment, please.
5. The music isn't loud enough! No one can hear it!
6. There's a lot to do. Someone's got to tidy up!

L **Relie les deux phrases qui se suivent:**

1. Is there anything to drink?
2. Can anyone help me?
3. Is there anything to eat?
4. How about bringing some CDs?
5. Don't leave the food on the tables.

A. We'll need some music.
B. I'm hungry.
C. Take it away.
D. I'm thirsty.
E. I can't do everything on my own.

So do I!

I like reading!

What do you read?

I read magazines but
I don't read books.

I often read in bed!

I never read.

I sometimes read the newspaper.

Don't you?

When do you read?

I read when
I want to relax.

I read when my teacher
says I have to!

PART 8

I think reading is boring!

Where do you read?

Neither do I.

I love poetry!

I like reading true stories.

I like science fiction best.

I like reading comics.

Do you?

THE MONKEY AND YOU

I am a monkey
In a zoo.
You stare at me
I stare at you.
If I swing by my tail,
Chatter, pull faces,
Go through the usual monkey paces,
Which I have learned
You consider your due,
Perhaps you'll throw me a peanut or two.

I am a monkey
In a zoo.
You stare at me
I stare at you.
You chatter, pull faces,
Hold out your hand,
You look intelligent enough
To make me think you understand
My monkey state
And are trying to communicate.

I am a monkey
In a zoo.
You stare at me
I stare at you.
Two sides to these bars there are.
What is life like over there
In your zoo?
At least you have peanuts to spare,
Who throws the peanuts to you?

Julie Holder
A Third Poetry Book:
Oxford University Press

Help Box

at least	*au moins*
go through... paces	*executer des pas*
hold out *(v.)*	*tendre*
monkey *(n.)*	*singe*
over there *(adv.)*	*là-bas*
peanut *(n.)*	*cacahuète*
pull faces *(expr.)*	*faire des grimaces*
side *(n.)*	*côté*
stare *(v.)*	*regarder fixement*
swing *(v.)*	*(se) balancer*
throw *(v.)*	*jeter*
to spare	*(avoir) de trop, de plus*

WHY IS IT?

Why is it,
That,
In our bathroom
It's not the dirtiest
Or the strongest
Who stays longest?
BUT
It always seems to be
The one who gets there
Just ahead
Of me.

Why is it
That people fret
When they're wet,
With loud cries
And soap in their eyes
And agonized howls,
Because they forget
Their towels?

Why is it that –
When *I'm* in the bath,
Steaming and dreaming,
My toes just showing
And the hot water flowing,
That other people
Yell and say,
'Are you there to stay
Or just on a visit?'

Why is it?

Max Fatchen
***A Third Poetry Book* :**
Oxford University Press

Help Box

ahead of *(adv.)*	*avant*	steam *(v.)*	*fumer (vapeur)*
cry *(n.)*	*cri*	toe *(n.)*	*doigt de pied*
flow *(v.)*	*couler*	towel *(n.)*	*serviette*
fret *(v.)*	*s'inquiéter*	wet *(adj.)*	*mouillé*
howl *(n.)*	*hurlement*	yell *(v.)*	*crier*
soap *(n.)*	*savon*		

Poems

TURN OFF THE TV

My father gets quite mad at me;
my mother gets upset -
when they catch me watching
our new television set.

My father yells "Turn that thing off!"
Mom says,"It's time to study."
I'd rather watch my favourite TV show
with my best buddy.

I sneak down after homework
and turn the set on low.
But when she sees me watching it,
my Mom yells out, "No!"

Dad says,"If you don't turn it off,
I'll hang it from a tree!"
I rather doubt he'll do it,
'cause he watches more than me.

He watches sports all weekend,
and weekday evenings too,
while munching chips and pretzels -
the room looks like a zoo.

So if he ever got the nerve
to hang it from a tree,
he'd spend a lot of time up there -
watching it with me.

Bruce Lansky
www.gigglepoetry.com
(Meadowbrook Press)

HelpBox

buddy *(n.)*	*copain*
catch *(v.)*	*trouver, attraper*
ever *(adv.)*	*jamais*
hang *(v.)*	*suspendre*
I'd rather *(expr.)*	*J'aimerais plutôt*
low *(adv.)*	*bas (bruit)*
mad *(adj.)*	*furieux*
munch *(v.)*	*mâcher*
nerve *(n.)*	*courage, toupet*
rather *(adv.)*	*plutôt*
set *(n.)*	*poste (de télévision)*
sneak *(v.)*	*marcher furtivement*
spend *(v.)*	*passer*
yell *(v.)*	*crier*

HALF ASLEEP

Half asleep
And half awake
I drift like a boat
On an empty lake
And the sounds in the houses
And streets that I hear
Though far away
Sound very clear;
There's my sister Betty
Playing by the stairs
Shouting like teacher
At her teddy bears.

I can hear Mum chatting
To Mrs Spence next door
And I feel the tumbler
Vibrating the floor.
And Alan Simpson
Plays his guitar
And his dad
Keeps trying
To start his car.
Dave, the mechanic
Who's out on strike
Keeps tuning and revving
His Yamaha bike.
From the open window
Across the street
On the August air
Drifts a reggae beat.

At four o'clock
With a whoop and a shout
the kids from St. John's
Come tumbling out.
I can hear their shouts
Hear what they say
And I play in my head
All the games they play.

Gareth Owen
A Third Poetry Book:
Oxford University Press

HelpBox

awake *(adj.)*	*éveillé*	shout *(n., v.)*	*cri, crier*
beat *(n.)*	*battement, mesure*	strike *(n.)*	*grève*
chat *(v.)*	*bavarder*	teddy bear *(n.)*	*nounours*
clear *(adj.)*	*clair*	though *(adv.)*	*quoique, même*
drift *(v.)*	*dériver, flotter*	tumbler *(n.)*	*sèche-linge*
keep *(+ V-ING) (v.)*	*ne pas s'arrêter de*	tumble out *(v.)*	*sortir en trébuchant*
rev *(v.)*	*faire tourner*	tune *(v.)*	*régler, accorder*
sound *(n. v.)*	*son, sonner*	whoop *(n.)*	*cri, quinte*

Fact or fiction...?

Bigfoot

In 1924, Albert Osman was on a camping trip in a forest near Vancouver, Canada. One evening, when he returned to his camp after a day's fishing, he found his backpack in pieces on the ground. He thought it was probably a bear, but in the middle of the night, a sudden noise woke him up. He was in the air in his sleeping bag in the arms of a gigantic monster!

He couldn't move as the animal carried him through the forest. Finally, the animal put him down on the ground. Albert opened his eyes and saw four enormous, hairy beasts – three adults and a child. They looked half gorilla and half human. Fortunately for Albert they did not attack him but he was their prisoner for six days.

On the sixth day, the oldest male took some tobacco from Albert's pocket and ate it. Soon he was very ill. While the other beasts tried to help, Albert escaped.

When he got back to Vancouver, local people told Albert that the beasts were "bigfeet". The first stories about these mysterious creatures date from over four hundred years ago and they are well-known in Indian myths. Native Americans call them "Oh-mah-ah" or "Sasquatch".

Legends say that a bigfoot is bigger than a Yeti (another mysterious beast that lives in the Himalayas) and some reports talk of bigfeet over 2.5 metres tall. Their footprints measure over 37 centimetres, and each foot has five toes, like a human foot. There are recent films and photographs of bigfeet but no one can really prove they are authentic. What do you think?

HelpBox

arm *(n.)*	*bras*	escape *(v.)*	*s'évader*
backpack *(n.)*	*sac à dos*	footprint *(n.)*	*empreinte de pied*
bear *(n.)*	*ours*	pocket *(n.)*	*poche*
beast *(n.)*	*bête*	sleeping bag *(n.)*	*sac de couchage*
carry *(v.)*	*porter*	wake up *(v.)*	*réveiller*

The hitchhiker

It was December and very late at night. The night was very cold but beautiful because there was a full moon and lots of stars in the sky.

A young man, Derek White, was on his way home on his motorbike. He was in the middle of the countryside, on an empty road, when he saw a young girl in a T-shirt and a summer skirt, by the side of the road. He was very surprised and stopped.

"Can you take me home?" she said. "I live in the next village." Derek said "Yes, of course!" and he gave her his jacket because she looked very cold. He took her home but when they stopped outside her house she didn't say goodbye but ran quickly to the front door.

The next day, Derek realised that the girl still had his jacket so he went back to the village and knocked at the girl's door. A woman opened it and when Derek explained why he was there, the woman turned very pale and then she said "Wait a minute please." She came back to the door with a photo. "Is this the girl?" she asked. "Er, yes," Derek replied. "That's my daughter," said the woman, "but she died in a car accident last summer. She's buried in the cemetery across the road."

Derek went to the cemetery and there, on the girl's tombstone, he found his jacket.

Help Box

bury *(v.)*	*enterrer*	hitchhiker *(n.)*	*autostoppeur/se*
by the side of *(expr.)*	*sur le bord de*	knock *(v.)*	*frapper*
come back to *(v.)*	*revenir à*	reply *(v.)*	*répondre*
countryside *(n.)*	*campagne*	stop *(v.)*	*(s')arrêter*
daughter *(n.)*	*fille*	turn (pale) *(v.)*	*devenir pâle*

A short story

The Speckled Band

adapted from a story by
Sir Arthur Conan Doyle

Episode 1

Dr Roylott lives in the country with his stepdaughter, Helen. The house has got an enormous garden. He keeps a lot of wild animals in cages in the garden – a cheetah, a baboon and other animals from India. A family of gypsies live in the garden too. They are strange, frightening people but Dr Roylott likes them. He's a strange man too. He's very violent and often has fights with people from the village. The house is very big and they need servants but servants never stay. They are frightened of the doctor, the animals and the gypsies. Helen has to do all the work in the house.

Help Box

baboon *(n.)*	*babouin*	gypsy *(n.)*	*tzigane, gitan*
band *(n.)*	*ruban*	speckled *(adj.)*	*tacheté, moucheté*
in the country	*à la campagne*	stepdaughter *(n.)*	*belle-fille*
fight *(n.)*	*bagarre, lutte*	wild *(n.)*	*sauvage*

Episode 2

Sherlock Holmes is a very clever private detective. He only investigates unusual crimes. He lives in Baker Street and shares his house with Dr Watson. Watson is interested in crime too. He often helps Holmes in his investigations and then writes about them. This is his report of the case of "The Speckled Band".

Very early one morning, a young woman arrived at the house in Baker Street. She looked worried and her face was very pale.

"You are trembling," said Holmes. "Are you cold?"

"No," she answered. "I am trembling because I am terrified."

"What is the matter? Please tell us."

"My name is Helen Stoner. I live in the country with my stepfather, Dr Roylott."

"And your mother?"

"She is dead. She met Dr Roylott in India. My father died when my sister and I were very young. He left a lot of money to my mother."

"So your mother married Dr Roylott in India?"

"Yes. Then, one day, he killed an Indian servant and went to prison. My stepfather is a very violent man, Mr Holmes."

HelpBox

investigate *(v.)*	*enquêter sur*
kill *(v.)*	*tuer*
stepfather *(n.)*	*beau-père*

"Then what happened?"

"When he left prison, we came back to England to his house in the country. But my stepfather didn't work. We lived on my mother's money. Then, eight years ago, my mother died in an accident."

Episode 3

"And Dr Roylott became very rich."

"Yes. He receives £1,000 a year. But if I get married he has to pay me £250 a year. That is in my mother's will."

"And your sister?"

"She died too. That is why I am here, Mr Holmes. When my mother died, my sister Julia and I were very lonely. We were frightened too," said Miss Stoner.

She explained about the gypsies and the wild animals. Then she said: "We didn't often go out but we sometimes visited an aunt in London. Julia met a young man there and he asked her to marry him. She died just before the wedding.

"How did she die?"

"We only use three bedrooms in the house. Julia's room was between mine and our stepfather's. The doors open on to the same corridor and the windows overlook the garden but there aren't any doors between the three rooms. One night, Julia came into my room and said: 'I can't sleep. Roylott is smoking one of those strong Indian cigars and I can smell it. And I heard a strange whistle. Perhaps it was a gypsy in the garden. I don't know.' 'That's strange,' I said, 'I didn't hear it.' We talked about her wedding, then she went back to her room and locked her door."

"Did she always lock her door?" asked Holmes.

"Yes, always. So did I. We were frightened of the gypsies and the wild animals. Later, I heard a scream. I ran into the corridor. I heard a whistle and a loud metallic noise – perhaps something fell, I'm not sure. I knocked on Julia's door and she opened it. She looked terrified. 'Help me, Helen,' she cried, 'I'm dying! It was the speckled band!' She fell into my arms. I called my stepfather and we tried to help her but she died."

Help Box

aunt *(n.)*	*tante*	noise *(n.)*	*bruit*
cry *(v.)*	*crier, pleurer*	overlook *(v.)*	*donner sur*
get married *(v.)*	*se marier*	scream *(n.)*	*cri*
knock *(v.)*	*frapper (à la porte)*	wedding *(n.)*	*(cérémonie de) mariage*
lock *(v.)*	*fermer à clé*	whistle *(n.)*	*sifflement*
lonely *(adj.)*	*seul, solitaire*	will *(n.)*	*testament*

Episode 4

"The police investigated but they couldn't understand why Julia died. After all, no one could get into her room because it was locked, and they didn't find any poison in her body. She looked terrified, Mr Holmes. Why did she die? What was the speckled band? It's a strange expression. Perhaps the band was a scarf – a gypsy scarf... I don't know."

Miss Stoner started to cry.

"When did Julia die?" asked Holmes.

"Two years ago."

"But why didn't you come to me immediately? Why did you come this morning?"

"Well, I am going to get married, Mr Holmes. Just like my sister, two years ago..."

"Ah, I see. And your stepfather knows, of course."

"Of course. I told him a week ago. Then, yesterday, I had to sleep in my sister's old bedroom because my stepfather wanted to repair my bedroom wall."

"How strange!"

"Yes, and I don't think the repairs are necessary, Mr Holmes."

"So, you slept in your sister's old room last night."

"Yes, but I couldn't sleep. I was too frightened. I remembered the night when she died. Then, in the middle of the night, I heard a whistle – the whistle I heard when Julia died! I lit the lamp but I couldn't see anything. No one was in the room. It was so strange. I got up, got dressed and took the first train to London. Please help me, Mr Holmes."

"I lit the lamp but I couldn't see anything."

Help Box

body *(n.)*	*corps*
scarf *(n.)*	*foulard*
sleep *(v.)*	*dormir*

Episode 5

Holmes and Watson visit the house with Miss Stoner when Dr Roylott isn't there...

We went into Julia's old room.

"Look, Watson, the bed is fixed to the floor," said Holmes. "It's impossible to move it."

There were shutters on the windows. Miss Stoner said Julia always closed them at night. No one could get in. Near the bed there was a servant's bell: a long cord hanging from the ceiling.

"Look at this," said Holmes, "It doesn't work. It isn't attached to anything."

"My stepfather put it there two years ago," said Miss Stoner. "I don't know why. And this too."

She pointed to a ventilator over the bed. It was between Julia's room and the next room – Roylott's room.

"Come along," said Holmes.

We went into Roylott's room. The ventilator was over a table in his room. On the table there was an oil lamp. Next to the table there was a metal cabinet and a chair. There was a bowl of milk on the cabinet.

"Have you got a cat?" asked Holmes.

"No, but there is a cheetah and a baboon."

On the bed there was a leather cord and the end was in a loop.

"We must spend the night in Julia's old room," Holmes said to Miss Stoner. "When your stepfather goes to his room tonight, unlock the front door and we will come."

Holmes and I went into the garden and waited. We saw the gypsies and the animal cages but everything was quiet.

"I knew there was a ventilator before we came here," said Holmes.

"How?" I answered.

"Because Julia could smell the cigar smoke. It means there must be communication between the two rooms."

"Do you know how Julia died?" I asked.

"Yes," said Holmes. "I know".

HelpBox

bell *(n.)*	*sonnette*	loop *(n.)*	*boucle*
cord *(n.)*	*corde, cordon*	oil lamp *(n.)*	*lampe à huile*
hang *(v.)*	*pendre, suspendre*	shutter *(n.)*	*volet*
leather *(n.)*	*cuir*		

Episode 6

It was about midnight when Miss Stoner unlocked the front door. She stayed downstairs and we went upstairs to Julia's old room. We turned off all the lights and I took out my revolver.
Suddenly, we saw a light in the ventilator tube. There was a smell of burning oil. Then we heard a hissing noise, like steam. Holmes hit the bell cord with his cane.
"Can you see it Watson? Can you see it?" he shouted.
But I couldn't see anything. Then we heard a terrible scream from Roylott's room. We ran into the corridor and opened his door.
He was in a chair with the leather cord in his hand and there was something around his neck - a speckled band. It moved, but Roylott didn't. He was dead.

There was something around his neck...

"What is it, Holmes?" I cried.
"It's a swamp-adder – the deadliest snake in India," said Holmes.
He took the leather cord, put it around the snake, pulled the loop tight and quickly pulled the snake from Roylott's neck. He opened the metal cabinet and put the snake inside and closed it.
"So that was the metallic noise!" I said.
"Well done, Watson!" said Holmes.
He explained everything: "Roylott didn't want to pay Julia £250 a year so he killed her, and he tried to kill Helen too."

"How did he do it?" I asked.
"He kept the snake in the metal cabinet. He took it out with the leather cord, stood on the chair and put the snake in the ventilator. It went through the ventilator into Julia's room and down the bell cord. His plan didn't work the first time. But, the second time, the snake attacked her. The same thing happened when Helen slept in the room."
"But the police didn't find any poison in Julia's body!" I said.
"It's a very rare poison, Watson. You can't detect it," answered Holmes.
"What about the whistle and the milk?" I asked.
"He whistled to call the snake. It came back and went immediately to the milk. Roylott then put the leather loop around the snake and put it back in the cabinet."

"You are very clever, Holmes," I said.
"Elementary, my dear Watson," said Holmes.

Help Box

deadly *(adj.)*	*mortel*
hit *(v. pret:* hit)	*frapper, taper*
keep *(v. pret:* kept)	*garder*
neck *(n.)*	*cou*
pull... tight *(v.)*	*serrer*
snake *(n.)*	*serpent*
steam *(n.)*	*vapeur*
swamp-adder *(n.)*	*vipère des marais*

GRAMMAR BANK

INDEX

1. LES MARQUEURS DE PERSONNES

A. Les marqueurs de personnes sujets

(on les appelle aussi « pronoms personnels »)

- **I** et **we** servent à prendre la parole.
- **I** s'écrit toujours avec une majuscule, même au milieu d'une phrase : **Am I late?**

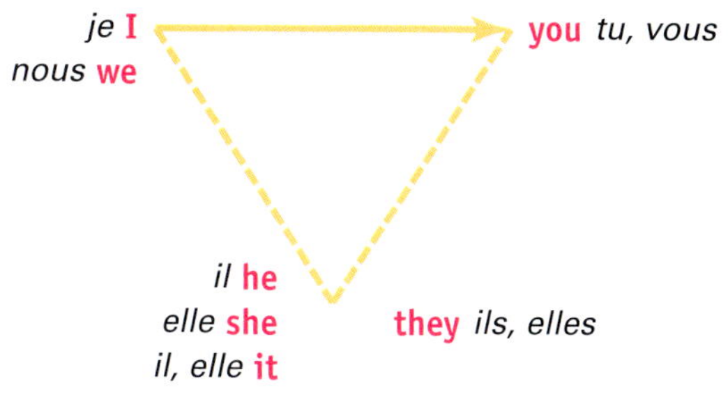

- **you** désigne la ou les personne(s) à qui on parle. En anglais on ne marque pas la différence entre « tu » et « vous ».

Are you at home?
Es-tu/Êtes-vous à la maison?

- **he** désigne un homme/un garçon.
- **she** désigne une femme/une fille.

He's at school. *Il est à l'école.*
She's in New York. *Elle est à New York.*

- **it** désigne une chose ou un animal, mais :
  - on emploie souvent **he** ou **she** pour parler d'un animal familier.
  - on peut également employer **it** pour identifier une personne.

It's in Australia. *C'est en Australie.*

He's my dog. *C'est mon chien.*
– Who is it? – It's Jerry!
– Qui est-ce? – C'est Jerry!

- **they** s'utilise pour parler de plusieurs choses ou de plusieurs personnes.

They're my shoes. *Ce sont mes chaussures.*
They're my friends. *Ce sont mes ami(e)s.*

B. Les marqueurs de personnes compléments

- On les emploie comme compléments d'un verbe ou d'une préposition. Ils se placent toujours après le verbe ou la préposition.
- Les marqueurs compléments **you** et **it** sont identiques aux marqueurs sujets **you** et **it**.
- Ils peuvent être compléments d'objet direct ou indirect (comme *nous* et *vous* en français). Note les différentes traductions de **me**, **her**, **him**, **you**, **them** ci-contre :

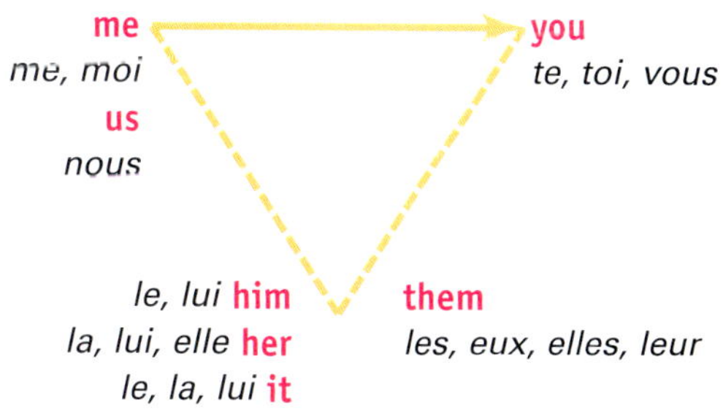

- Note l'ordre des mots lorsqu'un verbe est suivi d'un marqueur complément d'objet direct et d'un marqueur complément d'objet indirect :

Give it to me.
Send them to her.

Can you see me? *Est-ce que tu me vois ?*
Look at me! *Regarde-moi !*
Does he know her? *Est-ce qu'il la connaît ?*
Give her this book. *Donne-lui ce livre.*
We know him. *Nous le connaissons.*
Show him the map. *Montre-lui la carte.*
I can't see you. *Je ne te/vous vois pas.*
What about you? *Et toi/vous ?*
Let's invite them! *Invitons-les !*
Ask them a question. *Pose-leur une question.*

2. LES ARTICLES

NOTE : nous utilisons le symbole *(a glass of water)* pour les noms dénombrables et *(water)* pour les noms indénombrables.

A. L'article a/an

- **a/an** s'emploie avec tous les noms dénombrables singuliers. Pour identifier un seul élément, on utilise **a** devant une consonne et **an** devant une voyelle. Il n'y a pas, comme en français, de masculin et de féminin (*un, une*).

It's a book.
It's an English book.
It's an anorak.
It's a red anorak.

- Pour nommer le métier d'une personne on utilise toujours **a/an**.

She's an actress. *Elle est comédienne.*
He's a doctor. *Il est médecin.*

NOTE : I haven't got a map. *Je n'ai pas de carte.*

B. L'article the

- **the** s'emploie avec tous les noms. Il n'y a pas, au contraire du français, de masculin et de féminin et on ne marque pas la différence entre le singulier et le pluriel (*le, la, les*).

Look at the camera. *Regardez le camera.*
Listen to the song. *Écoutez la chanson.*
Write the words. *Écrivez les mots.*

- On emploie **the** lorsque ce dont on parle est clairement identifié par celui qui parle et aussi par celui à qui on parle. Compare la phrase avec **a** et la phrase avec **the** :

– **Where's Sydney? – Look at the map in your book.** *Regarde la carte dans ton livre.*
– **I don't know. Find a map.**
Je ne sais pas. Trouve une carte.

C. L'article zéro : Ø

- L'article zéro est un vrai outil en anglais. On l'emploie pour identifier plusieurs choses ou plusieurs personnes.

  Note que le symbole **Ø** apparaît uniquement dans les explications grammaticales.

- On l'emploie pour parler de quelque chose en général. Observe les phrases ci-contre où l'on exprime à la fois ses goûts en général mais aussi un avis sur quelque chose en particulier :

I love Ø chips but I don't like the chips in the cantine!
I like Ø cheese but I don't like the cheese in this sandwich!

- Mémorise les expressions ci-contre :

at Ø school, at Ø home
have Ø lunch/breakfast/dinner
on Ø Monday, at Ø night
by Ø bike/car/train/plane
leave/go/get Ø home
leave Ø school, get/go to Ø school
I speak Ø English quite well.

- Retiens également :
  I play Ø football. *(sport)*
  mais,
  I play the piano. *(instrument)*

  They're Ø roller skates.
  Ce sont des patins à roulettes.

  They aren't Ø ice skates!
  Ce ne sont pas des patins à glace!

3. LES NOMS

A. Le genre

- En anglais, la grande majorité des noms communs sont « neutres » *(ce ne sont ni des noms masculins, ni des noms féminins).*
- Cependant certains noms indiquent s'il s'agit d'une personne de sexe masculin ou de sexe féminin. Regarde les exemples dans l'encadré ci-contre.

a map	a child	a friend
une carte	*un enfant*	*un(e) ami(e)*

girl, woman	boy, man
sister, mother	brother, father
actress, policewoman	actor, policeman

- Certains noms communs prennent toujours une majuscule : les jours de la semaine, les mois de l'année, et, en général, les matières scolaires.

Are you coming on Wednesday?
My birthday's in June.
I like French but I don't like Maths!

B. Dénombrables ou indénombrables

En anglais, les noms communs peuvent avoir deux emplois :

- l'emploi dénombrable : lorsqu'ils désignent une chose que l'on peut compter,
- l'emploi indénombrable : ce qu'ils désignent ne se divise pas en unités que l'on peut compter.

dénombrables	indénombrables
glass (of water)	water
piece	cheese
minute	time
pound	money
bottle	milk

C. Le pluriel des noms

- Le pluriel de la majorité des noms est marqué par un -s final : **a boy → two boys.**
  Le -s final ajoute une syllabe aux noms qui se terminent en -se, -ce, -ge : **houses (Oo) places (Oo) bridges (Oo).**
- Mais il existe quatre autres façons de marquer le pluriel. Regarde les exemples ci-contre :

terminaison en :	singulier	pluriel
ss + -es	glass	glasses
sh/ch + -es	dish	dishes
x + -es	box	boxes
o + -es	potato	potatoes
en y → -ies	country	countries
	city	cities
en f/fe → -ves	wife	wives
	knife	knives
"central"	man	men
	foot	feet

D. Un nom peut jouer le rôle d'un adjectif

- Observe les phrases en anglais et leur traduction en français.

It's my phone number.
C'est mon numéro de téléphone.
It's a television programme.
C'est une émission de télévision.

4. LES ADJECTIFS

A. Les adjectifs sont invariables

- Ils ne s'accordent ni en genre ni en nombre avec le nom qu'ils qualifient.
- Ils se placent devant le nom qu'ils qualifient et ils se suivent.
- Ils peuvent être qualifiés par un adverbe.

She's got big blue eyes and long red hair.
Elle a de grands yeux bleus et de longs cheveux roux.

She's quite tall and very slim.
Elle est assez grande et très mince.

B. La forme comparative et la forme superlative

- La forme comparative :
  - si l'adjectif est court la construction est : adjectif + **-er** + **than**,
  - si l'adjectif est long la construction est : **more** + adjectif + **than**.

– A motorbike is faster than a scooter.
– Une moto est plus rapide qu'un scooter.
– But a motorbike is more expensive than a scooter!
– Mais une moto est plus chère qu'un scooter!

- La forme superlative :
  - si l'adjectif est court la construction est : **the** adjectif + **-est**,
  - si l'adjectif est long la construction est : **the most** + adjectif.

– I've got the biggest pizza.
– J'ai la plus grande pizza.
– Yes, but it's the most expensive!
– Oui, mais c'est la plus chère!

Adjectifs courts :
- ce sont la plupart des adjectifs d'une syllabe,
- mais aussi les adjectifs de deux syllabes qui se terminent par un **-y** (**heavy**, **happy**, **easy**...).

Adjectifs longs :
- ce sont les adjectifs de trois syllabes ou plus,
- et la plupart des adjectifs de deux syllabes.

ATTENTION ! Certains adjectifs d'une syllabe sont considérés comme des adjectifs longs : **tired**, **pleased**...

L'orthographe des adjectifs courts qui se terminent :

	comparatif	superlatif
– par -e		
nice	nicer	the nicest
– par -y		
heavy	heavier	the heaviest
– par une seule voyelle suivie d'une seule consonne		
hot	hotter	the hottest

C. Exprimer l'égalité ou l'inégalité

- Pour exprimer l'égalité avec un adjectif court ou long la construction est : verbe à la forme affirmative + **as** + adjectif + **as**.
- Pour exprimer l'inégalité la construction est : verbe à la forme négative + **as** + adjectif + **as**.

London is as interesting as New York.
Londres est aussi intéressant que New York.
New York isn't as big as London.
New York n'est pas aussi grand que Londres.

D. good

L'adjectif **good** a une forme irrégulière au comparatif et au superlatif :

	comparatif	superlatif
good	better	the best

5. LES ADVERBES

GRAMMAR BANK

A. Leur fonction

- Les adverbes sont des mots qui peuvent nous renseigner sur l'action du verbe :
  – quand ? *– comment ?* *– où ?*
  – à quelle fréquence ? *– à quel point…*

When? → **He left yesterday.**
How? → **She sings well.**
Where? → **He ran downstairs.**
How often? → **She never eats meat.**
How much? → **It's big enough.**

- Les adverbes peuvent aussi modifier le sens des adjectifs ou d'autres adverbes.

The film was quite funny
He speaks very fast.
He speaks too quickly.

B. Leur formation

- Le plus souvent, l'adverbe est formé à partir de l'adjectif du même sens auquel l'on ajoute -ly. Le tableau ci-contre indique les règles d'orthographe.
- Mais certains adverbes ont la même forme que l'adjectif. Par exemple :

fast	(adjectif)	**It's a fast car.**
	(adverbe)	**Don't drive too fast!**
early	(adjectif)	**I had an early breakfast.**
	(adverbe)	**I got up early.**
long	(adjectif)	**It's a long film.**
	(adverbe)	**We didn't stay long.**

ORTHOGRAPHE DES ADVERBES EN -ly

Adjectif	Adverbs
quiet	quietly
nice	nicely
lucky	luckily
easy	easily
real	really
possible	possibly

C. Les adverbes de fréquence

- Les adverbes de fréquence se placent, en règle générale, devant le verbe :

I always leave home at half past seven.
I don't often walk to school.

mais après le verbe be :
I am never late.
I'm not often late.

	Mon.	Tues.	Wed.	Thu.	Fri.	Sat.	Sun.
always	✓	✓	✓	✓	✓	✓	✓
usually	✓	✓	–	✓	✓	✓	✓
often	✓	–	✓	✓	–	✓	–
sometimes	–	✓	–	✓	–	–	–
never	–	–	–	–	–	–	–

6. EXPRIMER LA PROPRIÉTÉ

A. Les marqueurs de propriété déterminants

On les appelle aussi « déterminants possessifs ».

- Ils sont invariables. Observe les traductions dans le triangle.

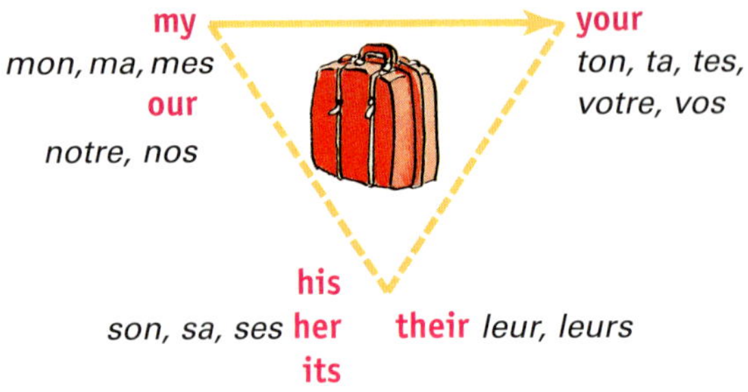

- Pour choisir entre **his, her** et **its** pose-toi toujours la question : *Qui est le propriétaire ?*

He's an actor. His name is Jerry.
She's my sister. Her name is Di.
It's a mixed school.
Its name is "Acland Burghley".

B. Les marqueurs de propriété pronoms

On les appelle aussi « pronoms possessifs ».

- Observe les traductions :
  It's mine. *C'est le mien/la mienne.*
  Il/Elle est à moi.
  They're yours. *Ce sont les tiens/les tiennes.*
  Ils/Elles sont à toi.

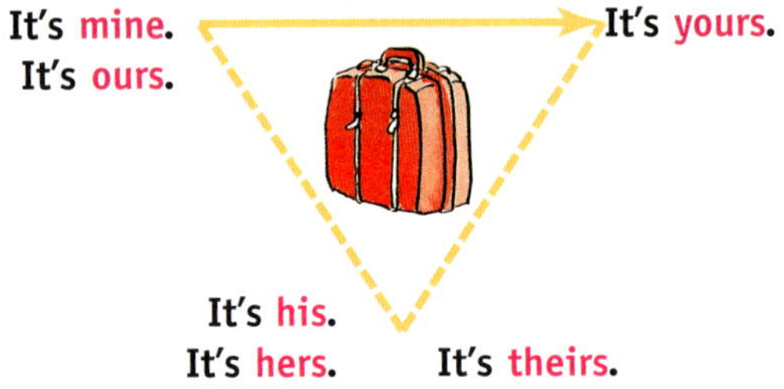

C. Le génitif : 's

- On emploie N + 's en anglais pour :
  1. marquer le propriétaire d'une chose,
  2. exprimer le lien entre deux personnes,
  3. l'identité de quelque chose.

1. **My mother's car.** *La voiture de ma mère.*
2. **Di's boyfriend.** *L'ami de Di.*
3. **Prince William's photo.** *La photo du Prince William.*

- N + 's joue le rôle d'un déterminant. On n'ajoute que l'apostrophe ' aux noms pluriels qui se terminent déjà en -s.

Déterminants	+ Nom
Her/Their	house
Sally's	house
The Hunters'	house

- Pour demander qui est le propriétaire, on emploie le mot interrogatif **whose** qui peut être déterminant (devant un nom) ou pronom (on l'emploie seul). Quand le nom apparaît déjà dans la question, on ajoute simplement 's ou ' au nom du propriétaire dans la réponse.

– Whose (mobile) is it? – It's Di's.
– À qui est le téléphone portable ? – Il est à Di.
– Whose (car) is it? – It's my parents'.
– À qui est cette voiture ? – C'est celle de mes parents.

- On applique les mêmes règles (nom singulier + 's, nom pluriel + ') pour traduire « chez ».

Let's go to Dylan's! *Allons chez Dylan !*
At the Tates'. *Chez les Tate.*
I'm going to the dentist's. *Je vais chez le dentiste.*

7. LES QUANTIFICATEURS

Les quantificateurs nous permettent d'exprimer une quantité (devant un nom singulier indénombrable) ou un nombre (devant un nom pluriel dénombrable).

A. some, any, enough : déterminants

- Le déterminant **some** s'emploie devant tous les noms
  – dans les phrases affirmatives,
  – dans les offres et les demandes polies.

There is some sugar on the shelf.
There are some raspberries in the bowl.

Would you like some sugar?
Can I have some raspberries?

- Le déterminant **any** s'emploie devant tous les noms
  – dans les phrases interrogatives,
  – dans les phrases négatives.

Is there any bread?
Have you got any serviettes?

There isn't any bread.
I haven't got any serviettes.

- Le déterminant **enough** s'emploie devant tous les noms et dans toutes les phrases : affirmatives, interrogatives et négatives.

There's enough steak. There are enough chips.
Is there enough steak? Are there enough chips?
There isn't enough steak! There aren't enough chips!

B. How much? How many? + N

Ces deux expressions veulent dire la même chose : *Combien de... ?*

- **How much? + N** indénombrable sert à se renseigner sur une quantité.

How much bread is there?

- **How many? + N** dénombrable pluriel sert à se renseigner sur un nombre.

How many pieces of toast do you want?

C. A lot of, lots of

Ces deux expressions veulent dire la même chose : *beaucoup de*.
On les emploie devant tous les noms.

There are a lot of people in the park.
There are lots of people in the park.
Can I have a lot of sauce, please?
Can I have lots of sauce, please?

D. Les quantificateurs « seuls »

- Lorsque le nom est déjà fourni par le contexte, les quantificateurs peuvent s'employer seuls. Ils sont alors des pronoms.

Regarde les exemples ci-contre :

There's a lot of cheese. Would you like some?
We'll need some potatoes. Are there any?
I'll get some milk. There isn't any in the fridge.
I've got some flour but there isn't enough!

8. LE VERBE "BE"

A. Les phrases affirmatives, interrogatives et négatives

- Observe les formes affirmatives dans le triangle.
- À la forme interrogative, **be** conjugué se place devant le sujet.
  Am I late?
  Is it nine o'clock.
- À la forme négative **not** se place après **be** conjugué.
  You are not (aren't) late.
  It is not (isn't) nine o'clock.

Forme affirmative

I am (I'm)
We are (We're)
You are (You're)
in New York.
He is (He's)
She is (She's)
It is (It's)
They are (They're)

B. Le prétérit de be

- Le verbe **be** a deux formes au prétérit : **was** et **were**.
- La forme contractée est possible seulement dans les phrases négatives :
  was not = wasn't, were not = weren't

I was
We were
You were
in London yesterday.
He was
She was
It was
They were

C. Les expressions avec be

- Attention à la traduction de certaines expressions avec le verbe **be**.
- Observe aussi ces deux traductions :
  I'm worried. *Je m'inquiète.*
  He's amused. *Il trouve ça drôle.*

How are you?	*Comment vas-tu?*
I'm fine!	*Je vais bien.*
How old are you?	*Quel âge as-tu?*
I'm fourteen.	*J'ai quatorze ans.*
I'm hungry.	*J'ai faim.*
I'm thirsty	*J'ai soif.*
I'm right.	*J'ai raison.*
You're wrong!	*Tu as tort.*
I'm cold.	*J'ai froid.*
It's cold.	*Il fait froid.*
It's fine.	*Il fait beau.*

D. There is, there are

- On traduit *il y a* par :
  there is (there's) + nom singulier
  there are + nom pluriel.

There's a taxi in front of our house.
Il y a un taxi devant notre maison.
There are taxis outside the hospital.
Il y a des taxis devant l'hôpital.

9. "HAVE GOT" – LE VERBE "HAVE"

A. Have got

- La forme verbale **have got** s'emploie uniquement au présent* pour :
  1. se décrire,
  2. parler de ce que l'on possède (ou non),
  3. parler de ce que l'on a sur soi (ou non),
  4. parler de son emploi du temps,
  5. décrire un lieu.

1. She has got long black hair.
2. They have got an American car.
3. I have not got my workbook!
4. We have got a test on Monday!
5. Central Park has got over 500,000 trees.

- **Have**/**has** est l'opérateur :
  – à la forme interrogative **have**/**has** se place devant le sujet :
  Have you got any brothers or sisters?
  – à la forme négative **not** se place entre **have**/**has** et **got** :
  I have not got a dog.

Formes contractées

I've got
We've got
You've got
a lot of friends!
He's got
She's got
It's got
They've got

B. Le verbe have

- **Have** peut également être un verbe « plein » et se comporte, dans ce cas, comme les autres verbes. Observe les différents sens de **have** dans les exemples ci-contre :

When do you have lunch?
Quand est-ce que tu déjeunes ?

I'm having a shower.
Je prends une douche.

Did you have a pizza for lunch?
As-tu mangé une pizza au déjeuner ?

No, I had an omelette.
Non, j'ai mangé une omelette.

Have a nice weekend!
(Passe un) bon weekend !

We're going to have a good time!
On va bien s'amuser !

* Comme tu as vu ci-dessus, la forme verbale **have got** s'emploie uniquement au présent.
Pour exprimer la même chose au passé on emploie le verbe **have** au prétérit.

She had long black hair.
They had an American car.
I didn't have my workbook!
We had a test on Monday.

10. PARLER DU PRÉSENT

A. Le présent simple

Le présent simple sert à donner des informations sur le présent qui sont vraies à tout moment. Il sert, par exemple, à parler de ses goûts, de ses désirs, de ses connaissances, de ses habitudes.

• La forme affirmative

On emploie la base verbale (V) à toutes les personnes sauf à la 3e personne du singulier où on ajoute un **-s**.

NOTE : les règles d'orthographe ci-dessous.

ORTHOGRAPHE

À la 3e personne du singulier :

- *on ajoute* **-es** *aux verbes qui se terminent par* **-o**, **-sh**, *ou* **-ch** *:*

go → go*es*	finish → finish*es*
do → do*es*	watch → watch*es*

- *on remplace* **-y** *par* **-ies** *pour les verbes qui se terminent par* **-y** *:*

worry → worr*ies*
hurry → hurr*ies*

Forme affirmative

I know
We know
You know
Boxer.
He know**s**
She know**s**
It know**s**
They know

• La forme interrogative

On a besoin de l'opérateur **do**/**does** :

Do you know "Smiles"?
Does Jerry live in New York?

Forme interrogative

Do I know
Do we know
Do you know
Boxer?
Does he know
Does she know
Does it know
Do they know

• La forme négative

On a besoin de l'opérateur **do**/**does** /

I **do not** (**don't**) watch TV very often.
Marsha **does not** (**doesn't**) live in Manhattan.

NOTE : **do** est aussi un verbe (*faire*).
Il peut figurer deux fois dans la même phrase.
What does he do? *Que fait-il ?*
When do you usually do your homework?
Quand fais-tu tes devoirs d'habitude ?

Forme négative

I don't know
We don't know
You don't know
Boxer.
He doesn't know
She doesn't know
It doesn't know
They don't know

B. Le présent avec BE + - ING

- **Cette forme verbale permet de commenter ce qui se passe au moment où on parle. C'est comme si on faisait un « arrêt sur image ».**
- On construit *toutes* les phrases du présent avec BE + -ING grâce à deux « outils » :
  – l'opérateur be au présent qui s'accorde avec le sujet,
  – la terminaison -ING qui s'accroche à la base verbale.

Forme affirmative

I am
We are
You are
He is
She is
It is
They are
having lunch.

> **ORTHOGRAPHE : V + -ING**
> - *Les verbes qui se terminent par une seule voyelle suivie d'une seule consonne, la doublent :* **sit → sitting** **run → running**
> - *Les verbes qui se terminent par un -e le perdent :* **come → coming** **have → having**

- Dans les phrases interrogatives avec des verbes qui introduisent leur complément par une préposition (look at, wait for, listen to), la préposition reste placée après le verbe.

Who are you looking at?
Que regardes-tu ?
What is he waiting for?
Qu'attend-il ?
What are they listening to?
Qu'écoutent-ils ?

Forme interrogative

What am I doing?
What is she buying?
What are they having for lunch?

Forme négative

I'm not listening to you.
He isn't wearing a jacket.
We aren't watching a film.

C. L'emploi du présent simple avec certaines constructions.

Dans certains cas, même si l'on commente quelque chose qui se passe au moment où l'on parle, on emploie le présent simple (et non le présent avec BE + -ING).

1. Avec le modal can et les verbes de perception : see/hear.

1. Listen! I can hear a noise!
Écoute ! J'entends du bruit !
Look! We can see Central Park!
Regarde ! On voit Central Park.

2. Avec les verbes feel, want, need.

2. I don't feel very well.
Je ne me sens pas très bien.
I want to go to bed.
Je veux aller me coucher.
I need an aspirin!
J'ai besoin d'une aspirine.

3. Avec le verbe look + adjectif.

3. You look ill.
Tu as l'air malade.

11. PARLER DU PASSÉ

A. Le prétérit simple

Le prétérit simple sert à parler d'événements passés, coupés du moment présent. Il ne correspond pas exactement à l'un des temps du passé en français, même s'il est le plus souvent traduit par le passé composé.

Rob went to Australia *two years ago*.
Rob est allé en Australie il y a deux ans.

His parents spoke to him on the phone *last night*.
Ses parents lui ont parlé au téléphone hier soir.

They talked about Di.
Ils ont parlé de Di.

• La forme affirmative

C'est le seul cas où le verbe ait une forme différente de la base verbale. Cette forme est identique à toutes les personnes.

– Avec les verbes réguliers (la plupart des verbes) on ajoute -ed ou -d à la base verbale:
walk → walked   **like → liked**

– Les verbes irréguliers font « bande à part ». Il faut retenir chaque prétérit.
Liste des prétérits irréguliers, pp. 160-161.

La forme affirmative: go

I went
We went
You went
to New York last summer.
He went
She went
It went
They went

• Les formes interrogative et négative

– On emploie dans tous les cas la base verbale du verbe, qu'il soit régulier ou irrégulier.

– On emploie l'opérateur: did (le prétérit de do) à toutes les personnes.
C'est lui qui porte la marque du prétérit.

La forme interrogative

When did you go to New York?
Did you visit Central Park?

La forme négative

I did not (didn't) see everything.
We did not (didn't) buy any souvenirs.

B. La forme passive

Tu as vu des exemples de la forme passive au prétérit.

• Lorsque l'on veut attirer l'attention sur l'agent, celui qui a accompli l'action, on construit une phrase active.
Observez les deux exemples 1.A et 2.A:
Henry Ford et **Paul McCartney** sont sujets du verbe.

• Lorsque l'on veut attirer l'attention sur l'élément qui a « subi » l'action, on construit une phrase passive. Observez les deux exemples. 1.B et 2.B:
The Model T et **The song "Yesterday"** sont sujets du verbe.

La forme active

1. A. Henry Ford produced the Model T.
2. A. Paul McCartney wrote the song "Yesterday".

La forme passive

1. B. The Model T was produced by Henry Ford.
2. B. The song "Yesterday" was written by Paul McCartney.

Pour construire une phrase à la forme passive:

• On commence la phrase par l'élément qui subit l'action.

• On forme le groupe verbal avec :
  – l'opérateur **be** (conjugué) qui porte la marque du temps (ici: le prétérit).
  – le participe passé du verbe (ici: **produced, written**).

• On introduit l'agent par la préposition **by**.

Liste des participes passés irréguliers pp. 160-161.

12. EXPRIMER LE FUTUR

A. Le présent avec BE + -ING

- Le présent avec **BE + -ING** s'emploie très souvent pour parler d'une activité future déjà programmée.
  Note qu'en français on emploie le présent de l'indicatif.

I am going to the concert on Friday.
Je vais au concert vendredi.
My parents are coming with me.
Mes parents viennent avec moi.
What are you doing on Saturday?
Que fais-tu samedi ?

B. Le modal will + V

- Comme tous les modaux, **will** permet à celui qui parle d'exprimer son point de vue et a la même forme à toutes les personnes. Ici il s'agit d'un avis personnel concernant le futur. Une phrase avec **will** est souvent introduite par :
  I think… ou **I don't think**…

I think life will be difficult in 2100.
Je pense que la vie sera difficile en 2100.
There will be too many people.
Il y aura trop de gens.
We won't have enough food.
Nous n'aurons pas assez de nourriture.
We'll have to live in space.
Nous serons obligés de vivre dans l'espace.
We won't be able to feed everyone.
Nous ne pourrons pas nourrir tout le monde.

- **will**/**won't** permet aussi de faire des hypothèses sur l'avenir.
  - La proposition où l'on fait l'hypothèse est introduite par le mot **if** et son verbe est au présent simple.
  - Dans la proposition où l'on imagine les conséquences à venir, on emploie **will**/**won't + V**.

What will we do if it rains?
If it rains, we'll have lunch in a café.
If it doesn't rain, we'll have a picnic.

C. be going + to + V

- Cette construction exprime ce que l'on a l'intention de faire ou ce que l'on a décidé de faire. Il peut s'agir :
  1. d'une décision que l'on vient de prendre,
  2. d'une décision que l'on a prise depuis un moment.

1. **I'm not going to do my homework straightaway. I'm going to watch TV.**
   Je ne vais pas faire mes devoirs tout de suite. Je vais regarder la télévision.
2. **Di's going to leave New York. She's going to work in London.**
   Di va quitter New York. Elle va travailler à Londres.

- Cette construction sert aussi à parler d'une action future que l'on considère inévitable.
- En règle générale, on n'emploie pas deux fois **go**.

Oh no! I'm going to miss my train!
Oh non ! Je vais rater mon train !
The weather's great! I'm going *(to go)* for a walk!
Il fait très beau ! Je vais (aller) me promener !

- **(be) going to** ou **will** ?
  Compare ces phrases :
  1. **The score's 6-0, 5-1 to Sally. She's going to win the match!**
     (On constate que quelque chose va se passer. C'est évident.)
  2. **I think Sally will win the match. She plays very well.**
     (On donne un avis personnel.)

GRAMMAR BANK

13. LES PRONOMS

A. someone, anyone, everyone, no one...

- Les pronoms **someone**, **something**, **anyone**, **anything** s'emploient suivant les mêmes règles que pour **some** et **any**.

Can someone help me?
Est-ce que quelqu'un peut m'aider?
I'd like something to eat.
J'aimerais quelque chose à manger.
Can you see anyone in the café?
Est-ce que tu vois quelqu'un dans le café?
I can't see anything.
Je ne vois rien.

- **No one** et **nothing**, comme **not anyone** et **not anything**, expriment la négation.

There was no one in the café.
Il n'y avait personne dans le café.
There was nothing to eat.
Il n'y avait rien à manger.

- Note les traductions des phrases avec **everyone**, **everything**.

Is everyone here? *Tout le monde est là?*
Everything's ready. *Tout est prêt.*

- Note les constructions: **something**, **nothing** + **adj.**

Let's buy something original!
Achetons quelque chose d'original!
There's nothing interesting on TV.
Il y a rien d'intéressant à la télé.

B. This, that, these, those

Ces pronoms démonstratifs servent à préciser la ou les chose(s) qui nous intéressent.

- **This** et **these** s'emploient pour indiquer ce qui est proche de celui qui parle.
- **That** et **those** s'emploient pour indiquer ce qui est éloigné de celui qui parle.

Singulier	Pluriel
What's this? 	**What are these?** 
What's that? 	**What are those?** 

- **This** et **that** s'emploient aussi pour désigner les personnes.

Pour présenter quelqu'un: **This is Tim.**
Pour identifier quelqu'un: **Who's that?**
Au téléphone: **This is Rob. Is that Sally?**

- **This**, **that**, **these**, **those** peuvent aussi jouer le rôle de déterminants. Ils se placent devant le nom qu'ils déterminent.

This <u>jacket</u> is Jerry's.
These <u>bags</u> aren't Marsha's.

C. one

On emploie le pronom one pour éviter de répéter un nom qui a déjà été mentionné dans un contexte.

– I like that photo.
– J'aime cette photo.

– Which one?
– Laquelle ?

– The black and white one. The one on the shelf.
– Celle en noir et blanc. Celle sur l'étagère.

D. Les pronoms relatifs

Une proposition relative est une phrase que l'on rattache à une proposition principale. Le lien entre les deux propositions est le pronom relatif.
Pour choisir le bon pronom relatif, il faut se poser deux questions :

- Quelle est la fonction du pronom relatif : sujet ou complément du verbe qui suit ?
- L'antécédent est-il
  – une personne ? (**journalist, writer**)
  – ou une chose/un animal ? (**newspaper, article, dog**).

Carole's the journalist who works with Rob.

The *Sydney Herald* is a newspaper that comes out every Sunday.

Boxer is the dog that was in the TV commercial.

Rob wrote the article Ø/that you read about Fred Dickinson.

Boxer is the dog Ø/that we saw in the TV commercial.

Tim is the writer Ø/that Di met on her first day in the studios.

E. what?, which?, whose?

- Ces mots interrogatifs peuvent jouer le rôle :

– de déterminants (devant un nom)

Déterminants
What <u>book</u> are you reading?
Which <u>film</u> do you prefer?
Whose <u>sweater</u> is this?

– de pronoms (seuls).

Pronoms
What are you reading?
Which do you prefer?
Whose is this?

14. QUESTIONS

A. Les mots interrogatifs

- Les mots et formules interrogatifs servent à poser des questions pour obtenir des informations précises :

Who?	→ identité	– Who's that actress? – *She's Di Hunter.*
Where?	→ lieu	– Where's Jerry? – *In his dressing-room.*
What?	→ nature	– What's that? – *It's your costume.*
		– What colour is it? – *Blue.*
When?	→ moment, date	– When's he leaving? – *Tomorrow.*
Why?	→ raison, cause	– Why are you late? – *Because the train was late!*
Which?	→ distinguer un élément	– Which one do you want? – *The big one.*
Whose?	→ identifier le propriétaire	– Whose mobile is that? – *It's Marsha's.*
How?	→ manière	– How are you going? – *By bus.*
How big?	→ grandeur	– How big is their flat? – *It's quite small.*
How far?	→ distance	– How far is Sydney? – *200 miles.*
How fast?	→ vitesse	
How heavy?	→ poids	
How old?	→ âge	– How old is Sally? – *She's fifteen.*
How tall?	→ taille	– How tall are you? – *One metre sixty.*
How long?	→ durée, longueur	– How long will it take? – *3 hours.*
		– How long is the lake? – *23 miles.*
How many?	→ nombre	– How many knives are there? – *Only five.*
How much?	→ quantité et prix	– How much time have we got? – *5 minutes.*
		– How much are the pizzas? – *£2.50*
What is/are... like?	→ description	– What's the weather like? – *It's sunny.*
		– What are your glasses like? – *They're red.*

B. Who? What? sujets du verbe

- Lorsque les pronoms **Who?** ou **What?** sont sujets du verbe, ils expriment déjà l'interrogation. L'ordre des mots est le même que dans une phrase à la forme affirmative.

Who <u>likes</u> science fiction?
Who <u>phoned</u> Di this afternoon?
Who <u>has got</u> a newspaper?
What <u>happened</u> during the rehearsal?
What <u>takes</u> place on 14th February?

C. Interrogatives indirectes

- L'ordre des mots dans une interrogative indirecte est le même que dans une phrase affirmative. On n'emploie donc pas les opérateurs **do**/**did**.
- Observe les transformations en questions directes.

Ask him if he is English.
→ Are you English?
Ask him if he can speak English.
→ Can you speak English?
Ask him where he comes from.
→ Where do you come from?
Ask him when he arrived.
→ When did you arrive?

15. QUESTION TAGS... AND SHORT ANSWERS

Les question tags à la forme négative		Réponses courtes
Jerry's an actor, isn't he?	→	Yes, he is. / No, he isn't.
We're going to Central Park, aren't we?	→	Yes, we are. / No, we aren't.
You're French, aren't you?	→	Yes, I am. / No, I'm not.
There's a cafe in the park, isn't there?	→	Yes, there is. / No, there isn't.
There are lots of people, aren't there?	→	Yes, there are. / No, there aren't.
He's got black hair, hasn't he?	→	Yes, he has. / No, he hasn't.
They've got a dog, haven't they?	→	Yes, they have. / No, they haven't.
Rob works in Sydney, doesn't he?	→	Yes, he does. / No, he doesn't.
They like vegetables, don't they?	→	Yes, they do. / No, they don't.
She went to New York, didn't she?	→	Yes, she did. / No, she didn't.
We'll be late, won't we?	→	Yes, we will. / No, we won't.
You can sing very well, can't you?	→	Yes, I can. / No, I can't.
You'd like to go to Florida, wouldn't you?	→	Yes, I would. / No, I wouldn't.
I have to wear a uniform, don't I?	→	Yes, you do. / No, you don't.
You were late, weren't you?	→	Yes, I was. / No, I wasn't.

Les question tags à la forme affirmative

Jerry isn't a singer, is he?

We aren't going to Central park, are we?

You aren't English, are you?

There isn't a café in the park, is there?

There aren't a lot of people, are there?

He hasn't got brown hair, has he?

They haven't got a cat, have they?

He doesn't work in London, does he?

They don't like fish, do they?

She didn't go to Australia, did she?

We won't miss the train, will we?

You can't dance very well, can you?

You wouldn't like to be famous, would you?

I don't have to wear a uniform, do I?

You weren't late, were you?

Les question tags

- Les **question tags** sont des questions accrochées à la fin de la phrase.
  - Si la phrase est à la forme affirmative, la reprise verbale est à la forme négative.
  - Si la phrase est à la forme négative, la reprise verbale est à la forme affirmative.
- Les **question tags** permettent :

1. d'exprimer un doute et de demander une confirmation. Dans ce cas, la voix monte à la fin de la phrase :

   Jerry's an actor, isn't he?

2. d'exprimer une opinion et de la faire partager. Dans ce cas, la voix descend à la fin de la phrase :

   You can't dance very well, can you?

GRAMMAR BANK

16. L'OBLIGATION

A. have + to + V

(l'opérateur : do/does)

- Cette construction exprime des obligations générales correspondant à une profession, à un règlement, à un emploi du temps, à une occupation régulière.

Di has to learn her words every morning.
Di doit apprendre son texte tous les matins.
He's a professional singer. He has to practise every day.
Il est chanteur professionel. Il doit s'entraîner tous les jours.
Do you have to wear a uniform?
Êtes-vous obligés de porter un uniforme ?

- La forme négative **don't/doesn't have to** exprime une absence d'obligation.

We don't have to wear a uniform at our school.
Nous ne sommes pas obligés de porter un uniforme à notre école.

B. Le modal must.

Les modaux (must, can, will, would...) sont des « verbes-outils », qui permettent à celui qui parle d'exprimer des opinions et des idées très variées. Un modal a la même forme à toutes les personnes. Il joue le rôle d'opérateur et se construit toujours avec la base verbale.

- Le modal **must** exprime une obligation que l'on impose à quelqu'un d'autre ou à soi-même. Il peut s'agir :

1. d'une opinion personnelle,
2. d'un règlement qui implique une conduite obligatoire.

I must eat something! *Il faut que je mange quelque chose !* (J'ai vraiment trop faim !)
You must get up! *Il faut que tu te lèves !* (Je pense que tu vas être en retard !)
You must stay calm! *Il faut rester calme !*

- La forme négative **must not** (**mustn't**) exprime une interdiction qui implique également une conduite obligatoire.

I mustn't be late! *Il ne faut pas que je sois en retard !*
You must not panic! *Il ne faut pas paniquer.*

C. have got + to + V

(opérateur : has/have)

- Cette construction exprime une activité ponctuelle qu'il est nécessaire de faire dans un avenir proche. Il s'agit généralement d'une activité personnelle programmée.

I have got to help Mr Blake tomorrow.
Je dois aider M. Blake demain.
We have got to get everything ready for the party.
Il faut que l'on prépare tout pour la fête.

- Compare la phrase avec **has to** (**1**) (obligation générale) et la phrase avec **has got to** (**2**) (obligation ponctuelle).
- Compare la phrase avec **must** (**3**) et la phrase avec **have got to** (**4**).

1. **Mr Hunter is a doctor. He has to get up early every day.**
2. **He's going to Scotland in the morning. He has got to get up very early tomorrow.**
3. **I must go to the dentist's!**
   Il faut que j'aille chez le dentiste ! (J'ai mal aux dents !)
4. **I have got to go the dentist's at four o'clock.**
   Je dois aller chez le dentiste à 4 heures.
   (J'ai un rendez-vous.)

NOTE : pour exprimer une obligation dans le passé, le prétérit de toutes ces expressions (**must, have got to, have to**) est **had to + V**.
Yesterday Dylan had to go to the dentist's and he's got to go back again today.
Di had to learn a lot of words this morning and she mustn't forget them !

17. CONSTRUCTIONS ET EXPRESSIONS

A. Donner un ordre

Affirmatif : V!

Be quiet! Close the door!

Négatif : Don't + V!

Don't talk! Don't open the door!

B. La permission

Can I go to the cinema? No, you can't!

Can I watch a video? Yes, you can.

C. Suggérer, proposer

Let's + V!

Let's go to the States!

Why don't we + V?

Why don't we go to Florida?

We can + V.

We can visit Sea World.

How about + V -ING?

How about flying to California?

I'll + V!

I'll get the tickets!

D. Exprimer une volonté, ses désirs

want + to + V

What do you want to do?

I want to go to the concert.

I don't want to work tonight.

would like + to + V

Where would you like to go?

I would (I'd) like to go to London.

What would you like to do there?

E. Exprimer ses goûts

like, hate, etc + V -ING

What do you like doing?

I like swimming but I don't like diving.

I hate cycling but I love skating.

F. Exprimer son savoir faire

can + V

I can play the guitar but I can't play the piano.

know how to + V

Do you know how to cook?

I don't know how to cook but I know how to make an omelette!

good at + V -ING

I'm very good at singing.

Are you good at acting?

I'm quite good at dancing.

G. Contredire

It's a real Picasso. – No, it isn't!

Di doesn't like Jerry. – Yes, she does!

James works in New York. – No, he doesn't!

Sally sang at the concert. – No, she didn't!

H. Exprimer les points communs

I'm quite good at English. – So am I.

I can't speak Italian. – Neither can I.

Di likes New York. – So does James.

Sally doesn't like Maths. – Neither does Dylan.

GRAMMAR BANK

18. LES VERBES IRRÉGULIERS

Trois formes différentes

Base verbale	Prétérit	Participe passé	
be	was/were	been	*être*
break	broke	broken	*casser*
choose	chose	chosen	*choisir*
do	did	done	*faire*
draw	drew	drawn	*dessiner*
drink	drank	drunk	*boire*
drive	drove	driven	*conduire*
eat	ate	eaten	*manger*
fall	fell	fallen	*tomber*
fly	flew	flown	*voler, piloter*
forget	forgot	forgotten	*oublier*
give	gave	given	*donner*
go	went	gone	*aller*
see	saw	seen	*voir*
show	showed	shown	*montrer*
sing	sang	sung	*chanter*
sink	sank	sunk	*couler*
speak	spoke	spoken	*parler*
swim	swam	swum	*nager*
take	took	taken	*prendre*
throw	threw	thrown	*jeter*
wake up	woke up	woken up	*se réveiller*
wear	wore	worn	*porter un vêtement*
write	wrote	written	*écrire*

Trois formes identiques

Base verbale	Prétérit	Participe passé	
cost	cost	cost	*coûter*
hurt	hurt	hurt	*faire mal*
put	put	put	*mettre*
read [ri:d]	read [rəd]	read [rəd]	*lire*

Deux formes identiques : la base verbale et le participe passé

Base verbale	Prétérit	Participe passé	
come	came	come	*venir*
run	ran	run	*courir*

Deux formes identiques : le prétérit et le participe passé

Base verbale	Prétérit	Participe passé	
bring	brought	brought	*apporter*
build	built	built	*construire*
buy	bought	bought	*acheter*
catch	caught	caught	*attraper, prendre*
feel	felt	felt	*(se) sentir*
fight	fought	fought	*combattre*
find	found	found	*trouver*
get	got	got	*obtenir*
have	had	had	*avoir, prendre*
hear	heard	heard	*entendre*
leave	left	left	*laisser, quitter*
lose	lost	lost	*perdre*
make	made	made	*faire, fabriquer*
meet	met	met	*rencontrer*
say	said	said	*dire*
sell	sold	sold	*vendre*
send	sent	sent	*envoyer*
sit	sat	sat	*s'asseoir*
sleep	slept	slept	*dormir*
spend	spent	spent	*passer, dépenser*
stand	stood	stood	*se mettre/tenir debout*
teach	taught	taught	*enseigner*
tell	told	told	*dire, raconter*
think	thought	thought	*penser*
understand	understood	understood	*comprendre*
win	won	won	*gagner*

Deux terminaisons possibles

Base verbale	Prétérit	Participe passé	
burn	burned/burnt	burned/burnt	*brûler*
dream	dreamed/dreamt	dreamed/dreamt	*rêver*
learn	learned/learnt	learned/learnt	*apprendre*

PART 1 lesson 1

A

a, an *(art.)* un/une 1.1
(be) able to (être) capable de, pouvoir 7.1
about *(adv., prép.)* environ ; au sujet de SYW1, 3.1
above *(prép.)* au-dessus de 2.2
abroad *(adv.)* à l'étranger 6.2
act *(v.)* jouer (la comédie) 3.3
actor *(n.)* acteur, comédien 2.1
actress *(n.)* actrice, comédienne 1.1
add *(v.)* ajouter 6.3
address *(n.)* adresse 3.4
admission *(n.)* (prix de l') entrée How to 3
adventurous *(adj.)* aventureux 3.3
advert *(n.)* une publicité How to 4
advice *(n.)* conseil(s) 7.1
aeroplane *(n.)* avion 5.3
after *(adv., prép.)* après SYW2, 7.4
afternoon *(n.)* après-midi 1.2
again *(adv.)* encore How to 1
against *(prép.)* contre SYW2
ago *(adv.)* il y a 5.2
agree être d'accord 6.2
air *(n.)* air 3.3
  air hostess *(n.)* hôtesse de l'air 3.1
airport *(n.)* aéroport How to 1
all *(pron., adj.)* tout(e), tous, toutes SYW1
  all around tout autour de SYW4
  all day/night toute la journée/nuit 3.2
  all over partout dans 3.1
  All right! D'accord ! 4.4
  all the rest tous les autres Sounds 4
alone *(adj.)* seul 4.4
along *(prép.)* le long de SYW3
also *(adv.)* aussi 3.3
although *(conj.)* bien que How to 5
always *(adv.)* toujours 1.4
amazing *(adj.)* étonnant 3.1
ambitious *(adj.)* ambitieux 7.1
American *(adj.)* américain 1.1, SYW3
amused *(adj.)* amusé How to 1
  He is amused Il trouve ça drôle
amusing *(adj.)* amusant SYW4
and *(conj.)* et 1.2
angry *(adj.)* fâché, en colère How to 1
announcement *(n.)* annonce How to 1
another *(dét.)* un autre 4.2
answer *(n., v.)* réponse ; répondre à 1.3
answering machine *(n.)* répondeur How to 7
any *(dét., pron.)* de/de la/du/des 2.1, 6.3
anyone *(pron.)* personne 7.1
appear *(v.)* apparaître How to 5
apple *(n.)* pomme 6.3
appointment *(n.)* rendez-vous 7.4
arm *(n.)* bras 5.2
around *(prép.)* autour de 1.4
arrival *(n.)* arrivée SYW3
as *(adv., prép.)* comme 5.4
  as ... as aussi ... que 4.3
ask (for) *(v.)* demander p. 11
  ask a question poser une question p. 11
asleep *(adj.)* endormi 1.2
assassinate *(v.)* assassiner 5.3
at *(prép.)* à 1.2
  at ... o'clock à ... heures 3.2
  at home à la maison, chez soi 1.2
  at school à l'école 1.2
  at Sally's chez Sally 2.2
attract *(v.)* attirer SYW4
attractive *(adj.)* attractif, joli 4.2
Australia *(n.)* Australie SYW4
Australian *(adj.)* australien 2.1
awful *(adj.)* affreux How to 6

B

bad *(adj.)* mauvais 2.3
bag *(n.)* sac 6.4
baker *(n.)* boulanger SYW5
ball *(n.)* bal, ballon How to 5, 4.3
  ball game jeu de balle/ballon 1.4
balloon *(n.)* ballon, montgolfière SYW3, SYW4
ballooning *(n.)* faire des ascensions en ballon SYW4
ballroom *(n.)* salle de bal How to 5
band *(n.)* orchestre, groupe 6.1
bar *(n.)* comptoir, tablette (de chocolat) 4.3, 6.4
bathroom *(n.)* salle de bains 2.2
be *(v.)* être 1.1
beach *(n.)* plage SYW4
beautiful *(adj.)* beau, belle How to 5
became *(prét. : **become**)* SYW5
because parce que 1.4
become *(v.)* devenir SYW5
bed *(n.)* lit **in bed** au lit 1.2
bedroom *(n.)* chambre à coucher 2.2

before *(prép., conj.)* avant (que) 2.3, How to 5,
behind *(prép.)* derrière 2.2
believe (in) *(v.)* croire (en) 3.3, 7.1
best *(n., adj.)* (le) meilleur 4.2
better *(adj.)* mieux, meilleur 4.3
between *(prép.)* entre 2.2
big *(adj.)* grand 1.3
bike *(n.)* vélo 2.3
birth *(n.)* naissance 5.1
  date of birth date de naissance 2.1
birthday *(n.)* anniversaire 2.1
black *(adj.)* noir p. 12
blew *(prét.:* **blow**) How to 5
blow out *(v.)* souffler 5.4
blue *(adj.)* bleu p. 12
board *(n.)* planche, tableau p. 12
boarder *(n.)* pensionnaire SYW2
boat *(n.)* bateau 1.4
book *(n.)* livre p. 10
boring *(adj.)* ennuyeux 7.1
born *(adj.)* né 5.1
  I was born je suis né
bottle *(n.)* bouteille 4.3
bought *(prét.:* **buy**) 5.2
bowl *(n.)* bol 6.3
box *(n.)* boîte 1.1
boy *(n.)* garçon p. 12
boyfriend *(n.)* petit ami 4.1
brave *(adj.)* courageux 3.1
bread *(n.)* pain 6.3
break *(n.)* pause, récré 2.3
breakfast *(n.)* petit déjeuner 3.2
bridge *(n.)* pont 4.1
bring *(v.)* apporter 7.3, SYW5
British *(adj.)* britannique 1.1
brother *(n.)* frère 1.2
brought *(prét.:* **bring**) SYW5
brown *(adj.)* marron, brun 1.3
  brown sugar sucre roux 6.3
build *(v.)* construire SYW5
building *(n.)* bâtiment, immeuble SYW5
built *(prét.:* **build**) SYW5
businessman *(n.)* homme d'affaires 5.2
but *(conj.)* mais
butter *(n.)* beurre 6.3
buy *(v.)* acheter 3.2
by *(prép.)* par **by bus** en bus 2.3
Bye! Salut!, Au revoir! 1.2

C

cake *(n.)* gâteau 5.4
call *(v.)* appeler, téléphoner 6.4, 7.3
  it's called cela s'appelle 1.4
came *(prét.:* **come**) 5.2
camel *(n.)* chameau 4.3
camera *(n.)* appareil photo, caméra 4.2
can *(modal)* pouvoir, savoir 1.4
Canadian *(adj.)* canadien 2.1
candle *(n.)* bougie 5.4
canteen *(n.)* cantine 1.2
car *(n.)* voiture 2.3
card *(n.)* carte 2.1
  birthday card carte d'anniversaire 2.1
career *(n.)* carrière 7.1
careful *(adj.)* prudent, attentif
  Be careful! Fais attention! 4.4
cartoon *(n.)* dessin humoristique How to 4
cat *(n.)* chat 2.4
celebrate *(v.)* fêter SYW3
celebrity *(n.)* vedette, célébrité SYW3
century *(n.)* siècle SYW4
chair *(n.)* chaise 7.4
character *(n.)* personnalité 7.2
charming *(adj.)* charmant 7.1
chatterbox *(n.)* moulin à paroles 1.1
cheap *(adj.)* pas cher 4.3
check *(v.)* vérifier How to 7
cheese *(n.)* fromage 3.3
cheetah *(n.)* guépard 4.3
chess *(n. sing.)* échecs 3.3
chicken *(n.)* poulet 3.3
child *(pl.* **children**) *(n.)* enfant 2.2
chimney *(n.)* cheminée How to 5
chip *(n.)* frite 3.3
chocolate *(n.)* chocolat 3.3
choose *(v.)* choisir 2.3
Christmas *(n., adj.)* Noël, de Noël SYW7
cinnamon *(n.)* cannelle 6.3
city *(pl.* **cities**) *(n.)* grande ville SYW1
classical *(adj.)* classique 3.3
clean *(v.)* propre 5.2
clever *(adj.)* intelligent Sounds 3
climate *(n.)* climat SYW6
climb *(v.)* grimper (sur) How to 5
clock *(n.)* horloge p. 13
close *(v.)* fermer p. 11

DICTIONARY

clothes *(n. pl.)* vêtements 1.3
cloudy *(adj.)* nuageux SYW1
clove *(n.)* clou de girofle 6.3
clue *(n.)* indication 4.2
coach *(n.)* carrosse How to 5
coast *(n.)* côte SYW4
coat *(n.)* manteau 5.2
cold *(adj.)* froid SYW1
  I'm cold j'ai froid How to 6
  it's cold il fait froid SYW1
colour *(n.)* couleur p. 12
come *(v.)* venir SYW2
  come in/into entrer 4.1, 5.2
  come back revenir How to 5
  come home revenir à la maison 4.4
  Come on! Allez!, Venez! 2.4
  Come up! Montez! 4.1
comedian *(n.)* comique 4.3
comma *(n.)* virgule How to 7
comment *(n., v.)* commentaire; commenter How to 4
commentary *(n.)* commentaire How to 1
commercial *(n.)* une publicité (à la télévision) 2.4
complete *(adj., v.)* complet; compléter 4.4
computer *(n.)* ordinateur SYW2
computing *(n.)* informatique SYW2
confident *(adj.)* confiant 3.3
Congratulations! Félicitations! SYW7
contestant *(n.)* concurrent 5.3
cook *(v.)* cuisiner, faire cuire 6.3
correct *(adj.)* correct, exact 5.3
cost *(v.)* coûter How to 3
could *(prét.:* **can**) 5.4
country *(n.)* pays SYW1
cover *(v.)* couvrir 6.3
Of course! Bien sûr! 2.4
crater *(n.)* cratère 7.3
craze *(n.)* mode, folie SYW4
crazy *(adj.)* fou SYW4
creative *(adj.)* créatif 3.3
cross *(v.)* traverser 4.1
crossing *(n.)* traversée 5.3
crowd *(n.)* foule 4.2
crowded *(adj.)* bondé 6.2
crumbly *(adj.)* qui s'émiette 6.3
cup *(n.)* tasse 3.2
custard *(n.)* crème anglaise 6.3
customer *(n.)* client 5.4
cut (into) *(v.)* couper (en) 6.3
cycle *(v.)* faire du vélo 1.4

D

Dad *(n.)* Papa 1.2
dance *(v.)* danser 3.2
dancer *(n.)* danseur 3.4
dangerous *(adj.)* dangereux SYW4
in the dark *(n.)* dans le noir How to 1
date from *(v.)* dater de SYW3
day *(n.)* jour p. 13
dear *(adj.)* cher ... 5.4
  Oh dear! Mon Dieu! 4.4
death *(n.)* mort 5.1
decide *(v.)* décider How to 5
decorate *(v.)* repeindre, décorer 3.3
deep *(adj.)* profond How to 7
defend *(v.)* défendre SYW5
definitely *(adv.)* certainement 6.4
degree *(n.)* degré SYW1
delicious *(adj.)* délicieux 6.3
deliver *(v.)* livrer 3.1
dentist *(n.)* dentiste 7.4
  at the dentist's chez le dentiste 7.4
depressed *(adj.)* déprimé 7.1
describe *(v.)* décrire 7.3
design *(v.)* dessiner, concevoir SYW5
destroy *(v.)* détruire SYW5
dial *(v.)* composer (un numéro) 4.4
die *(v.)* mourir 5.1
difficult *(adj.)* difficile How to 3
dining-room *(n.)* salle à manger 2.2
dinner *(n.)* dîner 2.3
  have a dinner party inviter des amis à dîner 6.3
direct *(v.)* contrôler, diriger 3.1
director *(n.)* metteur en scène 1.1
dirty *(adj.)* sale 5.2
disagree *(v.)* ne pas être d'accord How to 6
disappointed *(adj.)* déçu 5.4
discover *(v.)* découvrir 5.1
dish *(n.)* plat 6.3
dive *(v.)* plonger 3.4
divide (into) *(v.)* diviser (en) 3.3
do *(v.)* faire 1.4
  do the housework faire le ménage 3.3
doctor *(n.)* médecin, docteur 1.2
dog *(n.)* chien 2.4
door *(n.)* porte 2.4
downstairs *(adv.)* au rez-de-chaussée 2.2
drama *(n.)* art dramatique SYW2

drawing *(n.)* dessin How to 4
dream *(v.)* rêver 7.1
dress *(n.)* robe How to 5
dressing-room *(n.)* loge 1.3
drink *(n., v.)* boisson, boire 7.4
drive *(v.)* conduire 3.4
driver *(n.)* conducteur How to 3
driving instructor *(n.)* moniteur de conduite 4.2
during *(prép.)* pendant SYW5

E

each *(dét.)* chaque How to 1
each other l'un l'autre 1.1
ear *(n.)* oreille How to 5
early *(adv.)* tôt 3.2
earth *(n.)* terre 3.3
east *(n.)* est SYW1
Easter *(n.)* Pâques SYW3
easy *(adj.)* facile How to 3
eat *(v.)* manger 3.2
egg *(n.)* œuf 6.3
either ... or *(conj.)* ou ... ou 7.2
electric *(adj.)* électrique 5.3
embarrassed *(adj.)* gêné How to 1
emigrate *(v.)* émigrer 5.1
empress *(n.)* impératrice 5.1
empty *(adj.)* vide 7.4
end *(n., v.)* fin, finir Sounds 4. 5.4
English *(adj.)* anglais 1.1
enormous *(adj.)* énorme 1.4
enough *(dét., pron., adv.)* assez (de) 6.2, 6.3
fast enough assez rapide 5.4
That's enough! Ça suffit ! 7.3
entertainment *(n.)* divertissement SYW5
enthusiastic *(adj.)* enthousiaste 6.1
escape *(v.)* s'échapper How to 5
even *(adv.)* même SYW6
evening *(n.)* soir 1.2
every *(dét.)* chaque 3.1
everyday *(adj.)* quotidien 7.1
everyone *(pron.)* tout le monde SYW1
everything *(pron.)* tout 3.4
everywhere *(adv.)* partout How to 5
exactly *(adv.)* exactement 6.4
exchange *(v.)* échanger 5.2
exciting *(adj.)* passionnant SYW4
Excuse me, ... Excusez-moi, ... 1.1
exhibit *(n.)* objet exposé 1.4
expensive *(adj.)* cher 4.3
experienced *(adj.)* expérimenté 5.4
explain *(v.)* expliquer How to 1
explorer *(n.)* explorateur 5.3
extra-terrestrial *(n.)* extra-terrestre 7.3
eye *(n.)* œil 2.1

F

face *(n.)* visage 4.2
in fact *(n.)* en fait 5.4
fair (hair) *(adj.)* (cheveux) clairs, blonds 1.2
fairy *(n.)* fée How to 5
fall (off) *(v.)* tomber (d'un vélo...) 3.4
fall down s'écrouler How to 5
false *(adj.)* faux 4.3
family *(n.)* famille 2.2
famous *(adj.)* célèbre 1.4
fantastic *(adj.)* fantastique 3.3
far *(adj., adv.)* loin 5.4
far too... beaucoup trop... 5.4
fare *(n.)* prix (d'un billet de transport) How to 3
farm *(n.)* ferme 7.3
farmer *(n.)* fermier, agriculteur SYW6
fashion show *(n.)* défilé de mode 6.2
fast *(adj., adv.)* rapide ; vite 4.3
favourite *(adj.)* préféré 1.4
feed *(v.)* nourrir 7.1
feel *(v.)* (se) sentir 4.4
feeling *(n.)* émotion, sentiment 7.1
fell *(prét. :* **fall**) How to 5
felt *(prét. :* **feel**) How to 5
female *(adj.)* féminin; femelle 3.4
field *(n.)* champ 1.4
filling *(n.)* garniture 6.3
film *(n. v.)* film, tourner un film 3.2
finally *(adv.)* finalement 5.4
find *(v.)* trouver 1.3
fine *(adj.)* bien, beau
I'm fine! Je vais très bien ! 1.2
finger *(n.)* doigt 6.3
finish *(v.)* terminer 2.3
fire *(n.)* feu, incendie 3.3
on fire *(n.)* en feu How to 5

DICTIONARY

first *(adj., adv.)* premier; d'abord 1.1, 4.4
first name prénom 1.1
fish *(n.)* poisson 3.3
fix *(v.)* fixer 7.4
flag *(n.)* drapeau SYW1
flat *(n.)* appartement 2.2
flat *(adj.)* plat SYW6
flight *(n.)* vol How to 1
floor *(n.)* sol, étage 2.2
on the floor par terre 4.4
flour *(n.)* farine 6.3
flower *(n.)* fleur 4.2
fly *(v.)* piloter, voler 3.4
follow *(v.)* suivre How to 1
food *(n.)* nourriture 3.3
foot *(pl.* **feet***)* *(n.)* pied p. 12
for *(prép.)* pour; pendant 1.1, 5.1
found *(prét. :* **find***)* 5.2
free *(adj.)* libre; gratuit How to 3
French *(adj.)* français p. 10
fridge *(n.)* réfrigérateur 6.3
friend *(n.)* ami 1.2
friendly *(adj.)* aimable, gentil 2.4
frightened *(adj.)* effrayé How to 1
be frightened (of) avoir peur (de) How to 1
frightening *(adj.)* effrayant 4.2
from *(prép.)* de 1.1
front door *(n.)* porte d'entrée 4.1
in front of *(prép.)* devant 2.2
full stop *(n.)* point How to 7
fun *(n.)* **It's great fun!** C'est très amusant ! 3.1
funeral *(n.)* funérailles, obsèques 5.3
funny *(adj.)* amusant 4.2
future *(n.)* futur SYW5

G

game *(n.)* jeu, partie 1.4
games EPS (matière scolaire) 2.3
garden *(n., v.)* jardin, jardiner 2.2. 3.3
gas *(n.)* gaz 4.4
gave *(prét. :* **give***)* 6.4
generous *(adj.)* généreux 3.3
German *(adj.)* allemand SYW5
get *(v.)* obtenir, recevoir 3.2
get dressed s'habiller Sounds 5
get home arriver à la maison 3.2
get lost se perdre 7.3
get ready préparer 7.4
get to arriver à 3.2
get up se lever 3.2
(go and) get (aller) chercher 2.4
Get well! Bon rétablissement ! SYW7
ghost *(n.)* fantôme 5.1
giant *(adj.)* géant, gigantesque SYW3
gift *(n.)* cadeau How to 3
gigantic *(adj.)* gigantesque SYW5
girl *(n.)* fille 1.3
give *(v.)* donner 4.3
glasses *(n. pl.)* lunettes 2.4
go *(v.)* aller, partir 3.1, 7.4
go back to retourner à 7.2
go for it foncer 7.2
go home rentrer à la maison How to 4
go into entrer 4.1
go on holiday partir en vacances 6.2
go out sortir 7.1
go shopping faire des courses 4.3
go to bed se coucher 3.2
go to school aller à l'école 3.1
go wrong mal se passer 5.4
good *(adj.)* bon SYW2
Good! Bien ! 1.2
good at (+ N/+V-ING) fort en, doué pour... 3.4
Good morning! Bonjour ! p. 10
Goodbye! Au revoir ! p. 10
My goodness! Mon Dieu ! 2.4
grass *(n.)* herbe, gazon 1.4
Great! *(adj.)* Super ! 6.1
great-grandfather *(n.)* arrière grand-père 5.1
great-grandmother *(n.)* arrière grand-mère 5.1
green *(adj.)* vert p. 12
greeting *(n.)* salutation How to 1
greetings card *(n.)* carte de vœux How to 4
grey *(adj.)* gris p. 12
ground *(n.)* sol 7.3
on the ground par terre
gym *(n.)* gymnastique Sounds 3

H

had *(prét. :* **have***)* 5.2
hair *(n.)* cheveux, chevelure 2.1
hairdresser *(n.)* coiffeur 7.4
at the hairdresser's chez le coiffeur 7.4

half *(n.)* demi, moitié

half an hour demi-heure 4.1

half past... ...et demie p. 13

hall *(n.)* entrée 2.2

hand *(n.)* main 3.1

happen *(v.)* se passer 4.1

happy *(adj.)* heureux How to 1

happily *(adv.)* heureusement, dans le bonheur How to 5

harbour *(n.)* port How to 7

hard *(adj., adv.)* dur 3.1

work hard travailler dur/beaucoup How to 5

hat *(n.)* chapeau 1.3

hate *(v.)* détester 3.3

have *(v.)* prendre 2.3

Have a nice day! Bonne journée ! SYW1

Have a nice weekend! Bon week-end ! Sounds1

have a good time bien s'amuser 7.1

have a shower prendre une douche 4.1

have got avoir 2.1

have (got) to devoir, être obligé de 3.1, 7.4

he *(pron.)* il 1.1

head *(n.)* tête

headache *(n.)* mal à la tête 4.4

hear *(v.)* entendre 4.1

heard *(prét. :* **hear***)* How to 5

heat *(v.)* faire chauffer 6.3

heavy *(adj.)* lourd 2.4

height *(n.)* hauteur 2.1

helmet *(n.)* casque SYW4

help *(v.)* aider 1.1

her *(pron., dét.)* la, elle ; son/sa/ses (à elle) 1.2, 2.4

here *(adv.)* ici SYW2

Here's ... Voici ... 6.1

Here you are! Tiens !/Tenez ! 6.1

hers *(pron.)* à elle 1.2, 6.4

Hi! Salut ! 1.3

high *(adj.)* haut SYW5

him *(pron.)* le, lui 2.4

hire *(v.)* louer 6.2

his *(pron., dét.)* à lui ; son/sa/ses (à lui) 1.2, 2.4, 6.4

history *(n.)* histoire 1.4

hold *(v.)* tenir (à la main) 4.2

holiday *(n.)* vacances SYW3

summer holidays *(n.)* vacances d'été 6.1

at home *(n.)* chez soi, à la maison 1.2

homemade *(adj.)* fait maison How to 3

homework *(n.)* devoirs 2.3

horse *(n.)* cheval 3.4

hospital *(n.)* hôpital 1.2

hot *(adj.)* **It's hot.** Il fait chaud. SYW1

hour *(n.)* heure 7.3

house *(n.)* maison 2.2

housework *(n.)* ménage 3.3

how *(adv.)* comment 2.3

How about (going) ...? Et si on (allait) ... ? 6.2

How are you? Comment vas-tu ? 1.2

How big ...? Quelle taille ... ? 4.3

How deep ...? Quelle est la profondeur ... ? How to 7

How far ...? À quelle distance ... ? 7.3

How fast ...? À quelle vitesse ... ? 4.3

How heavy ...? Combien pèse ... ? 4.3

How interesting! Comme c'est intéressant ! 5.1

How many/much ...? Combien de ... ? 1.4, 6.3

How much is/are ...? Combien coûte(nt) ... ? 4.3

How old ...? Quel âge ... ? 2.1

How tall ...? Quelle taille ... ? 2.1

How wide ...? Quelle largeur ... ? How to 7

however *(conj.)* cependant 5.4

human being *(n.)* être humain 4.3

hundred *(n.)* cent 1.4

hundreds of des centaines de SYW6

I'm hungry! J'ai faim ! Sounds 6

I

I *(pron.)* je 1.1

ice-cream *(n.)* glace 3.3

ice-skate *(v.)* faire du patinage sur glace 1.4

idea *(n.)* idée 6.2

if *(conj.)* si 1.4

ill *(adj.)* malade 3.4

imaginative *(adj.)* imaginatif 3.3

in *(prép.)* dans p. 11

in Australia en Australie 1.2

in London à Londres 1.2

in the morning le/du matin 2.3

including *(prép.)* y compris 1.4

inhabitant *(n.)* habitant 1.4

injury *(n.)* blessure 4.4

inside *(prép.)* à l'intérieur de SYW7

instant *(adj.)* instantané 6.3

interest *(n.)* intérêt How to 6

interesting *(adj.)* intéressant 1.4

interrupt *(v.)* interrompre 7.1

into *(prép.)* en, dans 3.3

DICTIONARY

introduce *(v.)* introduire, présenter SYW5, 6.1
invade *(v.)* envahir SYW5
invent *(v.)* inventer 5.1
invite *(v.)* inviter 4.1
Irish *(adj.)* irlandais 2.1
island *(n.)* île 5.2
it *(pron.)* il, le/la 2.4

J

jacket *(n.)* veste 1.3
job *(n.)* emploi, métier, travail 1.2
jog *(v.)* faire du jogging 1.4
join *(v.)* adhérer à SYW4
joke *(v.)* plaisanter 7.2
juggle *(v.)* jongler 3.1
juggler *(n.)* jongleur 3.1
junk shop *(n.)* magasin de brocante 5.2
just *(adv.)* juste, seulement 6.4

K

keyword *(n.)* mot-clé How to 1
kick *(v.)* donner un coup de pied (à) Sounds 3
kid *(n. fam.)* gosse 3.1
kidnap *(v.)* enlever, kidnapper 7.3
kidnapping *(n.)* enlèvement 7.3
kill *(v.)* tuer SYW5
king *(n.)* roi How to 3
kitchen *(n.)* cuisine 2.2
knew *(prét. :* **know**) 5.2
knife *(pl.* **knives***)* *(n.)* couteau 6.3
know *(v.)* connaître, savoir 2.4
  I don't know je ne sais pas 2.4
  know how to savoir (faire quelque chose) 3.4

L

lady *(n.)* dame How to 6
lake *(n.)* lac 1.4
land *(v.)* atterrir 5.3
language *(n.)* langue 3.1
last *(adj.)* dernier SYW3
  last month le mois dernier 5.4
  last night hier soir 7.2
late *(adj., adv.)* tard ; en retard 3.2, 4.4
  I'm late je suis en retard 4.4
  it's late il est tard 4.4
the latest *(n.)* le plus récent SYW4
launch *(v.)* lancer 5.3
lazy *(adj.)* paresseux How to 5
learn *(v.)* apprendre p. 12
leave *(v.)* quitter ; laisser 3.2, 4.4
  leave home quitter la maison 3.2
left *(prét. :* **leave**) 5.2
left *(n.)* gauche 2.2
  on the left *(n.)* à gauche
Let's go (to)...! Allons (à) ... ! 1.4
letter *(n.)* lettre p. 12
library *(n.)* bibliothèque SYW2
life *(n.)* vie SYW2
light *(n.)* lumière 5.4
  light bulb *(n.)* ampoule 5.3
light *(v.)* allumer 5.4
light *(adj.)* léger 4.3
like *(v.)* aimer 2.2
  if you like si tu veux 6.2
  like (+ V-ING) aimer (faire quelque chose) 3.3
like *(prép.)* comme 6.4
  What is he like? Comment est-il ? 2.1
  What's the weather like? Quel temps fait-il ? SYW1
link *(v.)* lier SYW6
listen to *(v.)* écouter p. 11
little *(adj.)* petit
a little *(adv., pron.)* un peu (de) 3.4, 7.2
live *(v.)* vivre 2.2
living-room *(n.)* salon 2.2
look *(n.)* aspect, regard p. 12
look (at) *(v.)* regarder p. 11
  look *(+ adj.)* avoir l'air 4.4
  look after s'occuper de 2.4
  look for chercher 4.1
  look like ressembler à 4.4
  look out of regarder par 4.1
lose *(v.)* perdre SYW5
lost *(prét. :* **lose**) SYW5
a lot (of) *(n., adv.)* beaucoup (de) 1.4, 3.1
  a lot to do beaucoup à faire 7.4
  lots of beaucoup de 7.3
loud *(adj.)* fort 7.4
love *(v.)* aimer 3.3
lovely *(adj.)* beau Sounds 5
low *(adj., adv.)* bas, en bas SYW6
luck *(n.)* chance **Good luck!** Bonne chance ! 5.4

luckily *(adv.)* heureusement How to 5
lucky *(adj.)* chanceux 2.1
You are lucky! Quelle chance tu as ! 2.1
lunch *(n.)* déjeuner 2.3
lunchtime *(n.)* heure du déjeuner 1.2

M

made *(prét. & part. passé:* **make**) 5.2, 5.3
magnificent *(adj.)* magnifique SYW3
mail *(n.)* courrier 3.1
main *(adj.)* principal SYW6
make *(v.)* faire 1.1
make a decision prendre une décision 3.3
make an appointment prendre rendez-vous 7.4
man *(pl.* **men***)* *(n.)* homme How to 1
many *(dét., adv.)* beaucoup (de) SYW5
map *(n.)* carte
marry *(v.)* épouser 5.1
martial arts *(n.)* arts martiaux 3.4
What's the matter? Qu'est ce que qu'il y a ? 1.3
maybe *(adv.)* peut-être Sounds 4
me *(pron.)* me, moi 2.4
mean *(v.)* signifier, vouloir dire How to 2, 3.3
measure *(v.)* mesurer How to 7
measurement *(n.)* mesure How to 7
meat *(n.)* viande 3.2
meet *(v.)* rencontrer 1.1
met *(prét. :* **meet***)* 5.4
midday *(n.)* midi 3.2
(in the) middle (of) *(n.)* (au) milieu (de) SYW5
midnight *(n.)* minuit How to 5
mile *(n.)* = 1,6 km 3.1
That's miles! Ça fait des kilomètres (d'ici) ! 7.3
milk *(n.)* lait 6.3
Never mind! *(v.)* Ce n'est pas grave ! 6.4
mine *(pron.)* à moi 6.4
miss *(v.)* manquer 6.1
What's missing? Qu'est-ce qui manque ? 6.3
mix *(v.)* mélanger 6.3
mixed *(adj.)* mixte SYW2
mixture *(n.)* mélange 6.3
mobile *(n., adj.)* (téléphone) portable 6.4
money *(n.)* argent 5.2
month *(n.)* mois p. 13
moon *(n.)* lune 4.2
more... than plus... que 4.3
morning *(n.)* matin 1.2
motionless *(adj.)* immobile 4.4
motor home *(n.)* camping-car 3.1
motorbike *(n.)* moto 3.4
mouse *(n.)* souris p. 12
move *(v.)* bouger, deplacer 2.4
Mr Monsieur 1.2
Mrs Madame 1.2
much *(dét., adv.)* beaucoup (de) 3.3
not (very) much pas beaucoup 3.3
much more beaucoup plus 4.3
Mum *(n.)* Maman 1.2
museum *(n.)* musée 1.4
music *(n.)* musique 3.3
musical *(n.)* comédie musicale 7.2
musician *(n.)* musicien 5.1
must *(modal)* devoir, être obligé de 4.4
my *(dét.)* mon/ma/mes 1.1
mysterious *(adj.)* mystérieux How to 5
mystery *(n.)* mystère 5.2

N

name *(n., v.)* nom ; nommer, identifier 1.1, 5.3
natural *(adj.)* naturel 3.3
navigator *(n.)* navigateur 5.1
near *(prép., adv.)* près (de) 2.2, 2.3
need *(v.)* avoir besoin de 6.3
Neither ... I. Moi non plus. 6.2
never *(adv.)* jamais 3.2
New Year's Day *(n.)* le Jour de l'An SYW3
new *(adj.)* nouveau 1.1
news *(n. sing.)* nouvelles, informations 3.3
newspaper *(n.)* journal 3.1
next *(adj., adv.)* prochain ; après 3.4, 5.2
next to *(prép.)* à côté de 2.2
nice *(adj.)* agréable, sympathique 1.1
Nice to meet you. Enchanté. 1.1
night *(n.)* nuit 3.2
no one *(pron.)* personne 7.1
noisy *(adj.)* bruyant 3.3
north *(n.)* nord SYW1
nothing *(pron.)* rien 7.1
now *(adv.)* maintenant 2.2
nowhere *(adv.)* nulle part 7.3
number *(n.)* chiffre, nombre p. 13
nurse *(n.)* infirmière 1.2

O

occupation *(n.)* métier, profession 3.1

It's (8) o'clock. Il est (8) heures. p. 13

of *(prép.)* de p. 13

offer *(n., v.)* offre ; offrir 5.4, 7.2

office *(n.)* bureau 6.3

often *(adv.)* souvent 3.2

Okay! D'accord ! 1.4

Is it okay? Est-ce que ça va ? 1.3

old *(adj.)* vieux 2.1

on *(prép.)* sur 1.4

Once upon a time Il était une fois How to 5

the one *(pron.)* celui/celle 4.2

only *(adv.)* seulement 3.1

onto *(prép.)* sur How to 5

open *(v., adj.)* ouvrir ; ouvert p. 10, 1.4

opposite *(prép.)* en face de 2.2

or *(conj.)* ou 2.2

order *(n.)* ordre p. 13

ordinary *(adj.)* ordinaire 3.1

originally *(adv.)* à l'origine SYW4

other *(adj.)* autre SYW2

our *(dét.)* notre/nos 2.2

ours *(pron.)* à nous 6.4

outside *(adv.)* dehors 2.4

oven *(n.)* four 6.3

over *(prép.)* au-dessus de ; plus de SYW1, SYW3

on… own tout seul 7.3

P

packet *(n.)* paquet 6.3

paint *(v.)* peindre How to 6

painting *(n.)* tableau 3.3

pair *(n.)* paire 5.2

in pairs *(n.)* par deux p. 10

palace *(n.)* palais How to 5

panic *(v.)* panique 4.4

parachute *(v.)* sauter en parachute 3.4

parade *(n., v.)* défilé ; défiler SYW3

parcel *(n.)* paquet 5.2

part *(n.)* partie SYW1

party *(n.)* fête 3.3

pass *(v.)* passer, donner à 6.3

pass an exam réussir un examen SYW7

passenger *(n.)* passager 3.1

passionate *(adj.)* passionné 7.1

past *(n., prép.)* passé 5.1

it's ten past… il est… heures dix p. 13

pastime *(n.)* passe-temps SYW4

pear *(n.)* poire 6.3

peel *(v.)* peler, éplucher 6.3

people *(n. pl.)* gens 1.4

per cent *(adv.)* pour cent SYW4

perform *(v.)* se produire (sur scène) 3.1

perhaps *(adv.)* peut-être 3.4

person *(n.)* (une) personne p. 12

phone *(n., v.)* téléphone ; téléphoner p. 12

on the phone au téléphone Sounds 6

phone number numéro de téléphone 3.4

photographer *(n.)* photographe 4.1

photography *(n.)* photographie 3.3

pick up *(v.)* soulever, ramasser 5.4

picnic *(v.)* pique-niquer 1.4

picture *(n.)* image p. 11

piece *(n.)* tranche, morceau 3.2

pig *(n.)* cochon 4.3

pink *(adj.)* rose 1.3

place *(n.)* lieu, endroit How to 1

plan *(n.)* projet 7.1

plane *(n.)* avion SYW5

planet *(n.)* planète 5.3

play *(v.)* jouer 1.4

pleasant *(adj.)* agréable SYW6

please s'il vous plaît p. 10

pleased *(adj.)* content 5.2

police *(n. pl.)* police 7.3

policeman *(n.)* policier (homme) 4.1

policewoman *(n.)* policier (femme) 3.1

poor *(adj.)* pauvre 5.2

popular *(adj.)* populaire 1.4

poster *(n.)* affiche 3.4

postman *(n.)* facteur 3.1

potato *(pl.* **potatoes***)* *(n.)* pomme de terre 3.3

pound (£) *(n.)* livre (sterling) 6.1

powder *(n.)* poudre 6.3

practical *(adj.)* pratique 3.3

practise *(v.)* s'entraîner 3.1

present *(v.)* cadeau SYW 7

press *(n.)* presse How to 3

pretty *(adj.)* joli 3.4

price *(n.)* prix 4.3

prisoner *(n.)* prisonnier How to 3

probably *(adv.)* probablement 4.2
produce *(v.)* produire 5.3
producer *(n.)* producteur 3.4
product *(n.)* produit 4.3
professional *(adj.)* professionnel 6.1
programme *(n.)* émission 1.1
promise *(v.)* promettre 7.3
pronounce *(v.)* prononcer 3.1
pull *(v.)* tirer SYW5
pumpkin *(n.)* citrouille How to 5
pupil *(n.)* élève 1.2
push *(v.)* pousser 2.4
put *(v.)* mettre 7.4
  put down (on) poser (sur) 5.4
  put on mettre (un vêtement) SYW3
pyjamas *(n. pl.)* pyjama Sounds 5

Q

quarter past/to 8 8 heures et/moins le/quart p. 13
queen *(n.)* reine 5.1
quick *(adj.)* rapide How to 6
  Quick! Vite ! How to 5
quickly *(adv.)* rapidement 5.4
quite *(adv.)* assez, plutôt 2.1
quiz *(n.)* jeu, test 5.3
quizmaster *(n.)* animateur de jeu 5.3

R

rabbit *(n.)* lapin 4.3
rain *(n., v.)* pluie, pleuvoir Sounds 1
  it's raining il pleut SYW 1
ran *(prét. :* **run**) How to 5
raspberry *(n.)* framboise 6.3
react *(v.)* réagir How to 6
read *(v.)* lire p. 11
reader *(n.)* lecteur 3.3
ready *(adj.)* prêt 1.3
real *(adj.)* réel How to 3
realise *(v.)* se rendre compte 5.2
realistic *(adj.)* réaliste 4.2
really *(adv.)* vraiment 2.4
recipe *(n.)* recette 6.3
record producer *(n.)* producteur de disques 6.1
recorded *(adj.)* enregistré How to 1
recording studio *(n.)* studio d'enregistrement 6.1
red *(adj.)* rouge p. 12
  red (hair) (cheveux) roux 2.1
regular *(adj.)* régulier 3.3
rehearsal *(n.)* répétition 5.4
rehearse *(v.)* répéter 5.4
reign *(v.)* régner 5.1
relax *(v.)* se détendre 6.2
relaxed *(adj.)* détendu 7.1
remember *(v.)* se rappeler, se souvenir de SYW1
replace *(v.)* remplacer SYW6
result *(n.)* résultat 3.3
ride *(v.)* monter (à cheval), faire (du vélo), conduire (une moto) 3.4
right *(n., adj.)* droite ; bon, correct 2.2, 3.4
  Right! Bon !, Bien ! 6.3
  that's right c'est ça 1.1
  you're right tu as raison 6.4
ring *(v.)* sonner ; téléphoner 6.2
rink *(n.)* piste, patinoire 1.4
risk *(n.)* risque 3.3
river *(n.)* rivière, fleuve SYW4
road *(n.)* route 1.4
rollerblade *(v.)* faire du roller 1.4
Roman *(n., adj.)* Romain, romain SYW5
romantic *(adj.)* romantique 5.1
roof *(n.)* toit How to 5
room *(n.)* pièce, salle 2.2, 7.4
round *(adj., prép)* rond ; autour de p. 12
rub *(v.)* frotter 6.3
rule *(n., v.)* règle, régner 4.4, SYW5
run *(v.)* courir 4.4

S

salad *(n.)* salade, laitue 3.2
on sale en vente How to 3
same *(adj.)* même 4.3
sang *(prét. :* **sing**) 5.3
sank *(prét. :* **sink**) 5.3
saw *(prét. :* **see**) 5.2
say *(v.)* dire p. 13
scale *(n.)* échelle 4.3
scenery *(n.)* paysage SYW4
school *(n.)* école 1.2
scientist *(n.)* scientifique 5.1

score *(v.)*	marquer (un point)	5.3
Scottish *(adj.)*	écossais	2.1
scream *(v.)*	crier	4.2
scuba-diving *(n.)*	plongée sous-marine	SYW4
sea *(n.)*	mer	SYW1
seat *(n.)*	siège, place	How to 3
secretary *(n.)*	secrétaire	3.4
see *(v.)*	voir	1.4
seem *(v.)*	sembler, paraître	7.1
sell *(v.)*	vendre	5.2
send *(v.)*	envoyer	6.3
sensitive *(adj.)*	sensible	3.3
sent *(prét.:* **send)**		6.3
separately *(adv.)*	séparément	How to 7
sequel *(n.)*	suite	3.4
series *(n.)*	série	4.3
serious *(adj.)*	sérieux	How to 4
serve *(v.)*	servir	3.1
service station *(n.)*	station service	SYW6
share *(v.)*	partager	4.4
she *(pron.)*	elle	1.1
shelf *(pl.* **shelves***) (n.)*	étagère	6.3
ship *(n.)*	navire	5.3
shirt *(n.)*	chemise	1.3
shoe *(n.)*	chaussure	1.3
shop *(n.)*	magasin, boutique	5.2
shop *(v.)*	faire les magasins	3.3
go shopping	faire les courses	4.3
show *(n., v.)*	spectacle, émission; montrer	p. 12, 6.4
shower *(n.)*	douche	4.1
shy *(adj.)*	timide	3.3
sign *(n., v.)*	panneau; signer	4.4, 3.3
silly *(adj.)*	bête, stupide	4.4
sing *(v.)*	chanter	p. 12
singer *(n.)*	chanteur	2.1
sink *(v.)*	couler	5.3
sister *(n.)*	sœur	1.2
sit *(v.)*	s'asseoir	1.4
size *(n.)*	taille	4.3
skate *(n., v.)*	patin; patiner	p. 12
skateboard *(v.)*	faire de la planche à roulettes	3.3
skirt *(n.)*	jupe	1.3
skyscraper *(n.)*	gratte-ciel	1.4
slow *(adj.)*	lent	4.3
small *(adj.)*	petit	1.3
smell *(v.)*	sentir (une odeur)	4.4
smile *(n., v.)*	sourire	4.2
smoke *(n.)*	fumée	4.4
snow *(n.)*	neige	SYW4
So... I.	Moi aussi.	6.2
so *(conj., adv.)*	donc, si	SYW1, How to 3
sock *(n.)*	chaussette	1.3
sold *(prét.:* **sell)**		5.2
some *(dét., pron)*	du/de la/des, quelques; en	3.2, 6.3
someone *(pron.)*	quelqu'un	4.4
something *(pron.)*	quelque chose	7.1
sometimes *(adv.)*	quelquefois	3.2
son *(n.)*	fils	7.3
song *(n.)*	chanson	5.1
soon *(adv.)*	bientôt	SYW7
sore (throat) *(adj.)*	mal (à la gorge)	4.4
Sorry!	Désolé! Excuse-moi!	1.2
sort *(n.)*	sorte, genre	3.3
south *(n.)*	sud	SYW1
South Africa *(n.)*	Afrique du Sud	SYW4
space *(n.)*	espace	7.1
open spaces	grands espaces	1.4
spacecraft *(n.)*	vaisseau spatial	5.3
Spanish *(adj.)*	espagnol	1.1
spare time *(n.)*	temps libre	3.3
speak *(v.)*	parler	p. 10
Rob speaking!	C'est Rob à l'appareil!	5.2
spectator *(n.)*	spectateur	SYW4
speed *(n.)*	vitesse	4.3
spell *(v.)*	épeler	p. 12
spicy *(adj.)*	épicé	3.3
spot *(n.)*	endroit; tache; bouton	p. 12
square *(adj.)*	carré	p. 12
square kilometres	kilomètres carrés	1.4
stand *(v.)*	être debout	3.1
star *(n.)*	étoile, vedette	p. 12
star *(v.)*	être la vedette	3.4
start *(v.)*	commencer	2.3
state *(n.)*	état	3.1
state school	école publique	SYW2
the States	les États-Unis	5.1
statement *(n.)*	affirmation	How to 1
stairs *(n.)*	escalier	2.2
stay *(v.)*	rester	2.3
steamboat *(n.)*	bateau à vapeur	SYW6
stick *(n.)*	brindille	How to 5
still *(adv.)*	encore, toujours	SYW5
stone *(adj.)*	en pierre	SYW5
story *(n.)*	histoire	SYW5
strange *(adj.)*	étrange	How to 6
straw *(n.)*	paille	How to 5

strawberry *(n.)* fraise 1.4
street *(n.)* rue SYW3
stress *(n.)* accent tonique How to 6
strong *(adj.)* fort 3.3
subject *(n.)* matière SYW2
subway *(n.)* métro (USA) 3.2
suddenly *(adv.)* soudain How to 5
sugar *(n.)* sucre 6.3
summary *(n.)* résumé How to 5
summer *(n.)* été 1.4
sun *(n.)* soleil 4.2
sung *(part. passé :* **sing***)* 5.3
sunny *(adj.)* ensoleillé SYW1
sure *(adj.)* sûr 4.4
surname *(n.)* nom de famille 1.1
surprised *(adj.)* étonné How to 1
survive *(v.)* survivre 5.1
sweater *(n.)* pullover 1.3
swim *(v.)* nager 3.3
swimmer *(n.)* nageur 3.4
swimming pool *(n.)* piscine SYW2
switch *(n.)* interrupteur 5.4

T

table *(n.)* table ; tableau 3.3
  table football *(n.)* babyfoot SYW4
table-tennis *(n.)* tennis de table, ping-pong 3.3
tail *(n.)* queue How to 5
take *(v.)* prendre ; emmener 1.4, 2.4
  take a test passer un test SYW7
  take away enlever, emporter 7.4
  take… for a walk promener 2.4
  take orders recevoir des ordres 7.1
  take place avoir lieu 7.4
talented *(adj.)* talentueux 5.4
talk (about/to) *(v.)* parler (de/à) p. 11, 4.1
tall *(adj.)* grand ; haut 2.1, SYW6
tea *(n.)* thé ; goûter 3.2, How to 3
teach *(v.)* enseigner SYW2
teacher *(n.)* enseignant, professeur 1.1
team *(n.)* équipe p. 12
teaspoon *(n.)* cuiller à café 6.3
teenager *(n.)* adolescent 3.3
tell *(v.)* dire, raconter How to 4
temperature *(n.)* température ; fièvre SYW 1, 4.4
term *(n.)* trimestre 7.4
terrible *(adj.)* affreux 5.1
textbook *(n.)* manuel p. 11
Thank you. Merci. p. 10
  Thank you for coming. Merci d'être venu. 5.4
  Thanks a lot. Merci beaucoup. 6.1
  Thanks for phoning. Merci d'avoir appelé. 1.2
that *(pron., dét.)* ce, cela ; ce/cette… (-là) 2.1
  that one celui-là, celle-là 4.2
that *(pron., rel.)* que 5.3
the *(art.)* le/la/les 1.1
their *(dét.)* leur(s) 2.2
theirs *(pron.)* à eux 6.4
them *(pron.)* eux, les 2.4
then *(adv., conj.)* puis ; donc 5.4, 7.4
there *(adv.)* là 2.4
there is/are il y a 1.4
these *(pron., dét.)* celles-ci, ceux-ci ; ces… (-ci) 6.4
they *(pron.)* ils/elles 1.2
thing *(n.)* chose 1.4
think *(v.)* croire, penser 2.4
  Let's think about it. Réfléchissons-y. 6.2
  I (don't) think so. Je pense que oui (non). 7.1
I'm thirsty j'ai soif 7.4
this *(pron., dét.)* ce, ceci ; ce/cette… (-ci) 1.3, 2.4, 6.4
  This is… Voici … 1.1
  this one celui-ci, celle-ci 4.2
those *(pron., dét.)* celles-là, ceux-là ; ces… (-là) 6.4
thought *(prét. :* **think***)* 6.4
thousand *(n.)* mille 1.4
  thousands of des milliers de SYW5
throat *(n.)* gorge 4.4
through *(prép.)* à travers SYW1
throw *(v.)* jeter SYW4
tick *(v.)* cocher p. 13
ticket *(n.)* billet 6.1
tidy up *(v.)* ranger 6.4
tidy *(adj.)* bien rangé Sounds 3
tie *(n.)* cravate SYW2
time *(n.)* temps ; heure ; fois p. 13, 6.2
  on time à l'heure 3.2
  time zone fuseau horaire SYW6
  What time…? À quelle heure… ? 7.4
  What's the time? Quelle heure est-il ? p. 13
timetable *(n.)* emploi du temps 2.3
tired *(adj.)* fatigué 3.2
title *(n.)* titre How to 2
to *(prép.)* à 1.1
  It's ten to (8). Il est (8) heures moins dix. p. 13

DICTIONARY

today *(adv.)* aujourd'hui SYW1
together *(adj.)* ensemble How to 5
toilet *(n.)* toilette(s) 2.2
told *(prét. & part. passé:* **tell**) How to 5
tomato *(n.)* tomate 3.3
tomorrow *(adv.)* demain 2.3
tonight *(adv.)* ce soir, cette nuit 4.4
too *(adv.)* trop ; aussi 1.3, 1.4
  too many trop de 5.4
took *(prét. :* **take**)
at the top of en haut de 3.3
  (on the) top floor (au) dernier étage 2.2
tournament *(n.)* tournoi SYW3
tower *(n.)* tour 4.1
town *(n.)* ville How to 4
toy *(n.)* jouet p. 12
track *(n.)* piste 1.4
trainer *(n.)* basket (chaussure) 1.3
traffic *(n.)* circulation 3.1
travel *(v.)* voyager 3.1
traveller *(n.)* voyageur SYW6
tree *(n.)* arbre 1.4
trip *(n.)* promenade, voyage How to 3
  day trip excursion How to 3
  school trip sortie scolaire 6.2
trousers *(n. pl.)* pantalon 1.3
truck driver *(n.)* camionneur (USA) SYW6
true *(adj.)* vrai 4.3
try (to) *(v.)* essayer (de) 5.4
  try on essayer (un vêtement) How to 5
tube *(n.)* métro (UK) 2.3
turn down *(v.)* baisser le volume 7.4
turn off/on éteindre/allumer 5.4
TV *(n.)* télévision 3.2
twin *(n. adj.)* jumeau/jumelle 4.1
typical *(adj.)* typique 3.3

U

UFO *(n.)* **Unidentified Flying Object** OVNI 7.3
ugly *(adj.)* laid How to 5
umbrella *(n.)* parapluie SYW1
unblock *(v.)* déboucher How to 3
under *(prép.)* sous, en dessous de 2.2
underground railway *(n.)* métro SYW5
underline *(v.)* souligner 6.3
understand *(v.)* comprendre
  I don't understand. Je ne comprends pas. p. 10
unfortunately *(adv.)* malheureusement 5.2
unhappy *(adj.)* malheureux How to 5
unpredictable *(adj.)* imprévisible 7.1
until *(prép., conj.)* jusqu'à, jusqu'à ce que How to 5
unusual *(adj.)* hors du commun, inhabituel 3.1
upset *(adj.)* ennuyé, contrarié 7.2
upstairs *(adv.)* à l'étage 2.2
us *(pron.)* nous 2.4
usually *(adv.)* d'habitude 3.2

V

valuable *(adj.)* de valeur 5.2
vegetable *(n.)* légume 3.3
vegetarian *(n.)* végétarien 3.2
very *(adv.)* très SYW1
view *(n.)* vue 1.4
visit *(n., v.)* visite ; visiter 1.4
voice *(n.)* voix 5.1

W

wait (for) *(v.)* attendre 4.1
  Wait a minute! Attends un instant ! 4.1
waitress *(n.)* serveuse 5.4
walk *(n., v.)* promenade ; marcher, se promener 2.4, 2.3
wall *(n.)* mur How to 6
want *(v.)* vouloir 6.1
war *(n.)* guerre SYW3
warm *(adj.)* (temps) doux, tiède SYW1
watch *(v.)* regarder 3.2
water *(n.)* eau 3.3
wave *(v.)* vague 4.2
way *(n.)* chemin How to 4
  on the way sur le chemin 3.2
we *(pron.)* nous
wear *(v.)* porter (un vêtement) 4.2
weather *(n.)* temps SYW1
web *(n.)* toile d'araignée p. 12
week *(n.)* semaine 3.1
weekday *(n.)* jour de semaine Sounds 1
weigh *(v.)* peser How to 7

weight *(n.)* poids 4.3
welcome *(adj., v.)* bienvenu ; souhaiter la bienvenue 1.1
well *(adv.)* bien 3.4
Well done! Bien !, Bravo ! p. 10
Well? Eh bien ? 4.2
well-known *(adj.)* bien connu 2.1
went *(prét. :* **go**) 5.2
West Indies *(n.)* Antilles SYW5
what *(pron., dét.)* que, quel p. 10
What about you? Et toi/vous ? 2.1
What is it/are they? Qu'est-ce que c'est ? 1.3
wheel *(n.)* roue SYW5
when *(adv., conj.)* quand, lorsque 2.3
where *(adv., pron. rel.)* où 1.2, How to 5
which *(adj.)* quel(le) 4.2
which one lequel, laquelle, lesquel(le)s 4.2
white *(adj.)* blanc p. 12
who *(pron., pron. rel.)* qui 1.1, 5.3
whose *(dét., pron.)* à qui 6.4
why *(adv.)* pourquoi 1.4
wide *(adj.)* large SYW5
wife *(n.)* épouse 5.1
will *(modal):* **I will help** J'aiderai 6.3.
wildlife *(n.)* faune How to 3
win *(v.)* gagner 5.3
window *(n.)* fenêtre 2.4
it's windy *(adj.)* il y a du vent SYW1
winter *(n.)* hiver 1.4
wish *(n.)* vœu 5.4
best wishes meilleurs vœux 5.4
wish *(v.)* souhaiter SYW7
with *(prép.)* avec 1.2
wolf *(n.)* loup How to 5
woman *(pl.* **women**) *(n.)* femme How to 4
won *(prét. & part. passé :* **win**) 5.3
wonderful *(adj.)* merveilleux SYW4
word *(n.)* mot 3.2
work *(n., v.)* travail ; travailler, fonctionner p. 10, 1.2, 4.4
world *(n.)* monde p. 12
worried *(adj.)* inquiet How to 1
worry *(v.)* s'inquiéter 3.4
Don't worry! Ne t'inquiète pas ! 3.4
would *(modal)* : **I would like** j'aimerais 6.2
write *(v.)* écrire p. 11
write down noter How to 7
writer *(n.)* écrivain, scénariste 1.1
wrong *(adj.)* mauvais 4.4
you're wrong tu as tort 5.3
wrote *(prét. :* **write**) 5.2

Y

year *(n.)* an, année 2.3
yellow *(adj.)* jaune p. 12
yesterday *(adv.)* hier 5.3
you *(pron.)* tu/te/toi, vous 1.1, 2.1
yourself *(pron.)* toi-même, vous-même 1.1
young *(adj.)* jeune 3.1
your *(dét.)* ton/ta/tes, votre/vos 1.1
yours *(pron.)* à toi, à vous 6.4

CRÉDITS

Couverture

GRAPH'M – François Huertas

Cartographie

Gardes Coredoc, autres ABC

Textes

The Monkey and You : Julie Holder *in* A Third Poetry Book (Oxford University Press)
Why is it? : Max Fatchen *in* A Third Poetry Book (Oxford University Press)
Turn off the TV : Bruce Lansky *in* www.gigglepoetry.com (Meadowbrook Press)
Half asleep : Gareth Owen *in* A Third Poetry Book (Oxford University Press)

Illustrations

BD : V. Gibert et Ph. Sedletzki ; Chatterbox : Brunor ; pp. 10-11 C. Huerta ; pp. 42, 43, 70, 71, 132 et 133 Y. Lequesne ; p. 82, 90, 91, 106 et 107 F. Malenfer ; pp. 134-139 B. Cladères.

Iconographie

Photo page de couverture : Gettyone Stone
p. 7 : (8) Contact Press Image/P. Artinian ■ **pp. 14-15 :** (1) Pictor International, (2, 4) Jerrican/Fuste-Raga, (3) Réa/S. Attal, (5) Gettyone Stone ■ **p. 18 :** (1, 2, 3, 4) Coll. F. Morel (5) Pictor International ■ **p. 21 :** Gettyone Stone ■ **p. 24 :** (1) Diaf/L. Zylberman, (2) Gettyone Stone, (3) Corbis-Sygma/S. Attal ■ **pp. 30-31 :** (1,3) Gettyone Stone, (2) Kipa/Lewis, (4) Gettyone Stone, (5) F. Morel ■ **p. 32 :** (1) Kipa/P. Roncen, (2) Kipa/Lefranc-Baverel, (3) Kipa/Capital, (4) Gamma/Liaison/Godlewski ■ **p. 34 :** Coll. F. Morel ■ **p. 36 :** (1, 2, 3) © Acland Burghley ; (4, 5, 6) © Newstead Wood ■ **p. 37 :** (7, 8, 9, 10) © Millfield ; (11, 12, 13) © Trinity ■ **pp. 38-39 :** Coll. F. Morel ■ **pp. 46-47 :** (1) Hoaqui/de Wilde, (2) Hoaqui/Grandadam, (3) Gettyone Stone, (4) Vandystadt/Allsport/M. Boecch, (5) Hoaqui/Liaison int. ■ **p. 48 :** © Boehmers ■ **p. 49 :** (1) Rapho/Network/B. Lewis, (2) Keith Gibson, (3) Robert Harding ■ **pp. 52-53 :** (1, 2) Gamma-Liaison-Burrows, (3) Gamma-Liaison-Halebian, (4) the Image Bank-Archive/Lambert, (5) Gamma/R. Benali, (6) Gettyone Stone, (7) The Bridgeman Art Library (Yale University Art Gallery. New Haven) ■ **p. 54 :** Coll. M.B. ■ **pp. 62-63 :** (1) Hoaqui/Y. Gellie, (2) Sygma/B. Beirne, (3) Gettyone Stone, (4) Ph. Campos, (5) Hoaqui/Key/Voller Ernst ■ **p. 65 :** (1, 3) Keith Gibson, (2) Ph. Campos ■ **p. 66** : (1) Gamma/FSP, (2, 3) Kipa/Pa News/T. Melville, (4) Gamma/FSP/Eddie Mulholland ■ **pp. 68-69 :** (1) Robert Harding/R. Francis, (2) Vandystadt/Allsport, (3) Robert Harding/N. Servian, (4) Rapho/J. Pickerell, (5) Robert Harding, (6) Hoaqui-Liaison int./ B. Torrez, (7) Vandystadt/allsport/S. Munday, (8) Vandystadt/allsport/A. Want, (9) Hoaqui/Ph. Renault ■ **p. 71 :** (1, 2) Kipa/Capital, (3) Coll. F. Morel ■ **p. 74 :** (2) © Lion/J. Walter Thompson, (3) © The Express, (5) Ph. Campos ■ **p. 75 :** The Bridgeman Art Library (Bonhams, London) ■ **pp. 78-79 :** (1) Edimédia, (2) Gettyone Stone, (3) Sygma, (4) Roger-Viollet, (5) Collection Christophe L. ■ **p. 81 :** (1, 2, 3, 4) Roger-Viollet, (5) Sygma ■ **p. 82 :** (1) et (2) Gettyone Stone ■ **pp. 84-85 :** (1) Museum of London/R. Sarell, (2) Gettyone Stone, (3) © Peter Newark's Historical Pictures, (4) © London Transport Museum, (5) Keystone, (6) Magnum Photo/D. Stock, (7) P. Kennedy ■ **p. 87 :** (1) Jerrican/Fuste-Raga, (2, 6) Keystone, (3, 4, 5) Gamma ■ **pp. 94-95 :** (1) Stock Image, (2) Cosmos/S. Rapport/LFI, (3) Cosmos/S. Sibert, (4) Cosmos/J. Elk III, (5) Contact Press Images/A. Reininger ■ **p. 98 :** (1) DIAF-B. Regent, (2) Cosmos, (3) DIAF-J.-P. Garcin, (4) DIAF-D. Ball, (5) DIAF-A. Even ■ **p. 100 :** (1) Gettyone Stone, (2, 6) DIAF-N. Wheeler ■ **p. 101 :** (1) the Image Bank, (2) DIAF-IFA, (3) DIAF/TPC/C. Bowman, (4) Gettyone Stone, (5) Contact Press Images-D.Burnett ■ **pp. 100-101 :** Stock Image ■ **p. 102 :** Coll. F. Morel ■ **pp.110-111 :** (1 et 4) Cinéstar, (2) Gettyone Stone, (3) Diaf/Valdin, (5) La Photothèque SDP ■ **pp. 116-118 :** (1, 5 et 7) © Hallmark Cards.Inc. ; (3) © Camden Graphics Ltd. ; (4) © The Paper House Group ; (6) © The Ink Group ; (8) © Hartland Cards ■ **p. 123 :** (a) Rapho/Serraillier, (b) Gettyone Stone, (c) Réa/Lecker, (d) Réa/E. Grégoire.

We tend apologies to any author or publisher whom we have been unable to trace and whose rights may have been unwittingly infringed.

Cet ouvrage est imprimé sur papier mince.
Imprimé en France par Maury – 45330 Malesherbes
N° d'imprimeur : 78668 N° d'édition : 2706-01
Dépôt légal : Avril 2000

The Englis

CANADA
QUEBEC
THE UNITED STATES
The Atlantic Ocean
THE UNITED KINGDOM
IRELAND
The Bahamas
The Turks and Caicos Islands
Cayman Islands
Jamaica
BELIZE
Antigua and Barbuda
St Kitts and Nevis
Montserrat
Dominica
Saint Lucia
St Vincent/Grenadines
Grenada
Barbados
Trinidad and Tobago
GUYANA
GAMBIA
SIERRA LEONE
LIBERIA
GHANA
NIGERIA
NAMIBIA
The Pacific Ocean
The Atlantic Ocean
The Falkland Islands
Countries where English is the official language or mother tongue
Countries where English is one of the official languages or second language